I0550168

Lemon Custard
The Novella and Screenplay

Jack Remick

FOR HELEN

Quartet Seattle

ACKNOWLEDGMENTS

Robert Ray, Ryan Winfield, Stewart Stern, Joel Chafetz. Writers all who guided me on the journey. Thank you to the writers at Louisa's Bakery Cafe who, week after week, showed up to help me become a better novelist. Thanks to Susan Canavarro who built the cover of this volume using a real rose. Without your help, this book would not be. Thank you.

The Windmill

It was hot, no breeze. Sitting on the front porch, Olive rocked in the big white rocker fanning herself with the Chinese red fan Tim had bought at the State fair. She heard Toby cry out in his sleep. Hot and sweaty, Toby often cried out while Nan, beside him in her bed, never did. Olive went in to them, sat beside them. She fanned Toby until he stopped crying and then she looked at Nan, face turned toward her—calm, serene.

Olive returned to the porch and, in the still, hot air, she heard the thrum of the tractor on the front quarter where Tim was plowing. The diesel engine lugged as the plow bit into the ground. A familiar sound, just like all the other sounds on the farm—the owls, the shrill chirp of the killdeer, the distant rumble of thunder, the clank of the chain on the windmill.

Tucking the fan in the hip pocket of her jeans, Olive walked to the windmill and climbed the steel runged ladder up to the platform. The blades of the windmill hung quiet in the heat. On the platform, Olive looked out. The world was flat as far as she could see. Flat and black and moonless. In the sky, a dotted pinafore of stars spread out. It was quiet except for the distant, now faint throb of the tractor. Olive walked around the platform smelling the grease that oozed from the zerks where Tim maintained the machine. To the East, the front quarter stretched out black and empty and there, in the distance, she saw the twin beams of the tractor—tiny little yellow knives cutting the black. She imagined Tim in his cabin—the cool air conditioned cabin, and she remembered the sandwiches she had packed for him, the cold chicken leg, the potato salad he would eat without stopping and never a thank you. She remembered the sickening smell of diesel on his clothes when he came in.

And then, he turned and the lights vanished and Olive felt a cold grip in her chest, and her scalp tingled and her skin crawled.

She bent over, face in her hands, her body quivering as if a huge dog had hold of her, shaking.

She looked up, the blackness surrounded her, black and endless and silent. She peered over the rail of the platform at the water tank round and

1

flat, an endless hole and she felt the urge to drop into that hole.

She held the fan out over the tank, and let it go and it fluttered, spinning like a butterfly and then it disappeared against the black surface of the water and she listened but there was no sound. The platform under her feet felt like mush. She wobbled. She was floating, disconnected, rising up in the heat. Dizzy, head spinning, she felt like a top whirling out of control and then she pushed herself up, ready to go over the rail, but at the last second, she loosened her grip and leaned against the rail—it was the only thing holding her back. She knew then that she had to leave.

The blackness was too black, the silence too quiet. The sweep of the ground engulfed her and smothered her and trapped her in its vastness. She shook as she climbed from the windmill. She was afraid to look down and so she descended, eyes closed, until her feet touched the ground again. She knelt, hands in the dirt and she raised her hands and licked at the dirt on her palms. She tasted the soil, felt the grit in her teeth, smelled the dry dirt and she hated it.

Rising, she fled back to the porch, to the house, to the bedroom where Nan and Toby slept—the sheets kicked off in the heat—the smell of their small bodies acrid even to her nostrils and she knelt, pulled the sheet over Nan and then Toby and lay on the floor beside her babies and she closed her eyes and she dreamed of dying.

Sunlight inching through the shades of the room struck her eyes. She opened. Far away, she heard the dull hum of the tractor. Frantic, she flew to her bedroom, to the closet where she tossed skirts and blouses and shoes into a suitcase and then she packed Nan's little dresses and shoes and Toby's jeans and T shirts and tennis shoes. Finished, she carried her babies one at a time out to the Chrysler that stood beside the fence under the sycamore tree and she laid her babies down and then she loaded the suitcases into the trunk of the car.

As Olive started the engine, Nan sat up and she said,

Mommy, where are we going?

I'm taking you to Grandma Grace's sweetheart.

Nan lay back down and closed her eyes just as she muttered,

Mommy I have to pee.

But then she fell back asleep as Olive headed down the dirt road to the highway and as she drove, she looked in the mirror to see Tim riding up in his field truck, the dust like a swirling veil masking him. His hand out the window, he was waving, but Olive didn't stop.

At the highway, Olive punched the accelerator, felt the huge engine surge, forcing her head against the head-rest. She looked at the backs of her hands, saw the crust of sweat hardened dirt caked there, and under her nails, the brown grit. She heaved a sigh and blinked away the tears and the Chrysler obeyed her and rolled into the morning heat, the sun in her eyes already burning. Seventy, then seventy-five and up to eighty.

Grace and Paul

Olive: It'll just be for a while.

Paul: What happened?

Olive: Nothing. It's nothing, really.

Paul: What do you need?

Olive: I just need to leave Nan and Toby with you for a bit.

Paul: Where are you going?

Olive: Into Wichita. It'll just be for a while, Dad.

Paul: Have you talked to your brother?

Olive: No.

Paul: You're leaving Tim. You can't keep that away from Dean. He's coming this weekend to finish up the plowing.

Olive: Dean doesn't have to know.

Paul: I'll tell him, of course. Where will you be?

Olive: I'll let you know. I'll call.

Paul: What did you tell Nan and Toby?

Olive: I told them they were going to stay with you while I'm away.

Paul: Do you need money?

Olive: Oh Dad I don't know what I need.

Paul: Stay here till you get it worked out. I'll call Tim.

Olive: Don't do that.

Paul: He has a right to know.

Olive: You can't make it better.

Paul: You think I don't worry about you?

Olive: Don't worry about me.

Paul: You're leaving your babies while you run off looking for something you think you've lost, I've got a right to worry.

Olive: You're right, I'm just so confused.

Paul: Tell me about it.

Olive: I don't know what to tell you. Last night I climbed the windmill and I thought I was going to suffocate. I can't stand being out there anymore. I don't want to be there.

Paul: Has something happened with Tim?

Olive: I'll find something in Wichita.

Paul: You've been off the job market for a long time.

Olive: Dad, please. You have to let me work this out.

Paul: What do I tell Tim when he comes asking?

Olive: I don't want him to know where I am.

Paul: He's a good man. What do I tell him?

Olive: Tell him what you want.

Paul: He will come looking for you.

Olive: He can't leave until the work's done.

Paul: I don't like it.

Olive: I need to do this before I go crazy.

~~~

Olive: I won't be gone long, sweeties. While I'm away, Grandma will take good care of you and Grandpa will take you for lemon custard ice cream every Sunday. All right?

Nan: I guess so.

Olive: Oh, don't be that way, You have to look after Toby, you know. He'll need you to help him get dressed and brush his teeth.

Nan: I don't want to look out for Toby. He's such a baby.

Olive: He's your little brother and he needs you.

Grace: Did you bring clothes, Olive? I just did the wash.

Olive: Everything is clean but what they're wearing.

Paul: Come on you kids, I've got some new bugs to show you.

Nan: Bugs? Granpa, bugs are so yucky.

Toby: I want to see them.

Nan: You always want to see them.

Grace: They'll be all right, but will you?

Olive: Let's not talk about that now.

Grace: When do we talk about it?

Olive: Mom, please.

Grace: I wouldn't pry, Olive, you know that, but you show up here out of the blue, no phone call, so what am I supposed to think?

Olive: I told Dad everything.

Grace: Well, you can tell me too.

Olive: Mom, look. I'm really confused right now. I don't know. I feel like I'm in prison and everything is closing in on me and I can't breathe with Tim hanging all over me. I just can't stand it out there. I've got to get into town for a while or something. I don't know. I have to go.

Grace: How will we reach you?

Olive: I'll let you know when I get settled.

5

Grace: Let me pack you a snack.

Olive: I don't need a snack, Mom. I don't know what I need, but it's not a snack.

Grace: Kathleen Vernon's in Wichita. I'll call her and tell her you're coming, you can stay with her. I know she won't mind.

Olive: No you won't.

Grace: What's going on here, Olive? I don't understand this.

Olive: I can't be with Tim anymore.

Grace: So, you're leaving him?

Olive: I don't know. I think so.

Grace: For good?

Olive: Probably.

Grace: Hmmm.

Olive: Don't judge me, Mom. You don't know what it's like.

Grace: Don't I? I know what it's like being alone out here with three children. I know what it's like to be trapped. I know the feeling of not being able to catch your breath at night...I know, Olive...I know.

Olive: You never said anything.

Grace: Dad and I worked it out. You have to work it out or...

Olive: Or what, Mom?

Grace: Just that—You have to make a decision, that's what I'm saying.

Janey

It was tiny, even for a studio. A small twin bed, a table and two chairs, a kitchen nook with a tiny refrigerator. The bathroom was small, a small stool, small sink, a shower stall with a clear plastic curtain on a shower ring. The whole place smelled of Lysol. She opened the window onto the sound of a motorcycle whirring by. From the third floor window, she could see across the rooftops almost to the college where she had been a student. Olive said,

I'll take it.

You don't know what I'm asking yet.

It's just a place to stay.

You a student?

Not now. I was at Newman but that was a while back.

Huh. Get mostly students at State. This place wouldn't be open except it's August.

The woman held the door. The smell of cooked onions drifted in the air.

Two hundred, she said. First and last and a hundred deposit and no cooking in the rooms.

Olive pulled out her money clip and counted out five hundred in fifties.

The woman looked at the clip and she said,

You oughtn't to carry that much cash.

I don't have a checking account, Olive said.

You gonna pay cash every month?

I'll get a checking account.

The woman shrugged, took the money and, handing Olive the key before backing out into the smell of cooked onions, she said,

There's parking behind.

Olive set her suitcase on the bed and opened it and took out the two photos that lay on top and set them on the table. She looked at the pictures of her babies—Nan in a white pinafore, Toby in a blue sailor suit, both of them smiling and perfect. She took a deep breath, let the flutter in her chest slow to a steady thump and then she got up and went out into the August heat, through the smell of the onions, and into the street.

At the corner there was a newspaper box. Olive pumped in fifty cents for a copy of the Herald and walked to the café at the end of the block. Sitting in a booth, she searched the want ads as she watched the city unfold on the street—buses, a taxi, people and she liked it. She remembered the nights on the farm when there was total silence. She remembered the blackness of the sky.

She remembered the rushing in her head as she waited for something to happen but nothing ever happened except work and sleep and the babies. She looked up as the waitress, smiling, said,

What can I do you for?

Coffee?

Black?

Okay.

One sec.

The waitress left. Olive watched her walk away, watched her hips sway and her hair move like parts of a machine working in rhythm. Her skirt was short, her blouse scooped, the tattoo on her right shoulder was a flower. She returned with a cup and a glass of water. She said.

Looking for work?

Um huh.

What do you do?

I'm good with numbers.

If I was good with numbers I wouldn't be here slinging Adam and Eve on a shingle.

What? Olive said.

Nothing. Can I get you anything else?

No thanks.

Alone, Olive ran over the ads, came to rest on a small ad for part time people at GECU. She circled it and then she drank her coffee.

Eileen

Like all banks, the GE Credit Union office was glass and steel and plastic. The minute Olive walked through the door, she felt at home as if she smelled the numbers in the air and could roll on the balance sheets and hear the music of computer keys and see the theater on the computer screens where hope and dreams piled up as dollars in checking accounts.

She let the door close behind her with a slow deliberate rush of air. She knew that when it opened again, she'd be part of something again, no longer isolated in the middle of two square miles of wheat land. And that made her feel good.

The cool air inside the office swirled around her bare legs, pushed up the tunnel of her skirt and, like a small whirlwind, cooled the growing heat of her belly, cooled the sweat on her thighs, raised goosebumps on her arms.

She headed for the desk where a black woman wearing swoopy stylish glasses with bright red frames bent down like a swan feeding at a limpid lake. Olive stood, clutch purse in hand—still hot from the sun—and she waited until the woman looked up, the glasses framing eyelids touched with a light shade of purple. Her smile was honest and open and the lips, thick and arched like cupid's bows, said,

Yes?

I'm Olive Keller. I have an interview.

Ah, Miss Keller. Have a seat, please.

The woman rose, held out a very chic hand with long red polished nails and skin that had soaked up gallons of lotion. Olive took the hand, feeling embarrassed that her own skin was callused and hard, animal-like, rough from the udders of cows she had milked, hardened by the scoop she used to muck out the chicken coop. The chic woman wearing her fashionable glasses pulled her long tapered fingers away and sat facing Olive. In a husky, pleasant voice, she said.

Well, Miss Keller, what can you do?

I have a degree in accounting from Wichita State, Olive said.

Oh yes. I see from your résumé that you worked part time.

9

For three years I kept books at the Faculty Club at Wichita State.

The woman looked over her thin lenses and she smiled. She resumed reading and then, her voice dark yet clipped, she said,

There is a hiatus in your work history, Miss Keller.

After I got my degree, I got married and we had a farm outside of Plains for eight years.

Two children. Married?

In a way.

Something to be said for being married in a way. Why do you want to work for GECU?

Taken aback, Olive hesitated, rubbing her palms against the clutch purse, feeling the heat in the body like the heat in the skin of a butchered pig and she felt ashamed for the poverty of her skirt and the cheapness of her heels and the thinness of her blouse. She said,

I need a job and I'm good with numbers. I kept the books on the farm and you know that's not easy these days.

Ah yes. All the subsidies and shorting.

It's two sections, Olive said. Twelve hundred and eighty acres.

Oh my, the woman said.

We ran cattle. We had pigs. A small herd of dairy cows as well as the wheat land. I know the farm business.

The woman pulled off her chic lenses and studied Olive like a doctor examining a specimen and she said,

Well, a credit union, such as GECU doesn't have much business with agriculture, you know. We're more connected to...

I need the job, Olive blurted out. I can use a computer.

Again the woman studied her, in slow motion this time, eyes moving from Olive's frumpy hair to the thin white blouse that showed her bra straps. Olive looked away, embarrassed, felt the heat of rejection and the fire of shame beating at her and then the woman said,

Why are you leaving?

What?

Your husband. You're leaving him, aren't you?

Olive let the rush of truth sweep over her, glad for it coming out, but it was the first time it had been said in such a clear way. Yes, she was leaving her husband. Yes she was leaving her family. No, she didn't know why. There was no point in masking it. It was there. The truth. Olive felt a wave of relief rush over her.

Yes, she said. Yes I am.

And your children? The woman asked.

They're with my Mom and Dad in Hutch.

Hutch? I see. I have family in Hutch.

Grace and Paul Malone, Olive said.

Malone. Not a name I recall.

Do I get the job? Olive said.

Well, right now, we just have a part-time position, but it's not at the window.

The window?

Tellers. Front line. Face to face with the customer.

I'll do anything, Olive said.

The woman studied her again, taking her time. Again Olive felt the calluses on her hands and the roughness of her skin and she realized that unlike the woman across from her who smelled like a sweet floral perfume, she had no scent other than the raw sweaty odor of her anxious body.

The woman smiled. Olive stood.

She half turned, the clutch purse now wet and sticky in her hands and she looked down at her feet, naked, no stockings, her toe nails broken and snagged—how had she let that happen? How had she been so careless? She felt tears break out in her eyes. The woman said.

Can you start Monday?

Olive glanced up at this woman who had walked around the desk and was smiling at her. She was very tall and lean. She wore black pumps, her legs shapely, the feet almost delicate in their finery and the sob in Olive's throat turned to Oh. Monday.

The woman held out one of her polished and lotioned hands and in her fingers, delicate as butterfly wings, there was a card. Olive read it.

Eileen Norburg. Branch Manager. Olive smiled for the first time in weeks. She waited for her skin to crack. She wanted to laugh but was afraid it would hurt. Eileen Norburg said,

GECU has a dress code, Olive.

Olive let her own name wash over her. Coming from Eileen it sounded better than when she herself said it, as if there were hope in the name.

I don't know what that means, Olive said.

It means no bare shoulders, no tattoos showing, no skirts cut above the knee, pants are all right, no spiked heels.

Olive did laugh then. Tattoos? Spiked heels? I haven't worn spiked heels since I was in college.

Didn't we all? Eileen said. And everyone has tattoos these days. Do your tattoos show, Olive?

I don't have any tattoos or any marks that you can see.

Nothing to be ashamed of? Eileen said. Tattoos seem to be the thing to do these days.

She smiled. Olive watched the white teeth flash. She knew that her own teeth were yellow—intact, filled, drilled, cared for but yellow nonetheless and she pressed her lips over her teeth and again she tasted shame. She had a long way to go. But no spiked heels, no short skirts, no bare shoulders—that was easy. Very easy.

Nails

Olive rubbed her palms against her jeans and felt the calluses snag on the fabric. Shuddering, she glanced down at her cracked fingernails and the white circle where her wedding ring had left its mark. She thought about Eileen—her soon to be boss at GECU. Eileen whose nails were long, not shattered, nails painted and fresh. Eileen whose hands were soft. Olive was ashamed of the hardness of her palms where the calluses burrowed into her skin. Glancing down the street, she remembered the Rite-Aide at the corner. She walked there, went into the cool well-lighted interior and searched out the manicure section and found a Pedi-Egg guaranteed, it read on the package, to smooth out her skin. Olive bought it.

She bought hand lotion and nail files. She bought emery boards and fingernail polish—red, the same color Eileen wore—and as she paid for it, she couldn't remember a time when she had spent money on herself. She blushed as the clerk, an Asian woman with ink black hair and pale powdered skin and fingernails as long as scythes asked if she had found everything she needed.

I'm fine, Olive said.

She grasped the sack with her new hope in it and instead of heading back to the clothing store she had passed with its mannequin in the window, she walked to the Kiowa café at the corner, sat in the far corner away from the door and she laid out the first step in her reclamation project—get rid of her calluses.

Using the Pedi-Egg, she rubbed at the palm of her left hand. The cutters caught on her skin. She pressed harder, sanding at the hard ridges, each scrape grinding away a year of farm labor until a small mound of white gritty skin lay on the table in front of her. Then she rubbed her palm over her jeans and the slickness made her smile.

She worked at her right hand, the worst one, the hand that powered the scoop, the hand she used like a tool. In her efforts, she was clumsy, unbalanced. But she kept at it until a second mound of white grainy skin lay on the table. She was proud and a little bit free as she studied the results of her work—over the years, she had lost a side of her being—it had disappeared into the prairie night, disappeared like the flatness of her belly after Toby was born.

Olive scooped the twin piles of her past into the sack. She folded it. It wasn't thick or heavy.

And then she filed and sanded her snagged nails. The nails were cracked on top. Small dark cracks full of dirt. She didn't remember wearing gloves when she cleaned the hen house, didn't recall wearing gloves when she spread the manure in the vegetable garden, but she did remember the smells of that life and as she filed and trimmed her nails changed their shape like living animals evolving so fast it was hard to keep up and then, when she had smoothed away the cracks and ragged edges, she opened the bottle of red enamel and the smell was at once sharp and hopeful because it was the scent of a new beginning.

First the left hand, each nail a project because she didn't have a routine, no ritual of self to guide her to a finish—no, she had to find out by trial and error what to do. As she finished the small nail on her left little finger, she tried to recall the last time she had anointed herself in a pleasurable moment. It must have been when she was small. She didn't remember.

Then, using her left hand, she worked her right hand and her clumsiness made her smear polish on her skin and so she wiped it off and started over but dipping the brush into the small mouth of the bottle of enamel, she knocked it over, a splash of red bleeding out onto the table.

Here, let me get that, honey.

Olive glanced up at the waitress, a woman of 30, frizzy hair, pierced ears, short sleeved tank top with a single flower tattoo in red and blue and yellow on her right shoulder. She wiped up the spill with the deft swirl of a hand towel.

I'm sorry, Olive said. I'm so clumsy.

It's okay. I'm used to cleaning up messes. I been watching you.

I'm sorry. I'll go then.

No no don't give me sorry. You don't have to do that. Things are slow right now. Besides, you're not very good at it, are you?

What?

Nails. Polish. You're not very good at it.

She sat down facing Olive and she took the nail polish and worked at it like a pro until the nails were bright and perfect. Olive said,

It's been a long time since I've worn polish.

Yeah. Took me a while to figure out what you were up to. Where you from?

Plains, Olive said.

Oh yeah. I've been through there. I've got a brother in Liberal. He's a broker

for a co-op. He brokers sales to the big mills.

Oh.

You're running aren't you?

How can you tell?

You've got that free-at-last look in your eyes.

It's that obvious? Olive said.

That long blond pony tail is a dead give-away. Can I get you something? Iced tea is good today. We brew it with mint.

That's the way I made it at home. We always had a patch of mint around the water tank.

Mint's good in tea. Let me get that tea for you.

Before you go, Olive said, I need to buy some clothes.

You live around here?

In the brick apartment house on J Street.

You're just a couple of blocks from LouAnn's shop.

LouAnn's. I walked by there the other day.

She's got a good eye for last year's fashions. I need some stuff too, so I can take you over there if you want.

That'd be nice of you. I start a new job at GECU on Monday.

Oh yeah? Sounds good. Let me get you that tea. I'm Janey, by the way.

I see that, Olive said. I'm Olive Malone.

LouAnn

She didn't set the alarm but she woke up when the sun broke through the window. For a while, in a sleep-haze, and not remembering where she was, she flung her arm out but instead of landing on a warm body, it thudded into the mattress. The sun reminded her of every morning she had waked up on the farm—early on to get ready for school, later to milk the cows before going to school, and after that, eight years of getting up, feeling the urgency of things to be done, the chores that kept the farm running.

Olive rolled onto her side in the quiet light and listened to the sounds of the city—the muffled rumble of an airplane, the whine of a motorcycle on the street, a door slamming in the building around her. She remembered the grave-like stillness of the farm at dawn, the blue moment, her father called it—when the crickets stopped chirping, the moment before the birds started their chorus—an absolute death-like stillness.

She loved the small city sounds, each one a life, a person on the move, all that motion, that excitement, people going places, doing things, getting in trouble. She kicked off the sheet, luxuriated in her nakedness—the last few nights of sleeping nude made her feel alive because at home…back on Tim's farm…Nan and Toby always found a way to burst in on her. Surprise, they shouted as they leaped on the bed.

Standing, Olive ran her hands over her naked belly, her breasts and as she did, she watched her now bright red fingernails as if they were foreign objects, hands of a stranger. She remembered Janey and how she helped paint her nails. You ought to get extensions, she'd said. You've got really nice hands. But Olive protested that Eileen Norburg wouldn't approve of long nails—the dress code.

She walked to the bathroom—the tiny bathroom with its tiny tub and shower ring and its tiny sink and toilet and she wondered if a studio apartment meant one for tiny people. In the mirror, she looked at herself. It was the first time in eight years she had watched herself naked. She fingered the faint remains of the stretch marks snaking across her belly, lines so faint if you weren't looking for them you wouldn't see them. Some women, she knew, had deep scars that never went away. She was lucky. Six years after Toby, her marks were more of a memory than a fact.

She showered fast, dried, and slipped on clean panties that she kept in her suitcase under the bed because there was no closet in the studio. She laid out her jeans, white bra, and Levi shirt with red roses embroidered on the bodice. She dressed and went out into the street.

LouAnn's Consignment shop was small. The mannequin in the window wore a different dress than the day before—a blue frock with a sequined collar. She entered.

A Mexican woman was sorting clothes at a rack. She said,

So you came back? No Janey?

She had to pull an extra shift, Olive said.

Your stuff is in that box by the fitting room, the woman said.

Olive slid the blue silk dress over her head, the silk so smooth as it draped that she shivered. She took a deep breath, felt the fabric breathe with her as if it were alive. She also felt a quickening in her belly, an excitement like fingers stroking her thighs. She shrugged out of the blue dress, let it drop to the floor at her feet and, looking in the mirror, she watched the blush rise from her throat to her face and run up into her hairline like a runaway river of red.

She looked at the body in the mirror. Her body, flat belly, full breasts. She was no longer sure it was the same body that had come into the shop with her—the quivering in her legs grew more intense. She sat on the chair breathing hard until the shaking stopped. She could not remember a time when that rush of sex had swept over her so quick and hard. And from what? The slickness of the silk on her skin?

Standing, she reached for the yellow dress and held it in front of her, the yellow dress that buttoned up the front and as she slid it on, she felt herself changing again—she remembered how it felt then—making herself beautiful and sexy and she ran her hands over the front of the dress, felt her belly. Taking off the dress, she held it in front of her and it was no longer alive, but was just a dress, a yellow dress, an object, not a lover with silken fingers.

After hanging both dresses on their hooks, she reached for the skirt, the black skirt and she stepped into it, zipped it—skirts she could handle. It was a good fit, not a second skin like the magical yellow dress, but a practical linen skirt cut to the knees so it showed nothing, just the way Eileen Norburg had suggested—"No bare shoulders," she said, "no low cut blouses, no spiked heels, no tattoos exposed." Olive turned, the black skirt fitted not too tight over her hips and she stood on tip toes to watch her legs flex. They didn't look like the legs of a woman who'd had two kids. They weren't even the legs of the woman who'd slid off her jeans a minute before. They were the shapely legs of the woman who had slipped into the silk dress and found herself with goosebumps on her arms.

And then there was a sharp rap on the door. Olive said,

Just a sec.

She took off the black skirt, caught a glimpse of her dowdy white bra, covered herself again with the Levi shirt and stepped into her jeans—501s, a man's cut, tight at the waist and cinched with a man's leather belt—that had to go, that belt.

You need any help with anything? The woman said as Olive opened the door to the fitting room.

I'm okay, Olive said.

You like that yellow dress? The woman said.

It's silk, Olive replied.

I don't know about the yellow on you. I think you'd look good in emerald. All blonds look good in emerald.

Well, whatever, but I'll need some underwear.

Hmmm. C cup, the woman said. Black to go with the darks and yellow for that dress? Sure you don't want something in emerald?

I don't know the first thing anymore Olive said.

Don't you watch TV, honey?

No. I never had time to watch TV.

Where have you been?

The woman laughed, carried the pile of dresses, blouses, and skirts to the counter where she tallied them up on a calculator.

I guess I need some stockings, too.

Stockings? You mean pantyhose.

It's been a while since I bought anything except kids' clothes and jeans.

Well, with your shape, you can wear anything you want.

I look like a lumpy sack.

Sax Fifth Avenue.

A worn out lumpy sack.

You don't look old enough to have kids.

You just say that to everybody.

Well, I might stretch the truth to make a sale, but lie?

Two kids. A girl and a boy.

Yeah. Well. Okay. Three bras, 36C, right? And half a dozen pairs of panties...

Why do they come in sets of three? Olive said. There are seven days.

Um huh. That's how they get us, isn't it?

While the woman counted, Olive watched herself in the mirror on the door. Maybe she wasn't a wreck. She rubbed her belly. Maybe it didn't pooch out as much as she thought. And her breasts. Maybe she'd be okay after all.

You're into me for two hundred and twenty dollars, the woman said.

Ohh. Olive said.

The woman looked at her. Olive smiled.

You want to cut out something? Too much?

No, it's all right.

You can trade up anytime, except for the underwear. That's yours.

Olive reached into the hip pocket of her jeans for her money clip. The woman laughed.

A money clip? I haven't seen a money clip since the air base closed.

It's practical, Olive said.

You're going to need a purse.

I have a clutch.

From your high school prom, I'll bet.

You're making fun of me.

No. Just watching you. Where are you from?

Plains. But I went to college here in Wichita.

Hmmm. Not much there in Plains.

No. A drugstore. A barber shop. A gas station. Feed store and a new Wal-Mart but that's outside of town.

Yeah, Wal-Mart's everywhere now.

Olive counted out two hundred and twenty dollars. Two fifties, six twenties. The woman wrapped the clothing in two bags and slid them across the counter.

The woman said, Like I told you, you can trade up if you want.

I start a new job on Monday, Olive said.

Good luck. Olive, right?

Olive Malone, Olive said. She felt the rush come again. Malone. Not Keller. No longer Keller, just Malone.

Well, Olive Malone, we get new consignments every week if you need anything else.

Olive left the shop with her two bags and walked back to her studio. All she needed now was a couple of pairs of shoes. Sensible shoes like the pumps Eileen Norburg wore. Maybe three pairs. She was happy. She felt light. She felt free. She had just spent two hundred and twenty dollars on herself. The first time in eight years she'd bought more than one item at a time for herself. And colored underwear. She had never owned colored underwear. All her undies were white and all the elastic was worn out but still she wore them. All the stretch was gone from her bras making her sag and her legs had been bare for so long she had forgotten what stockings— no pantyhose—felt like. Her breath came easy as she walked on the balls of her feet, her hips swinging with a new, fresh rhythm.

In the studio, she tossed her packages down and stripped naked and pulled out the new bras and the new panties and unwrapped them from their plastic and she tried on black panties and a black bra and she stared at herself—She was enormous—she stood out like a statue—what would Eileen Norburg think of that? She embarrassed even herself with the brazen thrust. She closed her eyes. When she opened them, she saw herself still there, still thrusting. The cut of the panties was so skimpy that strands of her pubic hair stuck out from the legs. Olive gasped. She had pubic hair. She had forgotten she had pubic hair. She had forgotten she was a woman. But in the mirror, she was just that—a woman—and there was a lot of her.

Nineteen

Wow, honey, Janey said, you really did it. Talk about a change.

You like it?

A lot of guys like the pony tail 'cause it gives them something to hang on to.

What?

Nothing. I really like the new 'do. Not too short, not too long. Kind of foxy.

Olive patted at her hair and blushed. She couldn't remember anyone ever calling her foxy. She stirred the iced tea. Janey sat opposite her and wiped at the table with a clean white cloth. She said,

So, now that you're the New Olive with a brand new 'do and hot sexy clothes, you want to go out on Saturday?

Go out?

You know. Out. Dancing. Drinking. Slumming.

I don't know, Olive said.

Hey, sweetheart, look at you. Blushing. I play for the home team.

What?

Oh god, you are so pure. You know what a lesbian is?

Yeah.

Okay. I'm not one. And you don't have anything else to do, so let's go. I've got some places where I go hunting and with you as bait, I shouldn't have any trouble.

Hunting? What do you mean by hunting?

You really are just fresh off the farm, aren't you?

Janey frowned and pursed her lips. Olive fidgeted with her tea glass and then she smiled and said,

Why not.

That's the ticket. Look, I gotta get back to work. Can I get you something to go with the tea?

A salad, Olive said.

A salad. Gotta watch that figure, right? Don't worry, sweetheart, you could eat a horse and it wouldn't show. God I wish I had a figure like that.

Salad it is.

Olive sat looking at the nails on her hands. Then she opened her purse and took out the compact and studied her face in the mirror. Touching her lips, her eyebrows. Bait. And then she took out the two snapshots of Nan and Toby and leaned them against the sugar bowl. Janey came back with the salad. She said,

Those your babies?

Nan and Toby, Olive said. Nan is eight, Toby will be five.

Cute, Janey said. They look like you.

They're with my Mom and Dad.

Where's that?

Outside of Hutchinson. They have some ground there.

So, when are you bringing them here?

Olive scooped up the photos and returned them to her purse and jabbed a fork into the cherry tomato on top of the lettuce. She said,

I don't know. Do you have kids?

I don't want kids, Janey said. I don't have time for kids.

I wasn't ready to have kids, Olive said. I kind of fell into it but if you wait till you are ready, you probably won't never have them.

Yeah, well, I'll wait, Janey said. I got too much living to do. So we're on for Saturday?

Sure, Olive said. What time? Eight?

Eight? Nothing worth doing starts till midnight. I'll come over to your place around 11:30.

That late?

What? You need your beauty rest? Come on, you look nineteen. You really had two kids?

Beef

Just look at you, honey, Janey said. In a dress like that you're only gonna snag middle-aged perverts.

How do you want me to dress? Olive said.

Do you have anything...shorter? Tighter? You know, show me some skin?

Where is this place we're going? Olive said.

The Tomb, Janey said.

The Tomb? I don't know...

You gotta break loose kiddo, Janey said. See?

She twirled, her high heels like black spikes. Olive saw her tattoo—a single flower in blue and red and yellow.

Come on, Janey said, what do you have to lose?

All right, Olive said.

She opened her suitcase and spread out her skirts and blouses, the panties and the pantyhose. She said,

Show me.

Janey picked through the pile of clothing and came up with the short denim skirt and a blouse. She said,

This the best you've got?

The rest is for work.

At least this shows a little thigh.

I'm not bait, Olive said.

Sure you are. Put it on, it's better than the dress.

Why?

You'll see, Janey said. Just do it.

Olive took the blouse and skirt and went to the tiny bathroom and slid out of the yellow dress and stepped into the denim skirt and pulled on the blouse and fluffed at her hair and returned to Janey who sat on the bed, legs crossed.

Olive saw the floral tattoo on her bare thigh half covered by the hem of her short skirt. It was the pink freesia with a butterfly on it.

How's this? Olive said.

Now you're cookin'—You've got beautiful skin. We'll get you something better tomorrow and a real pair of high heels.

Olive drove. Janey guided her to an industrial section of the city out by the airport. Olive parked her Chrysler on the street in front of a building with a sign in red neon that flashed in a slow beat—The Tomb. Unsure, Olive gripped the wheel and looked at Janey who raised her eyebrows and got out. Olive followed. Janey led her to the door and knocked with a huge brass eagle's claw. Janey said,

They don't let just anybody in. Ohh, they'll eat you up, doll. God, I love your skin.

She touched Olive's bare shoulder sending a chill up into her hair. The door opened. A huge man in black barred the way. He was close to seven feet tall. Arms, thick as hams, splashed from wrist to shoulder with a lurid tattoo of snakes intertwined with the stretched out body of a naked woman. Riding on his beefy shoulder there was a motorcycle where another nude woman with unnatural pointed breasts lay spread eagled on the seat.

Hey Janey, the man said. Long time no see.

His voice was deep, cavernous. He stood aside, one huge hand planted in the middle of Janey's back.

This is my friend Olive, Janey said.

Uh huh, he said. Five bucks.

Give him five, honey, Janey said.

Olive dug out a bill from her sling purse and handed her money to the big man who raked her up and down with his eyes until she felt like a specimen on a pin. He closed the door and planted a hand in the middle of Olive's back just as Janey grabbed Olive's hand and pulled her down a dark stairwell into the throb of music unlike anything Olive had known before—a deep driving beat, loudness cut by high pitched guitar screeches like animals in pain and under the beat a chorus of voices chanted and on the dance floor bodies—all bathed in the red hue of overhead lights that flashed and flickered and in flickering turned the bodies first blood red then ash gray.

Olive felt another chill run up her back as Janey led her through the pulsating throng to a bar where the bartender—a woman with long straight hair—leaned on the top, her breasts leaping out of a tight leather bodice, her arms and neck ringed with tattoos and in her nose a gold ring. She shouted,

Janey, honey, where've you been?

You know, Janey sang out. This is my friend Olive. First time in the Tomb.

I can tell, the bartender said.

What? Janey said.

I can tell. She's a virgin.

Janey laughed. She said to Olive,

She sees all that unmarked skin, honey, and she knows you're pure. We gotta do something about that.

I don't know, Olive said. I don't know if I should stay.

And then Janey took Olive's arm and led her out into the sea of leather and skin and metal and tattoos and men with shaved heads and women in short leather skirts and black heels, bodies glued together in groups of two, three, four bobbing and weaving and Janey, facing Olive, raised her hands over her head and in the beat of the music Olive's head was spinning and she tasted thick smoke that was unlike anything she knew and the odors rising from the sweaty bodies around her were something she couldn't name, musky odors, oily, sticky, and Olive panicked. She felt dizzy, floating, cut loose the way she had been on the windmill platform in the dark, close to the edge, about ready to let go but then a pair of hands circled her waist and spun her and Janey was gone and in her place stood a tall man wearing dark glasses and a black leather vest, arms bare, tattooed, belly flat, muscled, wet with sweat. His lips were pierced with gold rings and in his ears, a line of gold studs marched from lobe to the tops and he pulled Olive against him and she smelled the scent of a man unlike anything she had smelled before—an animal odor, raw and yet sweet, hot and yet soothing and before she could stop herself she pressed into him and his hands played over her hips and he thrust against her and he was hard and big and his hands on her butt spread her legs and she was embarrassed for needing him and he held her to his body and she felt faint and limp and her head was still spinning, still floating and she was on the edge again but she was afraid to let go and then he leaned into her and kissed her neck and again the chill swept over her and she expected him to bite her, to suck her blood and then, she did let go, ready for anything, but he just looked at her, a half smile on his lips, and he backed away leaving her alone on the floor and she felt a hand on her back and she turned to face Janey who held out a glass, and as she took the drink, she heard Janey whisper in her ear,

Well, doll, you just lost your cherry.

Leading Olive to a booth, Janey sat her down and raised her glass and she said,

Let's drink to your initiation, babe.

Initiation into what?

You're one of his bitches, Janey said. He'll have you up against the wall next time so short skirt, no panties.

Are they smoking dope?

Dope? Janey said. They smoke just about anything that grows from a seed. If you're not high by now, you'll never make it. It's called a contact high. That's what your five covers.

They're all pierced, Olive said. Are you?

Janey took Olive's hand and slid it between her legs. She wore no panties. The skin between her legs was moist and slick, no pubic hair at all. Olive's fingers tangled in two metal rings, and she looked at Janey's glittering half-closed eyes in the red twinkling light.

Withdrawing her hand, Olive said,

I have to go pee.

Janey pointed to a hallway. Olive got up, went to the door with Crones on it, right beside the door with Grave Diggers on it. Standing, she slid her hand, still wet with Janey's moisture, between her legs and she too was dripping, so wet that fluids ran down her thighs and she touched herself, a light touch and she shuddered and closed her eyes and doubled over, her hand nested there in the heat and her breath came in sharp gasps and she was on the windmill again, spinning and spinning, dizzy, falling in a spiral and then she opened her eyes, looked at her reflection in the mirror. Her hands quivered, her knees trembled, the rush was a sensation she didn't know well though she knew what it was but it had been a long time since it had happened to her and it amazed her that it had happened here, in this way, but she knew things were different now, things had changed. Without washing her hands, Olive went back to the bar, to Janey still in the booth where a man now sat beside her, one arm around her shoulders, a hand between Janey's legs and Janey was smiling and nestled against him and her legs were open.

And then, Olive noticed that the music had changed. The lights had changed. The smells had changed and she no longer was afraid. She sat next to Janey, close, feeling the heat of Janey's body and Janey turned to her, her eyes dreamy and wet, a smile on her lips.

This is Kit, Janey said. He wants to take me home. You wanna make it a three-some?

After the Tomb

For a while after the evening at The Tomb, Olive didn't see Janey while but she did go back to LouAnn's where she found a short black skirt, a low cut blouse that showed the tops of her breasts—and she bought a pair of bright red high heels that at first were hard to walk in but once she got the hang of it, made her feel tall and alive and long and ready for anything. She avoided the café and started packing her own lunch. After work she came home to her tiny studio and showered and ate and looked at the pictures of Nan and Toby that she had pinned to the wall over the bed. She went to sleep sometimes dreaming about Nan and Toby, sometimes dreaming about Janey and Kit and in the dream they were naked and Olive was ashamed of herself as the images of her babies melded with the bodies in The Tomb and when she woke up, the pictures were always there and she thought she should take them down.

She remembered Janey telling her she had a lot of living to do and she had a lot to learn because she had lived a sheltered life with the cows and the chickens and the pigs and if what she said was true, she was right to leave Tim to his acreage because, Janey said, "You were just a head of livestock to him. A breeder if ever there was one."

Olive thought about Janey, but she didn't want to see her because seeing her reminded Olive of her orgasm standing in front of the mirror, reminded her of finding Janey with Kit, reminded her of the invitation to make it a threesome and why did she say no to that? What was a threesome? She could imagine what it meant and at that moment she had been afraid, watching Janey and Kit, watching his hands on her, watching Janey like a well-trained cow at the touch of a milker didn't shy away, but seemed to relish the touch as it made her blush and squirm.

Day after day, she came home from work carrying groceries, sometimes take-out, sometimes just a sandwich that she picked up in the store across the street from GECU.

One night after she showered and ate and went to bed but she didn't dream about Nan and Toby because the dream had changed and Janey was the one standing by the table and Olive was the one sitting with Kit's hand

27

on her leg, his fingers in her and it was Olive saying it was time for a threesome, and there she woke up and she was gushing wet between her legs and she was flushed and she realized that she had orgasmed again.

The more often she dreamed it, the more exciting it became and one Friday night, after work, two weeks after The Tomb, Olive came home with her sandwich and her potato salad and roll with its pat of butter and she ate and showered and then she pulled out her suitcase with her clothes from LouAnn's and she tried on the black skirt that cut her at mid-thigh, showing a lot of skin as Janey said, and she pulled on the blouse with the tight bodice that she couldn't wear to work and she looked at herself in the mirror.

She liked what she saw.

Hair cut asymmetrical and spiked, very modern, very chic.

It made her look ten years younger, the cutter had said, made her look very hot and sexy, Janey had said. Olive dabbed perfume behind her ears and she slipped into a pair of her colored panties—not panty hose—and she stepped into her new red high heels that made her legs look longer.

Picador

Leaving the studio, she got in the Chrysler and drove. She had no idea where she was going and she didn't care.

She drove until she came to a bar where the lot was full of BMWs and Porsches and Mercedes Benz and she parked her Chrysler and checked her face in the rear view mirror, dabbing at her lips. She stroked her cheeks—Janey was right—her skin didn't need much. Hers was skin that worked like bait, skin silky and smooth even after years in the sun on the farm.

And then, she went inside.

The music was soft, the lights softer. In the bar, a dozen tables scattered around. No skin, no tattoos, no leather skirts and open vests. No outrageous stilettos, no pierced lips or noses or tongues. Olive sat at the bar and ordered a Picador although she had no idea what a Picador was until she asked the bartender—a boy of 25—what his favorite drink for a single woman was, and he eyed her cleavage and smiled and brought her the Picador. She sipped it, tasted the bite of rum, the minty flavor of the crème de menthe. He said,

You like it?

It's good, Olive said.

Without the rum, it's a Stinger. You're new here.

Just slumming, Olive said.

He laughed. He said,

Yeah, well, you bring a lot of class to this slum.

Looking in the mirror, Olive watched herself sipping the drink. And then, she saw him watching her. Two stools down, one elbow on the bar, hand on his chin. Olive turned to face him, crossed her legs as he moved to the stool beside her. Leaning in, he said,

I haven't seen you in here before.

I haven't been in here before.

Can I buy you a drink?

I have a drink.

A girl like you needs at least two at a time, he said. He called the bartender and held out two fingers and pointed at Olive's glass.

29

It's a Picador, Olive said. Made with rum.

I like rum, and Picador is right up my alley.

The bartender said it's a woman's drink.

If that woman's hot for a bullfighter.

So you're a bullfighter? Olive said.

He smiled at her then, and, raising his glass to look through the clear pink liquor, he said,

Well, I know that if you mess with the bull, you get the horn.

Olive laughed. And already her head was spinning. She looked at him. He was tall, muscled with wavy black hair and very white teeth. He wore a pair of black slacks, a red shirt open at the neck. A gold chain blinked like a flashing beacon in the V of the shirt. Olive felt the gush between her legs and she remembered why she came there—this is a pickup, a man picking her up in bar, a man buying her a drink. He was talking to her, but she wasn't listening and then the bartender brought two more Picadors and Olive sipped at hers while he talked and she didn't listen but then after the third drink, Olive said,

I better be going.

She stood. Faced him. His hand settled in the small of her back and he led her out of the bar to a BMW parked at the curb.

My car is somewhere, Olive said.

Yeah. I'm sure it is.

He leaned her against the BMW and kissed her mouth, a light kiss, a test kiss and then Olive drove into him, hungry for what he had to offer her, having no idea where it was going or when or where, but he ground his body against hers and he whispered in her ear,

There's a place just down the street, Okay?

She nodded yes, head reeling. She felt giddy and free. She was doing what she wanted to do and he opened the door and she got in and he drove.

~~~

The motel was clean. Simple. It smelled of bleach.

under the skirt and she sucked in her breath as his fingers touched her and it wasn't Tim, it wasn't anything she'd ever felt before and her heart pounded and she bit her lip as he whispered,

Son of a bitch, you're just one wet mama. You want it, huh? You really want it.

Olive did want him in her right then.

She remembered Janey in the Tomb, Janey with her legs open and Kit's hands on her and Olive's need was so great she tore at his shirt as he scooted her skirt up to her waist.

30

Hey hey, he said. He laughed and he spun her around and pushed her down on the bed, her skirt up to her waist and he lapped at her between her legs, and she had never felt that electric before and his hands ran over her, under her blouse, under the elastic of the bra and he muttered Jesus, you taste like candy and Olive was at him again, biting him, hands grasping at his hair, her nails digging into him and he met her more than half way and the flood between her legs turned to a river and she was open, wide open, aching and open and hungry and he said Jesus Christ, what planet are you from and then he was in her, driving hard into her and she erupted, coming so hard her back arched until she ached and still she wanted more and again she came and still wanting more she clawed at him again and her legs wrapped around him squeezing, drawing him into her until she felt like he was going to disappear and then he sat up, breathing heavy, and pulled away from her and he said,

Look every guy wants a nympho, but you're one crazy bitch, aren't you? You'd eat a man's heart and not say boo. Okay. You got what you need, now it's my turn.

He rolled her onto her stomach and spread her legs and she didn't expect what he did next. She was so wet, so hungry, so on fire that she wasn't sure just when he penetrated her, she wasn't sure just what he was doing until the stab of pain in her bottom froze her and then he was grunting and heavy on her and she felt his sweat dripping on her naked back and she felt the beat of the gold chain slapping against her, so rough, as if there were sharp blades cutting into her, the scent of his cologne got stronger the harder he hammered into her and then he fell onto her, sticky and wet and reeking and he growled in her ear, his breath tangy, sharp with the residue of three Picadors.

You like that? You like taking it in the back door?

Olive gave in to the fullness, realizing what had happened, realizing why she ached, realizing that the fullness was the weight of him inside her. She, tried to free herself, but he said,

Oh no, you don't go anywhere till I get what I came for.

He held her then, arms pinned, pressing her into the bed, nailed down until he faded and the fullness went away.

She closed her eyes.

He got up. She heard him dressing.

Still lying on her stomach, Olive said,

Do you have a name?

Anonymous Sex, he said.

Do you want to know who I am?

Tell you what I know—I got what I came for, that's what I know.

You make a habit of that?

I'm a back-door man, he said. Yeah. Every chance I get. Wide-open bitch like you walks in, I can smell her a mile away. Tell what—you're the hottest lay I ever dragged outa that dive.

Do you have to talk like that?

Like you're the virgin princess who didn't know she was gonna get it?

Do you talk like that to all the women you do this to?

Just the sluts on the prowl.

She rolled onto her side to see him buttoning his shirt, tucking the gold chain inside the V of the red shirt. He slipped on his shoes. It was then that Olive noticed they were penny loafers that kicked off easy, slid on fast. He didn't say good bye. He left her on the bed. At first she was numb and she was floating and the bed throbbed and she felt nothing under her as if she were hanging on hot air but then she got up, wobbling as she touched the floor and went to the shower. She didn't look at herself in the mirror. In the hot water, she scrubbed. She washed her hair, scraped her skin with her nails. In the steam she smelled his cologne sticking to her. Spreading her legs, she touched herself where he had taken her and the twinge of pain made her bite her lips but it wasn't an unpleasant pain, more a jab of shame and she didn't know why. She didn't cry as she soaped her body and rinsed away the smell of his cologne. Standing in the hot running water, she peed and watched the stream leave her body, swirl around her feet. Drying off, she remembered her car. She knew she'd have to walk to her car. In the red high heels, it would be a long walk.

Tim

She leaned her head against the seat, head spinning. The burning sensation between her legs aroused her—the fullness was still there and now she needed to pee again—bad. Too many Picadors. Hand trembling, she got out, locked the car. She locked it now even after short trips to the store or to work. She remembered days on the farm leaving the windows open, keys in the ignition. No one ever touched it.

Headed for the door, she saw the pickup angled into the curb the way they did it in the small towns—and she knew it was Tim.

She stopped, making up her mind about whether to run or to wait. The burning in her bladder made the decision for her. She watched him get out of the truck as she unlocked the apartment door. He walked to her as she stepped into the foyer. He got to the door just a second before it closed. Olive turned to face him.

The first thing she noticed was his size. He was larger than she remembered, taller and wider and his shoulders were broader. He wore boots, his signature yellow cowboy boots with the rosettes cut into them. Boots that gave him added height. He held out a hand. He said,

Hello, Olive.

Tim, she said.

I called Grace and Paul. They're wondering.

Olive felt the urge to pee getting stronger along with the burning in her bottom. She clasped her thighs together. Climbing the stairs, she felt him behind her, matching her step for step. She let him in and then, dropping her purse on a chair, she dashed to the bathroom and closed the door.

The urgency left her and as she sat on the toilet, she remembered, years before, when, sometimes, after making love, Tim stood naked in the doorway to watch her, sometimes laughing at her for the way she folded the paper, wet it with a spot of water, a habit she still had, one that was part of her. She stood, stepped out of her panties that were wet and still smelled of sex, the odor of her body mingled with the scent of the man with the gold chain.

She soaked the panties in water, wrung them out, hung them on the shower ring then looked at herself in the mirror. She fluffed her hair, curled it under, then went back to the living room where Tim stood, hat in hand.

He looked gaunt and worn. She did not want to see him. She was impatient with him being there. She wanted to ignore him, as if by ignoring him she could dissolve him, turn him into dust, scrub him from her mind but he loomed very large over her and for a moment she felt insignificant. She said,

You talked to Mom and Dad?

Um huh, he said. They told me you hadn't called in a while. They told me the kids are asking when you're coming back.

Why did you do that, Tim?

They're my kids too, Olive.

Don't start, she said. I'm tired.

Are you drunk?

A little.

And dressed like that. Where've you been?

Out.

It's two o'clock.

She glared at him and he looked away and cleared his throat. He raised his eyebrows as he tracked back to her and then, waving his hand, he said,

Not much of a place you've got here.

It's just right.

Look, Olive. I know it's over between us. But the kids. Good god, you can't just run off and leave them.

Are they okay?

I don't understand that. What did I do? I mean, what did I say to burn you so bad?

I'm working now, Tim.

And that takes care of everything?

Almost.

Do you need money?

I don't need your money. I need to go to bed and get some sleep.

I had to hire a couple of hands to help me get the pigs to auction and a Mexican woman to clean the house.

Why are you here, Tim? Olive said again.

She sat down, smelled the odor clinging to her and in crossing her legs remembered she had no panties on. She shuddered. She had never sat down and crossed her legs while wearing no panties.

She squeezed her thighs tight, and looked up at Tim still standing, hat still in his hand. She noticed the circles under his eyes, deep purple pools of pain that oozed out of him and she hardened then, as the pity rose up in her and she had to bite her tongue to keep from calling to him.

I can't do it alone, Olive, he said. I can't farm and raise two kids by myself.

They'll be all right with Mom and Dad until I get settled.

You think that's fair?

They're five and eight, Tim.

I mean to Mom and Dad, Tim said. They're too far on to handle two little ones.

I'll take care of that when I'm ready.

Sure. You'll take care of it. What do I tell them?

I'll call.

You're going to bring them here? Not much here for two kids, Olive.

I'm working part-time, Tim, Olive said. When I get full time, I'll find a bigger place and I'll bring them here.

You're gonna manage that staying out till all hours? That's no way...

Don't try to herd me, Tim, Olive said. I don't want to herded. I'm not a cow or a horse or a pig.

Nan's gotta go to school in a month, Olive. And Toby's gotta start kindergarten. You think Mom can handle all that?

They're kids, Tim. I know that.

You're not acting like you know.

What do you expect?

I wish I knew but it looks like you abandoned your babies, Olive. How can a woman do that and still call herself a woman?

Is that why you're here? To remind me of that?

I'm out there sweating and I come in and you're gone. I didn't know what to think. You didn't tell Mom and Dad anything, you just dump the kids and take off and they're all worried, Jesus, hon, you don't just expect them to take care of our kids like that. They've been through it already.

I told you, I'll take care of things.

Well, you're not making much headway there, are you?

Olive watched him, saw the circles of sweat in his armpits, the beads of sweat on his face. She stood, walked to the window, slid it open and then turned on the small fan that blew a stream of warm air into the room.

I'm not coming back, Tim.

Aw, it's not so bad, is it?

I wear a skirt every day. I wear a blouse, high heeled shoes, and nylons. People call me Miss. I dress like a woman, not like a field hand. I haven't milked a cow in months and I haven't scooped wheat until my back hurts. That's why I'm not going back.

You got nothing here.

I had nothing out there. You were smothering me, Tim.
What do I tell Mom and Dad?
Tell them I'll call.
It's a long drive back tonight.
You can't stay here, Tim.
What?
I said You can't stay here.
You think that's why I'm here?
I don't care, why you're here, Tim. I just don't care.

Strawberry

She came awake in the heat sweating, short of breath. Lying on her side, she looked at a window smeared with dust and grease—a window as clouded as her brain. She lay there on the bed, waiting, not yet knowing where or when or who or what had happened. As her head cleared, she got flashes of where—a bar. A flutter of when—Saturday night. A flash of who—and there was a dark face, a sunburnt face with no eyes, no ears, no nose—just a mouthful of orange teeth, teeth the color of a Kansas sunset. And behind the face there was a blackness.

She slid off the bed, her feet landing on a gritty, cold, worn out linoleum with its color ground down to asphalt patches where shoes had walked—where were her shoes? And she said, Oh my god.

Her clothes were heaped on a chair beside the bed—the red skirt, the white blouse, pantyhose draped over the blouse like a long dead black worm. High heels spilled on their sides under a chair. She hunched her shoulders.

She didn't remember undressing, she didn't remember kicking off the shoes but it must have been in a hurry.

In a mirror, in a bathroom the color of a gray dream, she looked at herself. Her eye shadow was smeared. Her lips were raw and red. On her neck, she saw a red mark—teeth?—and at the top of her left breast, just above the nipple a deep splotchy bruise. She ran water in a rusty sink and smelled the sulfur in the water. She didn't drink. She splashed water on her face. The water was tepid, slow running, almost thick to her touch. She looked again at her face in the mirror. The silvering was long gone so her reflection was spotty, parts of her missing, her neck half there, her right shoulder gone as if a huge mouth that bitten off a chunk of her flesh. She covered her face with her hands and took a deep breath and then she returned to the chair, to her clothes and as she lifted the blouse, a hundred dollar bill fluttered free, rising then falling like a green breath. She snatched at it, felt a rush of heat rising from her body, burying the shame. Pantyhose, blouse, skirt—where were her panties? Again she muttered, Oh my god. She dressed.

The skirt seemed too loose, the blouse too daring. Her purse. She had a purse. She knew she had a purse. And then, under the bed, poking out from the iron frame, under the gray mattress with its twisted sheet and flat pillow, she saw her purse. She stooped to pick it up and she smelled herself—a scent she knew, a scent with its own history, a scent that in a few hours had turned rotten, and again the rush of shame spread over her— not because of what she had done, she knew what she had done, but because she couldn't remember with whom, she couldn't remember when, and she didn't want to remember where. The odor from between her legs was truth. Undeniable.

She stood.

She wanted to cry, but only a dry cough escaped from her throat, a hard hacking that she knew was the first hint of revulsion. She fled to the bathroom, to the toilet with no seat, and kneeling she vomited and even her own vomit smelled of shame and she tasted the residue of sex and smelled then the tincture of deodorant and fluids and sweat and the perfume she had smeared like a lure on her body—when? Saturday night. And in the smell, she saw the truth and for a moment, she considered just staying there, on her knees, over the toilet, until someone found her, until she died, until her corpse, bloated and rotted, was turned over to a coroner who would measure her worth by the fat in her belly.

She left the room. 306, it said. Third floor where? She walked barefoot, holding her high heels that now felt heavy and stupid instead of trim and neat the way they had felt when she first put them on. The corridor was rugless, dim lights cast orange sprays of light onto worn wood and at the landing, she waited, heard a cough from below. She glanced at her wrist, at the watch that read 5:30, its digital truth screaming at her.

5:30 Sunday morning?

She walked to the first floor, the sound of the wooden stairs grinding at her nerves, through an ascending cloud of cigar smoke and at the front desk, she saw a huge woman with frizzy blond hair and strawberry lips smoking a long black cigar without looking up as if she had grown used to the night trash—a woman barefoot and sick coming down alone, but when Olive reached the door, the woman said,

See you sweetheart.

She laughed a deep, throaty, diabolical laugh like someone who's seen it all and just waits for the innocent ones to fall. Turning, Olive said,

Where am I?

Well, sweetheart, if you don't know, who in the fuck does?

Did I come in alone?

The blond woman sneered.

I need to know, Olive said.

38

We all need to know something.

Please, Olive said, just tell me.

Oh for crissake. Let me look at you.

The blond woman lumbered to her feet and crooked a finger at Olive and Olive sidled up to the desk and she smelled the cigar stronger now and she smelled the odor of a huge fat woman who couldn't wash in all the creases and crevices of her huge body and the smell was sickening but close up, Olive saw the caring in the woman's eyes—pity? Trust? A motherly charm?—and she leaned both hands, huge hands with pudgy fingers, on the desk and she hunched forward and she said,

Oh yeah, you came in around midnight.

Alone?

No, sweetheart, you weren't alone.

Oh god, Olive said.

The blood rushed again to her face and her tongue swelled thick and hard and she looked at the fat woman's eyes and saw the pity there and she saw a woman who knew shame and sin and the fat woman said,

I'm sorry.

Did you see him? Do you know him? Did I know him?

There was two of'em both named Smith. Do you need a glass of water, sweetheart? You're kind of peaked.

Olive looked up and she saw the smile, a real honest smile. She said,

I don't know what I need.

You better get some help, sweetheart, you get lost again, you might not find your way back.

Olive left the hotel, didn't turn back to see the name, didn't want to know the name. She wanted the place and the bed and the fat woman to disappear. And then she stopped. Her car. Where was her car? She had a car, a Chrysler. A green Chrysler and she remembered driving it to the bar...which bar? She hobbled then into her high heels, the obnoxious high heels that hurt her feet but which she had bought because they made her legs look longer. Wobbling, she continued walking in the early morning light down a deserted street in a part of town she didn't know.

Sheila

The door opened sweeping in muggy air. Olive glanced up to see a tall thin red-headed woman wearing summer black—black short skirt, black voile blouse over a black bra and she wore black high heels but her legs were bare. She pulled off the chic sunglasses Olive had seen in a magazine and laid them on the desk by the door. She opened a black leather purse and using the pen at the desk, filled out a deposit slip.

Olive studied her from behind. She was bent over the desk. The sun breaking through the glass cast her in a golden aura. Then, she turned to face Olive and there was a flash of recognition followed by a puzzled look.

Olive went back to her stacks of paperwork—checking the tabs and entries, recording notes, deposits, and withdrawals as she looked for the smallest errors that always crept in—a transposed 1, a 3 read as an 8, a 9 as a 7. That was her strength, Eileen Norburg said, finding those small errors that added up at the end of the day.

Olive glanced up to see the woman in black standing in front of her desk, a sheaf of bills in her hand and the dark glasses crooked over a finger.

Hello, she said.

Yes?

It is you, isn't it? Olive Malone? The name plaque says Olive Malone.

Olive was shocked and pleased and she stood scattering a stack of slips on her desk. She said,

Oh my god.

I thought it was you. Sheila Masterson...Anderson...Remember?

Olive walked around the desk to put her arms around the woman she hadn't seen in ten years.

You look wonderful, Sheila said. You haven't added one year to that face—how do you do it?

Me? Olive said. You look like you just graduated from high school.

Oh come on. This face? I'm a million years old at least. How...what in the world are you doing here?

Just a part time thing, Olive said.

40

I didn't know you were even in town and I'll never forgive you for not calling me.

I've just moved back.

And Tim? Sheila said. Where are you hiding that hunk?

Olive circled Sheila's waist and guided her to a corner of the office beside the Xerox machine and she studied Sheila's face, caught the small etched lines at the corners of her eyes, the slight twist of sadness in her lips. She said,

I'd love to chat, but there's no time right now.

Let's get together, Sheila said. We can catch up. I can hardly wait to hear what you've been up to.

I can tell you're prospering, Olive said.

All appearances are lies, Olive. Oh my. This is such a thrill.

I really should get back, Olive said.

Oh I understand. Look. There's that French pastry shop out by the college. Do you remember?

The Éclair.

It's still there and the éclairs are still as fattening but now they're added espresso—it seems to be the next phase.

I remember.

Well, meet me after work...Ah...I can't today. So excited to see you though...Can't make it tonight but tomorrow? Saturday? You don't work on Saturday, do you?

I get off at noon.

Perfect. Just perfect.

Olive shooed Sheila to the door, hand in the middle of her back and she stood at the glass watching her get into a bright red Audi with a convertible top. Sheila waved as she drove away. Olive took a deep breath, then returned to her desk.

Eileen Norburg came to her, stood by her chair. She said,

Is Mrs. Masterson is a friend of yours?

From college, Olive said. We were roommates for a year.

Her husband finances a lot of his cars through the Credit Union.

Oh. He...

Runs a car dealership. Several actually. He's a good customer.

So you didn't mind?

Heavens no. It's good for business to work with people you know. I see there's more to you, Olive Malone, than you let out.

You mean do I have a secret life?

I'd be surprised if you didn't, Eileen said.

Catching Up

The first thing Olive noticed was Sheila's hair. Gone was the fashionable asymmetrical cut, gone was the red tint. In its place a wig that looked expensive, human hair expensive, the color of honey. Olive felt uneasy. Sheila looked graceful, her hands music on the table in front of her, her nails long and pointed and painted. Sheila smiled when Olive sat down. She said,

My god, it's you. I couldn't believe it when I saw you and you haven't changed one bit. So tell me, what are you doing back in Wichita?

Sheila patted at her wig with slender fingers and then said,

Before you ask, it is a wig. I have a dozen of them. It's my one absolute necessity these days.

A wig, Olive said. I remember you were raven-haired.

Raven-haired. I haven't been raven-haired for a long long time. The radiation killed every follicle on my head and would you believe I have nothing left—down there.

Down there?

She glanced up and around then leaned forward to whisper,

No pubic hair. It all fell out and it's never coming back. I'm one of the rare ones who stays that way and I have to live with it that way.

You had cancer, Olive said. I had no idea,

Have cancer, you sweet thing. I have cancer. It never goes away even when it's gone because your life is changed forever. You have no choice. Mine is uterine cancer. I went to the tumor review and saw the resected— the surgeons call it resection—uterus, it looked like mother of pearl.

I don't understand that, Olive said.

The tumor—when most people think of the tumor they think of a watermelon, but mine was a thin coral pink little gift from the cancer god. But enough about me. Tell me what you're doing and how did you get on at GECU?

Olive started to speak but the waiter came to the table. Sheila wanted a Danish and milk, would that be all right? And Olive said yes but coffee instead of milk and Sheila said she couldn't drink orange juice because acid is bad for cancer. You see, she added, once you're in the cancer club, you're a life-time member.

When the waiter was gone, Olive said,

I left Tim and I needed a job and I found part-time work at GECU. But I'm looking for something permanent and full time.

Oh my goodness, Sheila said. I thought you two were the perfect couple. Did he cheat on you?

Why do you say that?

They all cheat, don't they?

No, nothing like that, Olive said. I used to have big dreams, Sheila. But with Tim they just disappeared and I woke up and found myself ten years later on a farm with two babies and a husband who smells of diesel oil at night. I might as well be one of his pigs or a cow for the way he treats me. So I had to get away and Wichita seemed like a good place to start over and here I am. Ta-da

Oh my, Sheila said.

I feel awful talking about myself after what you're going through.

I'll survive, Sheila said. You and Tim had two babies?

Nan and Toby, Olive said. I left them with my Mom and Dad on the farm.

Wise move. This city is no place for children.

I'll go get them when I'm settled.

And how does Tim handle that?

Olive took a deep breath. Sheila was waiting for a confession. The intimacy of her problem that she shared without shame or fear emboldened Olive.

He wants me to come back, but I'm not going.

You look worried, Olive, Sheila said. Tell me what's wrong.

You mean besides the fact that I left my husband and abandoned my two children and I'm behaving like a slut?

A slut. Well, tell me every sordid detail.

Her eyes brightened and she smiled and Olive leaned away from the table as the waiter brought a tray with milk and pastries and a cup of coffee. Olive waited until he was gone and then she said,

I haven't been---chaste. I haven't been promiscuous, either but some things have happened.

Details, Sheila said. Tell me about the sex, in detail.

Sheila.

Listening to you is as close as I get to sex.

Why?

Sheila tore her Danish into small pieces with her fingers and dipped each piece in her milk before chewing and swallowing and Olive watched, admiring Sheila's nails and skin and make up that gave her the look of a cover girl with arched brows and full lips and eyes darkened with liner.

What did you do? Sheila said. And who did you do it with? Tell me, tell me.

A woman I met...a friend now, really, took me to a bar called The Tomb and, well, let's just say, I behaved like a silly little girl. I got so excited I went into the toilet and touched myself and it was the first time I've orgasmed in years.

That's all? Sheila said. That's behaving like a slut? You're lucky. I haven't had an orgasm...since...well...I don't remember when Daniel last touched me. I think he's afraid of hurting me or ashamed of me because after all, I am a disease.

No, that's not all, but that's where it started. Saturday night I went out alone, Olive said. I woke up in a hotel and I don't remember anything about it—not the bar, not the men, not what I did with them.

Men? More than one? Olive! Aren't you the one?

All I know is that I woke up naked in a broken down bed and there was a hundred dollar bill on a chair.

Oh my god. I hope you're on something.

What?

The pill? A patch? Birth control, of course.

Well.

Did they use condoms?

I don't know.

Oh my god, Olive. You were raped. You have to get tested.

Tested for what?

HIV. STDs. Remember in college? It happened to a lot of girls. Some kind of drug that kept them from remembering. And you have to see someone. Are you seeing anyone?

I live alone, Olive said.

No, no I mean a therapist.

Why would I see a therapist?

Because you were raped and you can't remember it.

I don't want to remember it.

Do you remember Rose Jorgensen?

Rose?

She taught psychology when we were in school. She's wonderful and she's in private practice now.

A psychologist? You think I need a psychologist?

Oh, she's more than a psychologist. She's a genius. She looks right into your mind and tinkers with all the little switches that turn you on and off.

I don't think I need that.

Let me give you her number at least, Sheila said. I can set up a meeting. She won't psychoanalyze you over a cup of coffee. And then, you're coming to dinner with Daniel and me. I have some friends you need to meet—to keep you out of trouble, or at least to upgrade the kind of trouble you get into.

Sheila laughed. She leaned across the table and kissed Olive's cheek. She said,

We'll take care of you. Oh god, I can hardly believe it's you.

You haven't changed, Sheila, Olive said. I'll never forgive you for hooking me up with Tim.

All I did was set the table, love. What you ate was your business.

Whatever I ate I wound up with two babies. And you? Olive said.

Sheila grimaced and wiped at her mouth with the napkin. She said,

No. This thing. This cancer. I have a hard time even saying it, but it was just a small piece of my problem. I couldn't...well...conceive...we tried, Daniel and I. The sex was good, but now I'm a wife in name only. ...maybe.. You haven't finished your Danish. You can...take it with you.

Sheila called the waiter, asked for a box for the pastry, and then Sheila paid even when Olive protested, but she was certain...she said,

After all, I have a rich husband I never see so I make myself feel good by spending his money any way I can.

Sheila stood. Olive looked at her. Flat belly, full breasts in a tight white top. She wore black slacks that fit her like wet leather. Olive said,

I can't get over how really good you look.

Window dressing, Sheila said. I'll call you about dinner. You can't say no.

All right, Olive said.

Sheila opened her purse and took out a cell phone and said,

Give me your number.

I don't have a cell phone, Olive said.

Well, you have to get a Blackberry at least, don't you? After all, you're a single woman living the dissolute life and you can't do that without a cell.

Digging in her purse, Sheila found a fountain pen with a gold nib. She wrote a number on a napkin and handed it to Olive. She said,

We're going out of town for ten days, but you call me when you're connected and I'll get in touch with Rose and set up something.

I don't know if I should.

Of course you should, Sheila said.

She slid her arm through Olive's and together they marched out into the morning sun.

Rose

The suite of offices lay just off 49th St. in a small complex across from the Woodland Market. Olive parked her Chrysler in the lot and entered the building and checked the note—Rose Jorgensen Suite 301.

Olive climbed the stairs and entered a small waiting room with brocaded furniture and a small stack of magazines on a low table. But before she could sit, an inner door opened and a middle-aged woman with iron-gray hair held out a hand. Long and slender. No extra meat on her bones. She said,

Olive? I'm Rose. Come in.

Her hair was done in a bun like the old fashioned school teachers Olive had seen in her mother's year books from high school. Rose wore a gray dress buttoned up to the neck. Glasses dangled from a gold chain on her chest. Olive watched the gold chain slither as if it were a snake. A distant warmth spread from her thighs to her bottom and she shivered. Rose closed the door.

The first thing Olive noticed was the cold. The room was chilly. Closed drapes turned the room into a dim cold cocoon. Two lamps stood beside two easy chairs—no couch. The lamps cast small halos of light in the darkened room. Rose stood at the door holding it while Olive entered.

Olive felt the chill deeper as Rose walked to one of the easy chairs. Olive hesitated—not sure she wanted to be there, not sure she had anything to tell this woman. Still standing, she looked at the yellow pencil tucked behind Rose's ear. Olive held back a laugh. Rose gestured to the chair with its own lamp. She said,

Please, sit down.

Chills ran up Olive's back. Rose's voice was thick and rich. A dark husky voice that held on as if it were coming from a deep place. Olive sat without question.

Rose smiled. She took her seat and pulled an afghan over her legs and tucked it in.

Olive noticed that Rose wore black flats—soft and sensible the way her mother liked them. And she was bare legged. Blue eyes, clear blue eyes like jewels in the planes of a face fine as sculpted marble. Rose said,

I keep the room cold. If you get chilly, there's an afghan beside you under the end table.

I don't need anything, thank you.

She watched the woman facing her. Eyes scanning her face, wrinkles in the long angular face, the skin marred with just a slight webbing of broken veins. A sharp nose. A full, rich mouth, unpainted. Olive said,

I don't know why I'm here.

And that's why you're here, Rose said.

Olive studied her, let her eyes travel the narrow face, glance at the thin fingers, no rings, no watch. Rose sat in patient silence, head tilted while Olive sized her up, offering who she was to full scrutiny without any discomfort. She was open. Then, Rose raised her eyes, lips in a smile. She said,

Your friend Sheila mentioned that you had a problem. We can talk about that if you want.

Olive glanced away from the face to the wall where four black and white abstract paintings hung like ciphers. Four large canvases—black paint, white background. Black and white. Pure and simple. On the wall behind Rose, three diplomas hung in heavy wooden frame. Olive couldn't make out the details on the diplomas and she squinted then glanced off, eyes not settling as she took everything in. Why was she here? Head spinning, she felt uneasy as if she needed to get up and run away, but then Rose said,

I'm over here.

I'm sorry? Olive said.

We can talk about why you're here.

I woke up in a hotel room naked. I don't know how I got there, I don't know who took me there.

Ah, Rose said. She retrieved a notebook from the table beside her chair and pulled the pencil from her hair. She made a note. Olive said,

Sheila thinks I need to talk about what happened.

No memory?

Nothing. I woke up and somebody had left a hundred dollar bill on the bed.

Ah, Rose said.

Is that all you say? Olive asked.

When I have something to say I'll tell you, Rose said. Tell me about your family.

Why?

I need to know.

But I was raped. That's why I'm here.

Let's talk about that then.

Rose crossed her legs, adjusted the afghan. Olive's skin was cold, she shivered, felt the heat of her thighs, wanted to tuck her hands between them. Rose looked at her, in silence, waiting. Olive said,

I don't know how this works. I do all the talking? Is that it?

I have a son, Rose said. He's a mathematician. I have one grand daughter who is half Chinese—her mother is also a mathematician. I have an MD, a PhD and I'm a licensed psychiatrist. My husband of 35 years died in April of lung cancer. It was hard, continuing without him.

Olive shifted in her chair and spread her hands on the arms. She glanced again at the diplomas on the wall...MD...PhD...Well. She said,

I have two babies—five and seven. I'm married to a man ten years older than I am.

Ah, Rose said. She made a note. And your mother and father?

I'm here because I was raped not to talk about my mother and father.

Drugged and raped, Rose said. Rohypnol is the preferred drug. There are others. You were drinking somewhere and you woke up in a hotel alone and now you're wondering what you did for one hundred dollars. So tell me about your mother and father.

They would both die if they knew I was here, Olive said. They're Catholic but they've never been to confession that I know of and they'd fall into a meat grinder before they'd ever admit to a stranger that they had a problem.

But here you are.

Yes, here I am.

You're married to a man ten years your senior, you have two children, but you go out drinking and you pick up men. Tell me more about that.

I'm leaving my husband. I've left him. And I left my babies with my mother and father.

Ah, Rose said. Now I see. So you're worried that you're pregnant?

I'm not pregnant.

Do you practice safe sex?

I take the pill.

The pill won't protect you from STD, Olive.

I don't think I've got anything...no, nothing seems to be wrong.

Still you should get tested. I have the name of a lab.

It's all right. I'm okay.

Tell me why you're leaving your husband.

He makes me sick, Olive said.

She cringed as she spoke. It was the first time she'd said that, the first time she'd thought it and she shivered again and rubbed her hands together and then she broke loose—

He kept me on a tether. For ten years, I've been pregnant or cooking or cleaning out chicken coops. He married me only because he wanted children and he needed someone to do the slave labor on his farm—it didn't matter who and I gave him two beautiful babies and then I went on the pill because I knew that it would never end if I didn't stop him some way. He just smothered me and I didn't spend anything on myself for ten years...I don't know...

Rose set down her notebook. Face stolid, not smiling, like a statue whose expression was fixed in time and space forever. She pulled the afghan off and she said,

Tethered. That's an interesting word. Tell me about that.

Dad used to keep horses on the farm. When they got loose, they went crazy because they didn't have any rope to hold them down. They went crazy and ran and ran until he corralled them and got the tethers back on them and that's how I am. That's how I am with Tim. I never had any time for me. Get up in the morning before dawn, cook breakfast, pack his lunch because he's out all day.

What does he do?

Oh. We own...he owns a farm. Two sections of ground. He works it most of the time by himself except during harvest when he hires...

Ah, Rose said. And you run the house?

I get the babies up, get Nan to school on the bus and then my chores. I milked two cows, fed chickens because he has to have fresh eggs. There's laundry, books, I keep the books because he doesn't trust anyone else with his money. I was going crazy. Then one night a few months ago I climbed the windmill. I was going to jump. I was going to get away one way or another because I was through being tethered like a brood mare or a farm animal.

Had you gone up? On the windmill? Before?

Sometimes, when the babies are asleep. I go up and look out. It's the only place I felt was really mine. You know...a secret place only I could go to.

But that time it was different?

Um huh.

Do you love your babies?

Of course I love them. I'll bring them to the city when I'm ready. That's my plan. But right now I'm trying...well...I have a job, I've got some money but I need a bigger place and a better job if I'm going to do that.

Have you gone back to the hotel?

There's no way I can go back there.

Are you ashamed?

49

How can I be ashamed? I don't know what happened. Maybe nothing.

But you know you were raped?

Oh. I'm sure of that. But, maybe...the thing is...I don't know because I don't know what I did...I just wanted to have some fun and maybe I am to blame...

No woman is to blame for being raped. No is no.

Maybe...I can't be sure.

Do you do that often? Go out drinking?

Does it matter?

Well, we can talk about that next time.

So we're finished? I feel a lot better right now.

Do you dream?

A little.

I want you to keep a dream book for me. Write your dreams down just as you recall them.

You think I should come back? I thought...

Of course, Rose said. Don't make a decision right now. Sleep on it and give me a call in a couple of days. If you decide to come back, I'll keep this hour open.

Rose stood. Set the notebook on the table. Stuck the pencil behind her ear. Olive didn't laugh this time. She looked up at Rose who now looked familiar, warm and open and accepting. Rose said,

Time is up.

How can you tell? Olive said. I don't see a clock.

I know, Rose said. Years of practice.

Olive looked at her own watch. It read 2:50. It had been fifty minutes to the beat since she entered the room.

Rose held out a hand. Olive stood. Took it. It was a hard hand but strong and forgiving. Rose said,

I'll see you next Wednesday. Same time.

I don't know, Olive said. I just don't know. I don't know if this is right for me.

You were drugged and raped. You woke up naked in a hotel bed with a hundred dollar bill and you don't want or need to talk about it?

Olive stood.

She felt herself lift off the ground the way she had the night on the windmill.

Her breath came in quick gasps as if she'd been running for a long long way and her legs trembled like the times after a rain when she had gotten stuck in the mud, thick mud unable to pull her feet from the muck and her hands were shaking so hard they wriggled like worms on her skin.

Rose beside her, not reaching out, not comforting, waited, her head very still, body very quiet, hands at her sides. Rose said,

Are you all right?

It's nothing. I get dizzy sometimes.

Let your dreams tell you what you need, will you do that?

Rose opened the door to the waiting room. Seated, thumbing through a magazine, a frizzy haired woman in a very short skirt, a low cut blouse, looked up. Her mouth was painted black. Her eyes thick with liner. Dangly ear rings twirled as she tossed the magazine onto the table. She stood. High heels, black stockings, thin legs, a red flower tattoo on the swell of her left breast. Looking straight at Rose as if Olive didn't exist, she said,

Hey doc, I know I'm early...

Larry

From her desk Olive watched Eileen Norburg standing at the teller's window. Even from across the office, even though Eileen was bent over talking, it was clear that she was angry. The way her thick black hair shook as she spoke, the way her hands punctuated the top of the counter as she spoke, the way she straightened all unmistakable signs and Olive felt a trace of guilt. It was her fault Eileen was angry.

She let the chill run up her back, but she returned to her figures—to the rows and columns of figures and she thought about the mistakes she had pointed out to Eileen earlier. The pages with each error circled in red, unmistakable errors. She expected to see the teller walk out, but after a few minutes, the talk slowed, the fingers on the counter top no long danced, and Eileen left the window and walked back to her desk.

Olive, careful not to leak her curiosity, watched Eileen's tall frame, thin and almost stark, her eyes still furious as she sat at the desk and crossed her legs and bounced her heel up and down like a piston. Then, turning to the teller, Olive saw him, Larry, a middle-aged man who was sloppy with his numbers. His face was red. He pretended to check his forms, but his hands trembled and his forehead glistened with diamonds of sweat. And then Eileen stood looking down at Olive. At six feet one inch, she was awesome and her fury hadn't faded yet. She leaned down, both hands on Olive's desk. Olive waited for the torrent. But Eileen said, Let's go get some lunch.

Olive sat back, leery of the tall black woman whose makeup was light purpose, her lips stained with a cocoa tint. Olive said,

Sure.

It was the first time in four months that Eileen had approached her. The first time Eileen had done anything except talk work—You're too good to be here, she said. Your talents are wasted here. You should be working for some corporation somewhere, not here.

Olive stood, grabbed her jacket from the back of the chair, collected her purse from the drawer in her desk and she followed Eileen out the door and into the crisp Fall air, into the street where Eileen plucked a cigarette from a pack of Pall Malls and lit it. She offered one to Olive who said not. Eileen said,

Sometimes I want to bite peoples' heads off, you? You'd think...

I know, Olive said.

Huffing, she tried to match Eileen stride for stride. High heels hammering on the sidewalk, they stopped in the parking lot and Eileen pointed to her Prius and Olive got in. She said,

We're driving?

There's time. I'm the boss. I'm mad. So yes, there's time.

She drove and as she drove, her skirt rode up on her thighs, the black stockings shimmering but she didn't adjust. Two men in a pickup pulled alongside. One of them rolled down a window and asked Eileen directions to her apartment. Olive waited, but Eileen said nothing until they parked in front of a small café a mile from GECU. Olive said,

Do you get that a lot?

It happens a lot more than it used to.

You've got great legs, Olive said. I'm sure it happens all the time.

You don't know the half of it, love.

The café was a potted palm and fern café with a dozen tables, most taken but the one at the back. The floor was Vermeer, the walls wainscoted. The music was canned, a woman making love to a piano. The smells were garlic and olive oil. Eileen sat the table by the window. She said,

Have you been here before?

No. I usually just grab a sandwich from the shop across the street.

I noticed that, Eileen said. Eating at your desk.

Well, you know...work work work.

A lot of women meet here from time to time. Are you looking?

Looking for what? Olive said.

A new job.

Well, yes, as a matter of fact, I am. But right now there doesn't seem to be anything popping.

The economy.

Right, Olive said.

You're sure you've never been here before? You fit right in.

I can't afford places like this yet.

How do you know?

I glanced at the menu in the window.

Maybe it costs less than you think.

Anything more expensive than tuna salad is out of my range.

I have friends here, Eileen said. So, are you all settled in?

Um huh, Olive said. I've got a place, looking for something bigger but can't go bigger until I land something that pays a little more.

Your kids, right? The bigger place for the kids?

Right, Olive said.

What else are you looking for?

I'm sorry?

You said you were looking for something bigger. What else are you looking for?

You sound like my therapist.

You're seeing a therapist?

Um huh, Olive said. You remember Sheila Masterson?

Of course.

She knows a therapist. I see her. I guess I shouldn't tell you that, huh?

So you have some issues?

Oh, I have issues.

You don't seem like the kind of person who sees a therapist.

Well. You know. It's kind of embarrassing to talk about it.

We all have secrets, Eileen said. Did I ever tell you I played ball at Wichita State?

Ball?

Basketball, Eileen said. We went to the regionals every year I was a starter.

You're tall enough all right.

Eileen looked at her then, an appraising look before turning away to stare out the window. Olive studied her profile—her eyes were almost shaped, just a hint of eye liner, her nose was sharp, her cheeks high and angular. Olive cleared her throat.

The waitress came with two glasses of water and a menu. She spoke to Eileen who smiled and patted her hand like an old friend without introducing Olive or even noticing her. Two chef's salads, no coffee, bread, no butter. When they were alone again, Eileen said,

You're not into sports?

'Fraid not.

I get together with friends on game nights to watch. Sometimes we go to the games, but that's not been happening much lately. So are you close to working it out with your ex?

My ex. Well.

Let me rephrase   Are you seeing some one?

As she spoke, Eileen fixed her eyes on Olive and pursed her lips and Olive watched the cocoa lipstick glisten as Eileen wet her lips.

No, Olive said. I've been out a couple of times with a friend.

A friend?

Janey. She works at the Kiowa Café.

Well, Eileen said. We'll have to get together sometime with Janey.

Really? Olive said. Can you do that?

Because I'm your boss?

Well. Aren't you?

You think I'll bite?

Nothing like that. I like you, Olive said. I've liked you from day one. But...

So I put the fear of god into you?

The waitress returned with the salads and the bread. She set the plates down and she smiled and said,

There you go. Anything else? Pecan pie is just out of the oven.

Pecan pie? Eileen said. Honey. I eat pecan pie and I'm high as a kite for a week, not to mention what it does to my waistline.

You could eat anything, the waitress said.

And I have eaten things you can't even imagine.

Sugarfree chocolate pudding then? The waitress said before she left.

Are you diabetic? Olive said.

No. Hormones go raging when I over do the sugar.

Eileen picked at her salad, set the tomato chunks aside then the slices of ham and cheese. She forked at the lettuce that she nibbled while watching Olive. Olive said,

That's how you stay so thin...eating like that?

How well do you know the night life in the City?

Olive choked on a slice of boiled egg. She coughed. She set her fork down and swallowed, then drank a mouthful of water. She said,

Well, I've been to the Tomb and a couple other places.

The Tomb. Now there's a place not many find on their own.

My friend took me. You know it?

Know of it, Eileen said. But it's not exactly my kind of place.

It was strange, Olive said.

I can show you another side of things sometime. If you'd like.

Olive finished her salad, finished half a slice of bread while Eileen leaned back in her chair, legs crossed and watched her. As she wiped her mouth with her napkin, Olive noticed that Eileen's eyes were fixed on a point that could only be at the center of her cleavage.

Worm

She woke up flat on her back, hands pressed into her belly and she was sweating. On the ceiling, shadow stripes stretched out long and black and the dream was still working as if she hadn't waked up at all and Sheila stood in front of her as solid and real as she had been in the pastry shop but she was silent and then she looked down at her feet and again glanced up at Olive and there was horror in her eyes and Olive followed her eyes back down to the floor where a long white worm was crawling from between Sheila's legs and curling on the floor and then, as if it had eyes, it streaked right at Olive, entwined itself around her and inched its way up to her crotch and Olive was helpless to stop it because her hands were paralyzed and as she stood there, her belly began to swell until it reached the size of a basketball and then it exploded sending a shower of white worms out like snow falling.

Still soaking wet, Olive got out of bed for a drink of water and standing at the sink, she trembled. The clock on the floor beside the bed said 2:35. At the window, she looked through the slats of the old fashioned Venetian blinds, looked out at the quiet and empty street with its lone street lamp. Sitting on the bed again, she looked at the wall where she had pinned the photos of Nan and Toby and in the gray light from the street, the pictures were flat gray splotches on the wall, but she knew they were there. They were safe with Grace and Paul. They were sound asleep in warm beds, snuggled down in warm blankets, and there was nothing that could harm them.

She pressed her hands over her belly again, pushed but felt nothing hard. STDs and HIV...Should she ask Rose about the lab? Should she get tested again? She'd ask Janey who would know about those things. It was dangerous, what she was doing, she knew that, but she didn't want to stop, not yet.

She watched the shadows change as a car drove along the street, headlights first marking the path like a scout, the moving shadows of light poles gliding along the sides of darkened building. In the grayness she saw herself in front of a fitting room mirror pirouetting, her body reflected over and over and she thought she didn't look bad, no she looked very good. Sheila was one of those whose hair would never grow back, while she was one of those whose body didn't show that she had given birth to two children. It was still young and soft and pliant. She imagined herself in a revealing bikini somewhere lying in the sun, her skin taking the heat, sweating, slick and wet as if she had just made love for an hour and she let her hands slide between her legs, let her fingers rub over the rise of her clitoris—hard and wet—and she closed her eyes and buried her fingers in her cleft, squeezing her thighs together until the dripping gush of her orgasm took her breath away and then she balled up, legs tight against her chest and let the throbbing ripple from her belly all the way to her bottom where again she felt the hardness of the man with the gold chain in her. And then she fell asleep.

Dean

What the hell are you doing, Sis?

We can't talk here, Olive said. I get a break in half an hour. There's a Starbux on the next block. I'll meet you there.

Dean turned and walked away. Olive watched his broad back until he was out the door then she glanced around—but all eyes were on the work. She let out a sigh of relief but noticed that her hands were trembling.

Checking the clock, she worked the rows of numbers until 11:00 o'clock, then she told Eileen she was on a break. Eileen nodded, rapt in her own paperwork, and waved good-bye. Olive scooted out the door and into the October heat. She walked to Starbux where her brother sat glowering at a cup of coffee. She sat down.

Three-fifty for a god-damned cup of coffee, Dean said.

He fixed his eyes on her. Olive felt the years melt away and she was back on the farm and Dean was eight and following her everywhere until she turned to throw rocks at him, but he didn't run off, instead, he dodged her bullets and kept his distance so that no matter where she was, he was there, fifty feet away.

I talked to Mom and Dad, Dean said. They're pissed off. They're not going to say anything because of the kids, but Jesus Christ, Sis, what you're doing is criminal.

You don't understand, Olive said.

Dean grinned then and he reached across the table and took her hand and turned it palm up and he said,

Just what in the hell don't I understand?

Why are you here, little brother? Olive said.

It's pretty clear why I'm here. But let's chit chat for a second. You look good. I expected you to look like hell, worn out, a tramp.

Thanks, brother.

And you've lost weight.

Put it on, actually, Olive said.

You look sexy, how's that? So now, tell me what the fuck is going on?

No judgments, Olive said.

Little brother judging Big Sis, Dean said, Not likely.

Olive stammered at first, the words coming in spurts and hollows, but then, as she told him everything, she found the beat and when she got to the part about standing on the windmill in the dark, Dean leaned away from her and lowered his eyes. He said,

So what you're telling me is that you run out on Tim and leave your kids because you had an existential moment on a fucking windmill? Jesus Christ, Sis.

You said you wouldn't judge, Olive said, but you are, you're judging me no matter what I say it'll never be all right.

If it's just you fucking up your life, Sis. No big deal. The city? I don't give a fuck. Do what you want. But you've got those babies. And Tim? Christ, I can't imagine what he's going through.

Or what I'm going through, Olive said. What about me?

Dean looked at her then, his hard blue eyes unrelenting and he twisted his mouth up like he'd just sucked on a sour lemon. He said,

Mom and Dad are too old for this kind of crap, Sis. They paid their dues with us and now you're making them double dip for your mistakes and that's not fair to them. They've got Toby in kindergarten in town and Mom drives him in every day and she drops Nan off at school and then drives back out to do her chores.

What do you want me to do? Olive said.

Do what you're supposed to do—be a mother.

I can't have them with me yet.

It's been four months since they even saw you.

Not yet.

Then you get squared away and you go back home and take those babies back to Tim and you set your ass down with that big lunk and you work it out because I'm not letting you fuck up those babies just so you can live the high life in the city like a princess. For god's sake.

Are you through? Olive said.

Yeah, hell yeah, I'm through. I told you what's on my mind so there you've got it.

Then leave, Dean.

You're more screwed up than a pig's turd. What's going on? Is there another guy? If there's another guy, you owe it to Tim to cut it off....

I don't owe Tim Keller anything.

You owe your babies and you owe Mom and Dad. You can't...

Olive sobbed. She sniffled and her eyes watered and she looked at her brother and his pinched and hateful face and she felt her body lift off, floating again, rising as if she had stepped out on that windmill platform

59

again, as if the sky had blanketed her suffocating her and she choked and her breath came in gasps. Dean reached for her, his hand on her shoulder digging hard, squeezing, but she felt no pain, nothing he could do would hurt her. She said,

I have to get back.

What do I tell Mom and Dad?

I'll call them tonight.

You haven't called in a month.

I have to get back to work.

You're really pissing me off now, Sis. All you have to do is what you should do and everything will straighten out. Why is that so fucking hard?

I can't do that, Olive said.

Okay. Okay. I've said my piece. I'll go back to Mom and Dad and tell them you're a fucking wreck, that you prefer...

Don't do that Dean.

Okay. I'll leave you with your petty problems and, Olive—I don't give a shit about you or what you do except I'm their uncle. They're blood, Sis. Blood and you don't just write off blood.

You said you were going, Olive said.

She stood then and Dean, facing her, scowled and she turned and left him at the table. She marched back to the bank, went back to work but the columns of figures moved like small dark dancers and she closed her eyes and she remembered Dean diving into the water tank under the windmill—naked—and he was eight and mop headed and cute and her Mom stood to one side shooting snap shots. She was younger then, and pretty. Laughing at Dean's antics in the water the way she would laugh at Toby when he was old enough to jump into the tank.

Olive got up and went to Eileen who was bent over her desk, pen in hand, signing papers. Olive said,

I need to take the rest of the day.

What happened in there?

Family, Olive said.

Your visitor?

My brother.

Bad news? Eileen said.

She reared back in her chair and looked at Olive with her liquid brown eyes and Olive wanted to tell her everything, but instead she said,

More than that.

Well, Eileen said, go ahead, take the rest of the day. I'll have to dock you.

I know, Olive said.

She returned to her cubicle and gathered her purse and sunglasses and left the bank and walked out into the October sun, her eyes burning but not from the strong light.

Cowboy

She searched for him like a starving wild animal on the hunt. She wanted it so bad her jaws ached. There were bodies in the bar, a lot of hot bodies showing a lot of hot skin and her eyes raked each one, but the ache in her jaws didn't ease up and so she sat at the bar crossing her legs as if she were an angel of death and the pit of darkness lay between her legs a trap baited and ready and waiting for the right moment.

She drank Picadors. She watched the bartender, the same young face she'd seen the night of the red shirted man, the man with the gold chain, the man who took her to the motel. The ache in her bottom made her flush with shame and desire and the wetness between her legs didn't want to wait and still he didn't come. On her third Picador, she motioned the bartender to her.

She took in the fresh young skin, the pale blue eyes with their frail lashes, took in the young mouth without a wrinkle at the corners. He said,

Hi. Saw you here the other night.

That's right.

He's not here, the guy you left with.

I'm not looking for the guy I left with. What time do you get off?

Fifteen minutes after I close out.

I'll wait, she said.

You might want to go easy on the Picadors.

Why should I?

Your lips'll go numb and you'll fall off that stool.

If I did fall would you pick me up?

I'd have to—you're the customer and the customer is always right.

Even is the customer is flat on her back?

Especially then. Can I get you a cup of coffee?

~~~

She waited and while she waited she tossed back the ones who came sniffing after her. She hauled them up beside her, weighed them the way a

62

butcher weighs meat on a scale and then hurled them, bruised and bleeding, back into the pack where they slunk away licking their wounds. But she wasn't ready to be had. She was hunting and to her taste right then, at that moment, still wet with memory, she wanted the hot young bartender with his soft eyes and still unhooked mouth.

~~~

She drove, in her Chrysler. He sat hunched against the door and she glanced at him as he sized her up. Parking at the motel, she pulled the key then turned to him. She said,

Get out. Room Sixteen.

She followed him, watching his butt, his back, his legs and she was wet as she approached the door. He said,

What now?

She opened, walked in and turned to face him. She said,

Come in, close the door and strip.

You get right to it, don't you?

Yes or no?

He unbuttoned his shirt, his chest was coated with wispy hair, his skin golden. He wore a single gold ring in his left nipple. Olive walked up to him, ran her hands over his chest, tugged at the gold ring. He sucked in his breath. She said,

Take it all off.

Yes ma'am, he said. He didn't mock her, didn't go sarcastic on her and she liked that, liked ordering him to do things. He dropped his jeans. A pair of black shorts, tight so his cock bulged out. Olive smiled. She said,

Go into the bathroom and shower.

He lowered his black shorts and stepped out of them and walked to the bathroom. Olive stayed close, smelling him as he walked, smelling the residue of cigarette smoke and alcohol drifting off him like a vapor trail. She admired his muscled back that flexed as he pulled open the shower stall door and leaned down to turn on the water. He glanced up at her. She stood against the door, her own wetness now dripping down her legs, her thighs sliding together as if a river of oil had burst loose. She watched him step into the water, watched him soap his body, his erection glistening wet. He tired to close the shower door, but told him to leave it open. Half turning away from her, he lathered. She told him to look at her. He looked down as he soaped his crotch, almost as surprised at his hardness. Olive laughed. He cupped his hands over his stiffness, but Olive said,

No. Don't do that. You're big enough.

When he had rinsed the soap from his body, he reached for the spigots. Olive said,

Hair too.

Okay, he said. He soaped his head, closed his eyes, and Olive looked at his erection standing flat against his belly and still shiny with soap and water. He shut off the shower and shook his head, ran his hands over his hair and scraped the water down over his body. Olive backed away, arms crossed, her river of slickness sticky on her legs as she sat on the edge of the bed, waiting. She said,

Don't cover up.

All right, he said from inside the bathroom.

He came out, body hair slick against his golden skin, head hair spiked from using his fingers like a comb. His erection held steady against his belly and then he looked down. In the dropping of his eyes, Olive saw hesitation and not a little fear. She felt his uneasiness, his wariness. He raised his eyes to hers, helpless, and she held his gaze, unblinking, until he trembled, waiting for her to tell him what to do. The burning in her crotch spreading up into her belly, Olive pressed her thighs together until the rising of her orgasm made her shudder and then, holding back her pleasure, she released him with a whispered, throaty, husky voice saying,

I want you to come standing there.

He glanced away, at the door—his escape—at his clothes, his refuge. Then, he smiled and knowing what she wanted of him, the nervousness flowed away and he touched his erection, gripped it with his right thumb and two fingers and stroked, all the while watching her as she peeled off her skirt and blouse, unhooked her bra and slid her panties off just as he doubled over grunting, his semen arcing out and he gasped and Olive strode to him and took his hand and slid it between her legs— dripping, running with her own orgasm. She smelled his ejaculation—so much of it—and it did not smell acrid, it did not smell sharp, it did not stink. It smelled sweet and clean. She said,

I want you to kneel now and lick me.

~~~

Dressing with slow deliberation, she stood at the foot of the bed slipping into her red panties and then the short skirt. She took her time snugging her breasts into the red bra and she watched his eyes as they flickered over her body. She buttoned the blouse and then, standing first on one foot then the other, she stepped into her high heels. Raising her arms to smooth at her hair, she smelled her own sweat, smelled the scent of his come on her wafting up through the neck opening of her blouse.

She left him on the bed, naked, his cock flaccid on his belly, his face wet, his body slick with sweat. At the door, she turned. She said,

You'll have to walk back to the bar.

Yeah, he said. I figured as much.

Do you have a name, cowboy?

Without waiting for his answer, Olive spun out the door and got into her Chrysler and drove to her apartment. It was 4:00 AM and she was very sleepy.

Wings

She sat on her chair in her chilly corner of the office and she clutched the hem of her skirt, nails digging in because today, for the first time, the curtains were open and the light rushed in like an endless waterfall. There had to be a reason why the curtains were open. She looked at the black and white paintings on the wall. She tried to make out the images—were they birds? Or insects? The painting on the right looked more complete than the one on the left as if the painter had started on the left and worked to the right where he finished the job—but still...Birds? Or Insects? When she looked at the paintings from the corner of her eye she saw a pair of wings—beating wings.

Across the street, at the Wheatland Market, a woman got out of a black BMW SUV and guided her two children—a boy and a girl—into the store. Olive felt a lump collect in her throat, a dry lump, and she groped again at the hem of the skirt, a fingernail gouging into her thigh—a sharp pain, but she didn't move her hand.

She glanced at Rose wrapped in her afghan, Rose who watched her, blue eyes open, innocent as if she had already seen everything and had become not cynical but clean and pure again—a virgin at 57 experiencing everything for the first time. Rose wore her glasses on a gold chain around her neck. Olive's chest tightened as her eyes fixed on the chain. She squeezed her thighs tight. Rose said,

Are you all right?

I haven't been open with you, Olive said. I haven't told you everything.

I know.

How do you know?

For the first time, Rose said, you're facing me right on instead of turning away.

I do that?

When you're holding back, you turn your profile to me, cross your legs and use your thigh as a shield.

Well, I've been dreaming again—two dreams. One about those

paintings behind you—they make me nervous—and the other is about Tim.

Olive twisted the hem of her skirt into a ball and looked down at her heels where a scruff from a stumble getting out of her Chrysler marred the leather, and she noticed the tops of her thighs, her knees lined up straight at Rose. Her fingernail digging into her thigh felt wet as if she'd opened a wound. Rose, still watching, held her pencil off the notebook page, waiting. Olive said,

In my dream, the paintings are there.

What about them?

Nothing. They're on the wall, behind you, but you're not in your chair. I see the paintings. That's all. The other dream is more gruesome. I'm strapped to the windmill and I'm naked and Tim is standing over me— he's huge, he's really huge—and he won't let me go and when he touches me I want to vomit. There are leather straps cutting into my wrists and no matter how hard I twist, I can't get free. And there's a saddle on the ground and I think he wants to put it on me.

What is he doing to you? Rose asked.

He's holding something—like a leather club that he rakes between my legs and then I start gushing blood like the heaviest period I've ever had and then he pulls back. There's disgust on his face like I'm something horrible. Then, I wake up. In the dream I feel like I've been eaten by a cannibal. I can't explain that.

Olive straightened her skirt, let go of the hem, saw the twisted fabric where she had held it so tight her sweat had dampened the wool. She looked from Rose to the paintings that now seemed to have changed shape—no longer bird wings, no longer trees bending in a heavy wind, but slender threads like veins coursing black blood.

Across the street, the woman at Wheatland Market was settling her children into her SUV. She strapped them into their car seats, closed the door, then drove away.

Olive felt nothing. No lump in her throat, no pain in her chest. Rose was writing in her notebook, head bent, silent as she was most of the time and then Rose, still looking down at the page, said,

And did you write it down?

Yes. All of it.

Good, Rose said. Leave your book with me, will you?

Why do you want to read this stuff?

It's what I do, Rose said. Now, tell me the rest of it.

The rest of what?

What you're masking.

Olive's eyes landed on the gold chain holding Rose's glasses again. Her chest tightened and she smelled, ever so faint, the odor of the man's cologne and felt the tapping of his gold chain against her back. She said,

A few weeks after Janey, my friend, took me to the Tomb, I went out by myself. It was a mistake.

We all make mistakes, Rose said. We're the sum of our mistakes.

You've never made a mistake in your life, Olive said.

Rose looked at her, eyes clear, no smile on her face. Then she stuck her pencil behind her ear and retucked the afghan around her legs. Olive hadn't asked for an afghan. She liked the goose bumps from the chill, she liked to feel her sand papery skin rough from the cold. She said,

I met a man in a bar. I guess you could say he picked me up but I didn't fight it. I drank too much, we went to a motel…we had sex.

Olive stopped as her head spun and she felt herself floating again, disconnected again, as if in a dream again and she was back on the windmill, on the platform, floating and then she smelled his cologne again, stronger this time, and the slow beat of his gold chain on her back landing like a whip.

Where are you? Rose said.

Olive jerked. She said,

On the windmill again, for a second. I could smell him.

What does the windmill have to do with the man?

I don't know. It wasn't pretty. I don't know why I keep doing this. I have to stop. But I can't. When I'm on the windmill, I see the water tank down there—it's a horse tank. We don't have horses anymore but the tank is still there for the livestock. When I'm spinning I fall sometimes, but I never hit bottom.

This man, Rose said.

He wore a red shirt and he had a gold medallion around his neck. His cologne was so strong I couldn't wash it off for a week. It made me ill.

What did he do to you?

Well, he used me in a way that confused me.

Say it, Olive.

Is the time up yet? Olive said.

Put words on it. If you don't say it, you won't get free of it.

She stood, walked to the window. At the Wheatland Market, a beer truck was backing into loading dock. Olive wondered if the glass of the window would shatter if she rushed at it. She turned to Rose who still sat like the sphinx, waiting. She said,

He entered me from the rear.

Anal sex, Rose said.

Yes.

Own it, Olive. You have to take control of it.

Okay. We had anal sex, okay. We had anal sex and then he left me on the bed like a whore he'd just paid for and I don't know his name and he doesn't know mine.

Where do you feel that? Throat? Heart? Belly?

What?

Are you angry? Afraid? Disgusted? Ashamed?

I'm not sure...

Ah, Rose said. Tell me more about that.

There's another dream, Olive said. I didn't write it down. In the dream, I'm huge. I'm pregnant. Huge as a cow. I give birth to these bloody awful things that burst out of me and they're covered in blood. I can't tell if they're human or not.

You're a mother.

I hate being a mother.

You are a mother.

I can stop mothering.

Is that what you need?

Why are the curtains open today? Olive asked.

I forgot to close them.

Why did you forget to close them?

Sometimes, when I leave for the night, I open them.

Olive said: I'm not sure I didn't like what he did to me.

Rose made a note in her book then, and she looked up at Olive. Tucking her pencil behind her ear, Rose said,

Are you ashamed of that feeling?

Butterfly

The stairs were steep. The air cool. The sound of her footsteps echoed back like hammer blows. She stopped on the second floor landing when she heard a door slam. She froze. And then, face pressed to the wall, she noticed the small brown swirl on the plaster. It looked like a butterfly wing or an insect wing that had been ripped off. She glanced up the stairwell, listening for footsteps—never arrive early, she had learned after the run-in with the woman in Rose's waiting room. You don't want to come face to face with the next crazy person on the stairs. She was now a crazy woman meeting with a psychiatrist to sort out her issues. She leaned against the handrail, remembered the railing of the windmill, remembered floating, her head spinning and the black water at the bottom in the tank.

She pulled back and as she pulled back, she smelled cologne. Reeking cologne, the cologne of the man in the red shirt and the gold chain. She shuddered. Her bottom tightened. She looked at the insect wing again. She touched it. It broke free from the wall and fluttered out, spinning until it fell on the floor.

Kneeling, Olive wet her finger tip and touched the fragile wing. It stuck to her finger. And she blew on it and again it flew away. She heard another door click and then there was silence.

She skipped up the stairs and into Rose's waiting room to find the door to Rose's office already open and Rose standing by her chair. She said,

Come in, please.

Rose took her seat, spreading the afghan over her legs. The afghan was red and black, yellow and blue—the colors of a butterfly wing. It reminded Olive of the afghan on Grace's bed, a quilt Grace's mother made as a wedding gift. Rose plucked her pencil from behind her ear. Olive sat in her chair in the cold room, goose bumps rising on her skin like small grains of sand. Rose said,

How have you been?

Okay, I guess.

But you're not sure?

I went hunting again.

Rose said Ah and she made a note then looked at Olive.

You're going to think I'm a slut, aren't you?

How you think about it is what's important, Rose said.

Well, I think I'm a slut but I can't stop right now.

But still you go out drinking and hunting. With your friend, Janey?

No. Alone, Olive said. He's a bartender. I took control of him. I used him, made him do what I wanted him to do.

And what did you want him to do?

I didn't want him to control me.

Are you leaving something out, Olive?

Rose made a note in her book then she looked at Olive and she asked why Olive was censoring and Olive said,

When I have control it's easier. He's young. He's beautiful. I picked him up and I took him to a motel where I'd been before and we had sex. When I finished with him, I got dressed and left him naked on the bed. I don't know his name and he doesn't know mine.

Is that important?

It had to be anonymous to get even.

The hundred dollars? Rose said. The anal sex?

The woman at the hotel, Olive said, the desk clerk, she had the strangest color hair. Like strawberries. But her skin was grotesque. She smoked big black cigars and she stank. She was laughing at me because I was so stupid. I felt so stupid

Ah, Rose said.

Olive said: I keep dreaming about it but I can't remember going there. I can see myself coming down the stairs but I never see myself going up them. The room was so old the linoleum had worn in spots. It was dirty. She was dirty. Everything about her was dirty.

Looking again at the paintings, Olive saw trees bending in a heavy wind, almost breaking. She broke out in a sweat and her underarms were sticky and she said,

The dirt in the country is clean.

I didn't know that, Rose said.

It's clean, Olive said. You plant seeds in the soil and they grow. Wheat, corn, soy beans, flowers. You can grow flowers, all kinds of flowers. You go out and you work and you get dirty and you wash off the dirt and you feel good, but here, what can you grow in this filth?

But you left the country. You go hunting. How do you feel coming back from one of your expeditions?

If I get what I want, I feel good.

What do you want?

71

I don't want to be bored. Most men are boring. Tim was boring. I hate being bored. Do you know how dark it is in the country?

That's why you came to the city? To keep from being bored?

The city is filthy and it's stupid to think about bringing kids here but it's not boring. Still, when I come home from work no matter how hard I wash I just can't get clean.

Is it just coming home from work that you can't get clean?

You mean is the sex dirty?

Is it?

Rose held her pencil off the page. She looked at Olive, her face smooth, blue eyes calm, mouth relaxed. Olive said,

You look so peaceful.

My hunting days are over, Rose said. Now tell me—why can't you get clean?

I'd rather talk about Tim.

All right.

Tim inherited the farm from his father who was a family friend. He used to help Dad with the harvest. But then his father died and Tim came to Wichita—it was my senior year—and he asked me to marry him in my dorm room. I was 21 and I was still a virgin.

How did you manage to stay a virgin after four years of college? Rose asked.

I was in a religious school. I took it seriously.

But you're not religious now, are you?

No. I didn't go out much but every time I made out with a guy I'd hear my mother saying if you lose your virginity you won't be worth much as a wife.

And how did you react to his proposal?

I was scared. He was so much older and he is so big, it was hard to say no. He said he'd talked to my folks. Of course they all like him because he works hard and he has his own ground. I didn't know what else to do and when I talked to my mother, Grace, she just thought it was wonderful that I had a man who wanted me, a man with a place of his own.

You have someplace to go, she told me. So, the day I graduated, we got married. We didn't have a big wedding, just Mom and Dad and a minister—Tim isn't Catholic. After that, no honeymoon, I went to his farm. It was a mistake. The first night we had sex I got sick because Tim's semen smells so strong it gags me. He'd come in me and for days I smelled him every time I peed or squatted to gather eggs or sometimes just driving to town I'd smell it and I'd have to pull over and vomit. Just from the smell.

And that's why you're abandoning your babies?

I don't know why I'm abandoning them.

Did you have oral sex with Tim?

He wouldn't know what oral sex was, Olive said. The bartender, that boy, that kid, he already knows everything—he did everything I told him and his semen smelled sweet. I didn't think it mattered, but it was sweet.

Olive plucked a Kleenex from the box beside her chair and she wadded it up, staring at it and then she wiped her nose and dropped the Kleenex in her lap. She said,

I always wiped myself with Kleenex. I'd use half a box after Tim had finished. But with the bartender, I just let him come on me, It was different. If my mother ever heard me telling you these things she'd disown me. She had three babies but to look at her you'd think she is still a virgin.

Our mothers are special, Rose said. You're a mother. Remember how special you are the next time you phone your babies. Are they in your dreams?

No. A little. I don't know why they're not.

Are you writing in your dream book?

There's something else I need to ask you.

Our time is up, but if you're quick.

There's this woman at work, Eileen Norburg, my boss. I don't know about her...

Daniel

He wore the same red shirt, the same black slacks, the same black penny loafers without a coin in the slot. Standing at the door, Olive smelled his cologne, the same cologne that had stuck to her skin while Sheila, looking glorious in blue, said,

Olive, this is my husband Daniel.

He smiled and held out a hand.

Sheila ushered Olive in, closed the door and Daniel led them into a living room of white—drapes, furniture, walls, white except for twin splashes of blue—one a huge monochrome painting in brilliant cobalt that linked to an enormous carpet of the same color.

Daniel offered Olive a martini.

I've never had a martini, Olive said.

She watched him at the bar mixing drinks, listened to the click of glassware and metal while Sheila asked how she'd been and they'd had a marvelous trip to Zihuatanejo had she ever been there. Feeling uneasy, Olive shook her head no as she looked at Sheila who was gracious and talkative. She said,

And this is Harold.

Olive, fixated on Daniel and his red shirt, had not seen the man with blond hair sitting on the white sofa until he uncoiled a tall frame, taller than Tim, six-five or more and held out a soft hand the color of honey. He said,

Sheila's told me about you, Olive. Glad you could make it.

His voice was deep and modulated, like a radio announcer's rich and thick with practice. His grip was firm. She said,

Harold.

Call me Hoddy, everyone else does.

Hoddy?

It's a long story—a nickname from when we were kids.

I see, Olive said. I've never heard that before.

You weren't one of nine kids, he said.

Olive smiled as Daniel approached with four glasses on a glass tray and, looking right at Olive, said,

I hope you like gin because that's all we drink in this house.

Olive took the glass, sipped at it, and followed Sheila to a pair of easy chairs and as Sheila sat she looked like a flower in the cup of the white chair. Olive said,

You look just absolutely beautiful.

The Mexican sun, Sheila said. Curative.

Olive watched Daniel who held forth with Harold, Hal as he liked to be called.

Hoddy's an engineer at Boeing. He designs things.

You're bad, Sheila.

I'm just looking out for you, sweets.

I can look out for myself.

Of course you can, but three at a table feels unbalanced. He's divorced.

What does Daniel do?

Daniel? Oh, he sells cars. Well, more than sells, he owns four agencies. I have no idea what kind. All I know is that his cars are expensive and Hoddy drives one of them. It's an Audi TT, I think. It's sporty anyway. You'll have to ask him.

Is this your way of telling me Harold has money?

Can't you tell by looking? MIT, I think. He didn't lose everything in the divorce because his Ex had her own. Oil rights, I think. Well, now that we've oiled our tongues with Daniel's liquor, let's go eat.

Sheila stood, swooping like a butterfly and gripped Olive's hand sloshing the remains of her martini.

Oops, Sheila said. Maybe tongues aren't all that's oiled. Enough, Daniel. The roast is ready...go...all of you...sit.

Olive at her place across from Harold listened but didn't hear a word as she watched Daniel carve a standing rib roast and serve it all the while bantering about Kansas City beer.

And what do you do, Olive? Harold said.

Me? Olive broke out of her reverie then. Uh. I work in accounting.

I told her they're always hiring at Boeing, isn't that right, Hoddy?

He latched his clear blue eyes on Olive and he said,

Yeah, I think so. Are you looking?

I'm always looking, Olive said. Sheila tells me you drive an Audi TT. I might be in the market for one of those. Does it have a large back seat?

Back seat? Harold said. Not really...

Daniel, with a hunk of meat in his mouth coughed. Sheila said,

Are you all right, Danny?

Careful man, Harold said. You'll choke on that Kansas City beef.

75

I'm okay, Daniel said. He set his fork down still with the meat stuck on it. He rose and poured wine all around and then, standing beside Olive, he said,

So you're looking for a TT, huh? Think you can handle a muscle car like that?

If it's expensive and exciting I can handle it, Olive said.

What does one of those TT thingies cost, Danny? Sheila asked.

A lot, babe.

Danny'll give you a break on the price, Harold said. He never sticks it to his friends.

Daniel laughed, sat down, and eyed Olive. He said,

They come in raw at thirty-five.

Raw? Sheila said.

Stripped. With all the extras it runs upwards of forty-five if you get the leather option.

Hear that, Olive? Sheila said. The leather option. Sounds depraved.

As Olive nibbled at her Kansas City beef, she listened but heard nothing because she smelled Daniel's cologne, the same cologne he wore the night she met him and every time she looked up he was watching her and there was a smile on his face and his eyes sparkled and when Sheila cleared the table, Olive followed her into the kitchen. Sheila said,

I wouldn't call you rude, Olive, but Harold is definitely interested and you keep staring off into space.

He keeps looking at my breasts.

You are spectacular, you know. You always were. That rosy skin is enough to make any man stare.

I'm not feeling well, Olive said.

The migraine of convenience? Give him a chance.

Dessert was sponge cake soaked in rum. Olive felt her heart hammer when Daniel poured coffee. She smelled his cologne again, his sweat again and she could look only at his hand with the diamond ring on it, the ring she knew hadn't been there the night in the motel.

Her head spinning again with disconnected feelings of revulsion and self-hatred sweeping over her every time she caught Daniel's clandestine leers, Olive stood. She said,

My headache's getting to me, Sheila. I'm going to have to go.

Me too, Harold said. I'll walk you to your car.

Daniel, on his feet, started to speak but Sheila held up a hand and he turned and Olive saw Sheila's smile. She went to her and kissed her.

We'll just have to do it again, Sheila said.

Then, face to face with Daniel, she looked him in the eye and he held her gaze and she said,

You have a beautiful home.

He took her hand, it was clammy, and then she looked into his eyes and his worry was written there. Olive said,

I wasn't serious about wanting a TT.

I didn't think so, but let me give you my card in case you want to take a look at my inventory.

Hell's bells, Danny, Harold said. Don't give her your card, give her a break on the price and maybe she'll come looking for you. That's what a woman needs.

Sheila laughed then and walked to the door. She whispered,

See? I told you. I can tell when a man likes you.

On the street, Olive felt the floating again as if her feet had lifted off the ground. Her head was spinning and she felt light enough to blow away. Harold said,

Are you all right?

Hmm?

Nice people Sheila and Danny. He's swell when you get to know him. He'll give you the shirt off his back.

I'm sure, Olive said.

Look. You want to have dinner with me next Sunday?

What?

Dinner. You and I. There's this great barbecue place out by the airport that you'll really like if you like ribs and burnt ends. They make a great burnt end sandwich. Are you okay?

I'm okay.

Let me call you then, Harold said.

He opened the door to Olive's Chrysler and he watched her get in, and she saw that his eyes weren't on her face but were fixed on her breasts as she leaned forward to key in the ignition. He said,

A Chrysler 300. Nice vehicle, get Danny to give you a price and you can trade it in for something faster and then you'd be in the club.

Olive said: I have two children.

Harold said: Say yes.

Olive said: All right.

Harold

I have a little place down on the river, he said. It's not much, just a couple of rooms but it's got a piece of beach and it's isolated so no one can hear you scream and there's a little deck because I like to kayak in the summer. They say it's good for the heart, kayaking and it works out the tension.

Olive listened to him talk and as she listened, she looked at the pile of BBQ rib bones on the table, dismembered, scattered a wreck of an animal and she felt ill, even bloated as she took in Harold's speech about the benefits of exercise and the human brain and she decided she didn't like engineers. She said,

Have you ever butchered a steer?

He looked at her as if she had just dropped in from another planet and didn't speak English. He said,

What?

Butcher a steer. Kill the thing you eat? Have you ever seen a washtub full of blood? Or the guts of a pig falling in to a vat? Bones aren't white when they're smeared with blood.

What are you talking about?

Meat, she said. Raw meat. On the farm, you do two things to live— you grow your food and you kill things. Have you ever killed anything, Harold?

He leaned elbows on the table and in the candle light, his eyes twinkled. He cupped his chin in his hands and he said,

You're a fascinating woman, you know that? I've been out with half a dozen of Sheila's friends and not one of them ever talked about butchering a steer. And no, I've never killed anything except fish because if you don't kill them, they just die out of water. And how humane is that?

Sort of a mercy killing, Olive said.

Yeah. Sort of.

Well, I don't think this is going anywhere, Harold.

Hoddy, remember?

I don't know you well enough to call you by your pet name.

Pet name? Come on. Give me a chance. What's good for Danny is good for his pals.

Stunned, Olive sat back, hands falling into her lap. She looked at him and he was smiling, his blue eyes now vicious and leering with a perverted innocence. He said,

You think I don't know?

Know what?

Danny tells me everything. Christ, I could write a book about his conquests. The man is a real animal. He told me about a woman he picked up in a bar—you—and he gave me every detail. We like the same things. So. How about it? My place or yours?

Olive laughed. Catching her breath, she looked around at the patrons in the restaurant and then she picked up the water glass and poured it into Harold's lap until the glass was empty then she set it down. She said,

How's that?

He didn't flinch, or shout, or even pull away. He just smiled and his eyes twinkled like a little boy and he said,

We can go to my place on the river or we can go to a motel. Danny says you're real good on a motel bed.

Tell me something, Olive said.

Anything.

Does Sheila know about this little club of yours?

Sheila doesn't live on this planet, he said. Her idea of sex is reading a Harlequin romance.

So she has no idea that you and Danny share everything?

You mean have I ever had her. No. Never did.

So what makes you think you can have me?

Look at you. You look like a tramp with those tits hangin' out, you smell like a tramp, you go down like a whore so Danny tells me.

Like I said, Harold, this isn't going anywhere so I think I'll call it a night. When Sheila told me you were divorced, I have to admit I felt sorry for you. But you're just another pig, Harold.

Oh come on. What's Danny got that I can't give you?

When I was a girl, I helped my Dad slaughter pigs. I know the smell of blood and I know the feel of a knife cutting gristle and, Harold, I know a pig when I see one.

So that's a no?

That's a no, Olive said.

She stood then and opened her purse and dropped a twenty dollar bill on the table.

What's that for?

You'll need to buy some hog slop, Harold. Maybe you can invite

Danny out to your place on the river and wallow in the trough together but believe me, you'll never touch one square inch of the skin on my body.

Olive left him at the table. She walked out to her Chrysler and she sat for a while relaxed and calm. Breathing slow, she felt her heart beat and she tasted the sweetness of the BBQ sauce left on her lips. She leaned back in the seat and she remembered Daniel's grin the night Sheila had invited her to dinner. She had walked into the slaughterhouse like an innocent. He hadn't recognized her at first, and then, as the light came on, he had leered at her until she left and poor Sheila, caught up in her cancer trap hadn't seen a thing. Then it made sense. Her confession about being a wife in name only. Her isolation.

Danny had talked to Harold about his women and Sheila knew nothing about any of it and the two men wrapped up in their little pornographic trysts shared like little boys splitting a Hershey bar.

She started the car, switched on the lights and was startled to see Harold standing in front of her.

He walked to the door, opened it. Slid in. Looked at her. He said,

I'm sorry. I was a little over the line back there.

I'm leaving now.

Give me another chance.

I don't think so.

Harold grabbed her hand and she let him pull her to him and then when he tried to kiss her, she reached across her body and she raked his face with her nails—long and hard—but he didn't grunt or groan the deeper she dug, the more he grinned.

Is that all I get? He said. I can take anything you've got.

Gold Chain

She opened the door.

He stood there carrying flowers.

Red roses in a red foil wrapper.

He wore those black penny loafers, a pair of black slacks, a belt with a chrome buckle. He wore that red short-sleeved shirt open at the neck, a gold chain dangling in the V.

Olive stepped back, recoiling as if he had hit her. She held up a hand like prey warding off a vampire. He held out the roses. She looked at them, then at his face. A smile. He said,

Shall we try it again?

Olive glanced over his shoulder into the empty hallway. She said,

Are you out of your mind?

We need to talk.

We have nothing to talk about.

I think we do, he said. What are you going to do?

You mean am I going to kill you?

About Sheila, he said. How am I supposed to know you're pals?

Then you mean am I going to tell her you...

Can I come in? It's kind of smelly out here.

He drew back the flowers and he leaned against the door frame. Olive smelled his cologne, the same cologne he wore the night she picked him up, the same cologne he wore at dinner. Chills ran up her back. She stood aside then and let him in and she closed the door and retreated to the window leaving him in the center of the room holding his red roses. He looked around at the tiny studio, at the bed then at Olive who pointed to the chair at the table. He sat. She leaned against the wall, waiting.

I'm sorry, he said. I should have called.

It is a coincidence.

Yeah, well, where do we go from here?

We don't go anywhere, Daniel.

Don't be that way. It's not like I don't know you.

He stood, advanced on her. She held out a hand keeping him away because she knew what he wanted. He stopped, facing her, looking her up and down, he said,

God, you're lovely.

Tell it to your wife.

Look, he said.

No, you look. It was a mistake.

It was terrific, he said. I've never had sex like that and I know I didn't treat you right and I'm sorry for that but I didn't think I'd ever see you again.

I want you to leave.

She crossed her arms, the barriers up. She was angry then that he had come begging and she felt strong, like she had wrested control from him and she studied his eyes, pinning him in place the way he had pinned her, drunk, to the bed and she smelled his cologne and remembered his sweat dripping on her bare back as he penetrated her, remembered his grunts and guttural groans as he came in her, remembered the feel and taste of him in her mouth. She said,

I know you—you're the kind who can't let well enough alone,

Look, he said. You know why I'm here.

Um huh, she said, and it's not going to happen.

He inched closer to her, touched her hands crossed over her chest—he looked at her face, a plea in his eyes and she laughed. She controlled him now. She could make him do what she wanted. It was a new feeling, a great feeling and she said,

What did you tell Sheila?

What did I tell her?

Did you tell her you were coming here for a repeat of Saturday night or did you just slip out while she's asleep?

I didn't tell her anything. We're adults.

And you're married to Sheila.

Let me explain.

There's nothing to explain. Married. Wife with cancer. Plain and simple. Get out.

Do I have to beg? I've never had anyone like you.

Do you say that to all your pickups?

As I remember it, you were having a hell of a good time.

I didn't enjoy it, she said. I felt humiliated and dirty and I hated the smell you left on me and I hated myself for letting you do it that way...to me.

That's not how I read it, he said.

Leave.

Aw come on, Olive. I can't stop thinking about you.

You know my name but that night you didn't ask. Anonymous Sex, that's what you said. A little anonymous sex no strings no complications. When you can't find a slut on the prowl for dick what do you do? Does Sheila know you go to bars and pick up women and have anal sex with them?

That was the first time.

You are a terrible liar, Olive said. My granny would say you'd climb a tree to tell a lie when you could stand on the ground and tell the truth. Now. Go.

Damn it, he said. I...you...we...

Don't even try to make anything of it. When I saw you at that table with that nasty grin on your face I knew you were back in that motel room and I knew you were enjoying humiliating me again.

You're not going to say anything to Sheila, are you?

Olive shrugged. She liked watching him grovel. She liked his abject humiliation. Liked seeing the pain on his face.

Look, I can help you out here. This place? How much rent do you pay?

So you're now offering me money?

What do you want?

Let me see your wallet.

Without a hitch, he tugged his wallet from his hip pocket and handed it to Olive. She pulled all the cash from the case and counted it. She said,

Sheila told me you were rich. This isn't rich. This is paper boy money.

Hell, I'll write you a check right now. What a thousand month?

You want to see me again? Olive said.

Yeah. I really do.

Five thousand a month because I'll need a new apartment and you can buy me an Audi.

An Audi?

An R 8. A guy came into GECU the other day for a loan. He wants to buy an Audi R 8. I want an R 8.

Christ, that's a lotta dough.

So you don't want to see me.

He reached for her, hand on her waist. He still held the roses. He tried to kiss her, but the smell of his cologne gagged her, gave her flashes of him pressed into her naked back and she turned aside and pulled away. He insisted, but she twisted loose and stood, holding his cash, his wallet.

Ask me out on a proper date then.

He stiffened, his face blanching. He looked at her, breathing through his mouth.

A date?

83

If you want it bad enough, you'll find a way. Just tell her, your wife, Sheila, my friend, tell her you're taking me to dinner and then we're going apartment hunting.

We do this, you can't see Sheila anymore.

Olive walked to the door, held it open. Breathing hard, he chased her. Stopped. Olive tossed his wallet and the cash out into the hallway. Then, planting a hand on his chest, she shoved him over the threshold. Still holding the roses, he stumbled, turned, looked back at her. As Olive closed the door, he said,

You can't see her. You hear me.

Hands trembling, knees quaking, Olive leaned her forehead against the door. She was floating again, her feet had lifted off the floor and she was in the dark, disconnected, adrift again and alone and very much afraid of what she was feeling. More than anything, she needed a shower to wash the stench of his body from her hands.

Wheatland

I don't know where to start, Olive said. I feel like I want to run away and die.

The words were heavy as they left her mouth, each one peeling loose a piece of her pain until the hole in her chest was deep and dark and dangerous.

Rose, as usual, sat in her quiet chair, the blue and red afghan tucked around her legs like a protective sheet. Not once—in months—had Olive asked for a quilt. She preferred the chill as her skin danced in the cold air of the office. She glanced out the window, into a shaft of sunlight breaking through the winter clouds—the gray and light as complex as the four paintings on the wall behind Rose. In the parking lot of the Wheatland Market, Olive watched a meat truck unloading boxes—too far away to tell what was in them—but the two men in white coats worked hard and fast. Turning back to the paintings on the wall, Olive looked at Rose in the middle—two paintings behind each shoulder as though all five of them were connected somehow with Rose at the center. She said,

After Dean, my younger brother came to see me, I went crazy. He didn't let up on me but kept hounding me to go back to Tim, to the farm, but I can't do that. Not now.

Rose tapped her notebook with her pencil. Waiting. Olive watched her the way she always watched her, waiting for Rose to leak judgment, to condemn her, but Rose always held her ground, eyes clear, waiting.

Then, Rose raised her pencil. She said,

You never talk about your other brother. Why not?

He'd dead, Olive replied. There are just the two of us now.

I see, Rose said. How did he die?

He was killed in the desert. An IED, they call them. Explosives...He and three others.

I'm sorry.

He was two years older than I am.

I am sorry.

I don't want to talk about that today, Olive said. I'm confused.

85

Rose made a note. Olive took a deep breath. She said:

Sheila invited me to dinner.

Good, you're getting out to new places.

She was in Houston for a while. She has cancer. She came back and invited me to dinner. I met her husband, Daniel.

Olive looked at Rose, waiting, and she felt the thumping in her chest, the fast and powerful beating of her heart and she stood, walked to the window, looked at the Wheatland Market where now the two men from the meat truck were leaning against the wide of the building smoking cigarettes. They looked assured and solid as they gestured. Then, one of them crushed his smoke on the ground and got into the truck and drove away. The other man then carried a box of meat to his van before re-entering the back door of the market. Turning to Rose, Olive said:

Daniel is the man with the gold chain I had sex with. The man in the motel. The man I had anal sex with.

Rose held her pencil on top of her notebook. She glanced up. Her face was open, but there was a slight pinching of the forehead—a reaction.

Daniel is Sheila's husband, Olive said. I want to die, but how could I know? The minute Sheila opened the door, I smelled his cologne—it's burned into my brain now—and when I saw him, he was wearing his red shirt and black pants like a uniform and, Rose...

Olive stopped. She stood looking down at her witch doctor, her mind healer, at Rose, calm and peaceful. Olive said.

At first he didn't recognize me. I was a stranger he'd never seen before but then something triggered him and he recognized me. Now I have a problem.

Rose said: Has anything come of it?

You mean have I told Sheila? No. I haven't told her, but he came to see me at my apartment on J Street one night. I tossed him out. I need to tell Sheila. I'm bound to tell her. I have to.

Have you talked to her since?

We've gotten together twice since then, but she's so worried about her health she can't talk about anything else except how she thinks I should be interested in a friend of theirs, Harold, but that's not going to happen. She knows something's troubling me.

Well, Rose said, this is a big thing.

It was a coincidence and it's eating me alive.

Are you feeling guilty? Rose asked.

How can I feel guilty if I didn't know?

Olive sat down, felt a rush of blood to her face. She said:

All through dinner, I smelled his cologne and it was making me sick.

Why do you think smells affect you that way, Olive?

I don't know. But every time I smelled it I remembered being with him and how he felt in me and there he was and I remembered every word he said. Damn it. And the gold chain. The same gold chain I felt beating against my back when he...took me...and I couldn't help wondering how many others there have been and there was poor Sheila the gracious hostess all smiles, her husband having sex with me in a motel room while eating roast beef. It was a nightmare. I have to tell her.

How do you feel right now? Rose asked. Where does it lock up? Where do you get tight. Chest? Heart? Neck? Throat?

In my stomach. I can't explain it.

Try.

I get a warm feeling in my bottom. If I'd stayed any longer, I'm sure I'd've thrown up. I can still taste his skin and it's making me sick.

You're reliving it right now, Rose said. Breathe. Relax.

Olive closed her eyes, let the full feeling own her for a few seconds, then she tasted vomit rising in her throat but she held on, held it back until Rose said:

Why do you need to tell her?

I need to confess if I ever want to get clean. It was a mistake.

How much do you value her friendship?

What?

What will happen if you confess all this to her?

I don't know.

The coincidence, Rose said. It was a coincidence.

Yes, the coincidence, He was just a face. A body. But still, I think I should tell her.

Do you need to tell her for you or to make yourself feel better.

I can't carry this around and still be friends with her. I have to open up.

We'll have to talk about this some more but right now, how are your dreams? Do you dream about him?

About him? About Daniel? No, but I have a nightmare about my babies. I see them and they're dead. Their faces are covered with dirt and when I try to wash them their skin falls off and I wake up.

Where are you feeling that right now? Rose asked.

Olive wanted to speak, but the words jammed up in her throat and she felt her mouth open and close like a fish gasping. Then, she was floating, the treacherous, nebulous floating as if she were lifting off, losing her footing, drifting away she was so light, and she clutched at the arms of the chair and she gasped, and she looked at Rose, a spasm jolting her chest like an electric shock.

Olive, can you hear me?

Umm, Olive whispered.

Show me where you're feeling this.

I'm suffocating, Olive said. Floating, choking just like I did on the windmill.

Ah, Rose said. The windmill. We always come back to the windmill, don't we?

Lemon Pie

She noticed right off that the café smelled like lemon pie. The smell reminded her of her mother Grace's kitchen in harvest-time—fried chicken, fresh butter, biscuits and lemon pie. The sweet citrus scent of lemons and sugar wafting from the kitchen and the faint haze of smoke with sunlight drifting through the plate glass window of the café set off ribbons of haze that drifted like waves as Janey came to Olive's table. She sat down, fanning herself with her order book. She said,

Didn't hear you come in.

I just got here.

Where have you been?

Busy.

Doing what?

Olive set the newspaper on the table open to the want ads where half a dozen jobs were circled in black ink. She said,

I need a new job.

What's wrong with the bank?

It's never going to let me go full time.

Why do you need full time?

My kids. Remember?

Sure, I remember, Janey said, I thought you'd forgotten.

Janey looked away. Olive watched her in the sunlight, the almond shaped eyes, the straight nose, full lips. Janey was more than a waitress. Olive remembered the Tomb the night they first went out together. She wanted to ask about the man Kit, but instead, she turned back to the paper. Janey said,

Anything turning up?

Same stuff I'm doing now. Let me ask you a question, Olive said.

Ask away.

Why do you stay here?

Here? You mean Wichita?

No. I mean here at the Kiowa Café. You're smart, you're beautiful, you've got tons of personality.

And a high school diploma that's backed by straight C's.

Don't you want something more?

Like what?

I don't know—more. A car.

Janey leaned across the table that intimate closeness of secrets and she laid a hand on Olive's hand and she said,

Look, Olive. You've got two kids, you've got a degree, you've got a future waiting out there. The way I see it, I grow up, I grow old, I die and that's that.

Don't you think about what comes next?

Like if Jesus will save my soul? All I want is to have a good time, get high, get laid, buy sexy underwear.

No, I don't mean that...I mean...you know...If you stay here, what comes next?

What comes next is what comes next and you're freaking me out. What's got into you?

You could go back to school.

On the tips I make here?

Olive studied her, let her eyes rove over Janey's angular face, the eye shadow, the lips the color of cherries, the hair that was so black it shattered the light like a prism. She said,

I worry about you, Janey.

Max just baked a couple of lemon meringue pies.

I thought I smelled pie.

They're still hot. You want a piece?

I like it cool, Olive said. You know. So the sugar weeps through the skin.

Weeps, Janey said. See, I'd never have called it weeps. Not in a million years.

You know what I mean, the little sugar...

I know what you mean.

Janey slid out of the booth. Olive turned back to the papers, to the want ads but nothing had changed. She felt lucky to have the job at the bank.

As she folded the paper back to the front page, she wondered if she had made a mistake coming to the City, leaving her babies, leaving Tim. She felt a shudder in her shoulders and the urge to cry but she held on—for what?—a one room studio with no closet and a tiny bathroom big enough only for someone under four feet tall. She remembered Toby—how cute he was, tow-headed, and small and she remembered how he smelled when he got out of the bath tub. She made a note to call and then she looked up and saw herself reflected in the plate glass window. A shaft of sunlight burning through the lemon meringue haze and she saw her face lit as if by a flood lamp. She watched herself for a long time. Her asymmetrical hair cut was snow white in the light. She raised her painted fingernails, touched her lips. Sitting up straight, she watched her body, the tight top, her breasts. She was very much a city girl now. She watched her reflection until the sunlight shifted and she disappeared into blackness.

She took a deep breath and closed the paper—maybe tomorrow an opening would come up—something just right—full time—that would let her rent a bigger place, big enough for Nan and Toby.

Janey set a plate on the table. She said,

There you go.

Olive jerked back, looked at the pie, smelled the tang of lemon and it was as if she had just emerged from a long sleep. She was spinning again. Floating. Her body rising like smoke. Janey said,

What's the matter? You okay?

Uhh. Olive muttered. She reached for the fork and cut the pie and then she let it go with a click because she couldn't hold it. It was too heavy. The dab of lemon filling on the fork had been the last straw making the fork too heavy to hold. Janey said,

Did you ever get tested?

What?

You know. Tested for HIV after your creepy thing with that sick fuck.

No. Yes. I'm okay.

You gotta carry condoms, Janey said. Those guys are totally irresponsible. I had the clap before I started carrying my own. You'd think. You can't be too careful these days. By the way, you remember Kit?

Um huh.

What do you think? He wants me to move in with him. But I don't know.

Olive picked up the fork again and tasted the lemon on it. It was just right—tangy, sharp with just enough sweet to mellow out the lemon. She licked the fork then cut a bite and ate it. Janey said,

What do you think?

Think about what?

About moving in with Kit.

If you wanted to move in with Kit, you wouldn't be asking me.

What're friends for?

This is good pie.

We've got to get you out more, Janey said. There's a rally this weekend in Hutch.

What kind of a rally?

Bikers, Janey said. It's a draw. Not quite Sturgis but they get maybe a

91

thousand bikers that weekend.

You want me to go to a biker rally?

Do you want to get laid?

Not bad enough to go to a biker rally. Jeez, Janey. What are you thinking? That's dangerous.

No it's not. Those guys are very cool—free pot, free booze, free sex—everything a girl needs.

They're bikers.

They're better than some of the clowns I've gone down on at the Tomb.

I can't do that, Olive said. I'm a mother of two.

The pie any good?

Terrific. Tell Max he's a good chef.

He knows. He's a biker, Olive.

He is.

Yeah. He and his old lady go to all the rallies. So what are you going to do?

I'll stick to his lemon pie, Olive said.

You're no fun anymore, you know that?

Olive licked the last of the pie from the fork. Without a word, Janey took the plate and the fork. Olive thought about what it would cost to bring Nan and Toby to the city and there was just no way she could afford it. She needed a sugar daddy. A man with a big house. A man who knew what he wanted.

Worry

From the window looking down into the parking lot of the Wheatland Market, Olive watched the woman pack a cartload of groceries in the black SUV. Her flaming red hair hung in ringlets to her shoulders. She wore a black warm up suit with white trim and white running shoes. She pushed the grocery cart to a return station and then, standing beside the SUV did a frantic search of her purse for the car key before realizing she had stuck it in the pocket of her warm up jacket. A big sigh. Olive said,

She goes shopping every week at the same time. I wonder if she dreams about leaving her babies. I wonder if she hates her husband enough to poison his biscuits.

You look nice today, Rose said. Is that a new outfit?

Turning, Olive watched Rose stir, arrange the afghan to cover her knees. Long bony fingers, skin sallow and thin, nails clear—no polish—sun spots mottling her skin to a brownish tinge.

Olive said: There's a man who comes into the bank. I know he wants to ask me out.

Will you go if he asks?

I don't know if I can.

You've reformed?

Because he's a little man, shorter than I am. There's something magnetic about him though—like he sees me for who I am. The problem is that he excites me. He smells good. I wonder what he'd be like but he's small. Tim is huge. I'd forgotten how big he is—huge—and this man is small.

Why should his size bother you?

Should I sleep with him?

Do you think that's what I mean?

He smells like flowers.

Rose stirred, moved the afghan covering her knees.

Olive watched her through half open eyes, misty as if in a dream, the Technicolor afghan spread out in a haze like a rainbow in field of flowers. Rose with her penetrating but kind eyes, a wise woman who already knew

93

everything Olive was going to say, who already knew the feelings she was hiding, who could see into her far deeper than anyone had ever seen, the eyes ripping off the lies like tissue paper from a Christmas package. Olive sat up straight, closed her knees together. She said,

He's kind of like you.

Like me?

He sees through me.

You think I see through you?

I don't know.

Let's talk about your dreams.

Olive closed her eyes and told Rose that she had dreamed about Nan and Toby on the farm riding with Paul on a tractor, wearing straw hats and red bandanas around their necks and she heard the rumble of the tractor's engine as it lugged when the plow bit deep and she watched the babies taking turns sipping from the water jug Paul kept beside him out of the head and she watched her mother, Grace, driving across the plowed field to bring sandwiches and she smiled as she watched her father open the lunchbox and hand sandwiches to each of her babies—bologna and cheese, lettuce, tomato and mayonnaise and she watched her father wipe a spot of mayonnaise from his chin just before he leaned down and brushed a fly from Toby's sandwich just before he bit into it and when she opened her eyes, Rose was looking down at her notebook and the flashes of black lightning linking the four paintings danced in front of Olive's eyes. She said,

I'm a mess, a total mess. I can't bring them here—not now, maybe not ever.

Rose said: A child's greatest fear is that it's mother will abandon it.

Well, I guess I've done that.

Where do you feel it when I talk about that? Abandoning your babies?

I told you already—I'm ashamed and maybe a little bit afraid of what will happen, but I can't go get them.

Do you want to get them?

I worry about them, Olive said. I worry but I can't bring them to the city.

Farm life wasn't right for you, how do you know it will work for them?

Being a kid is one thing, Olive said. Being a pregnant animal is another. They'll be all right. I'm just not ready...

Will you ever be ready? Rose said.

I don't know.

Olive clasped her hand over her mouth. She didn't want to talk anymore so she stood and paced the room to the window glancing at Rose, the Sphinx, wrapped in her afghan, cold, as if she had no heat in her body. The woman from the black SUV returned to the car holding a grocery sack. Only one. No children with her. A red car, a very sporty car with a convertible top pulled into the slot beside the SUV and a man got out. Over the top the car, he talked to the woman who was still holding her grocery sack. She looked around, the man said something, and then she got in her car and drove away. Olive sat on the edge of the chair and faced Rose. She said,

Men are messy. I hate having to clean up. I hate the feel and smell of a man's come on me. I hate the grunting and the sweat.

And the short man at work? Rose said.

Maybe he'll be different. But I haven't made up my mind about him yet.

But you want to?

Yes. I think so.

Are you masturbating? Rose said.

Sometimes. Not much. Just sometimes. A few months ago, I'd have lied to you. But now? No. I enjoy it. Gee. If my mother heard me say that to you, she'd...I don't know...wash my mouth out with soap? I just can't imagine my mother masturbating no matter what...

Ask her sometime she might surprise you.

You're kidding. She's never had a sexual thought in her life.

Still, Rose said. Your hunting seems to have slowed down.

I haven't been out for while.

How are you feeling about that?

I think I'm addicted to orgasms.

There are different forms of addiction—drugs, alcohol, sex. Can you control it?

What do you mean?

At work do you run to the restroom to masturbate?

No, it hasn't gotten that far...Sometimes, after I shower...Do you think I should masturbate more?

Are you ashamed of it?

No. Not a bit. And you think I should sleep with the short guy to show I've got an open mind about shorties?

I can't make that decision for you, but you can have sex with yourself and not feel guilty about it. That's progress. Have you thought about a wand?

A wand? Like a princess wand? Not since I was six when I had a part in a school pageant and wore a pink dress with a diamond tiara.

We're a little beyond pink dresses and diamond tiaras here. No. It's a special kind of vibrator you can use to help yourself orgasm.

Where do I get something like that? Olive asked.

Rose made a note in her notebook and tore the sheet in half and handed it to Olive. The address was for a store called Love Season. Olive held the paper and studied Rose's face. She said,

Will this turn me into a complete woman?

Spending some time alone with your wand can open some doors, Rose said.

Clifford

He was short. He was fat. He was bald but he made her laugh. He turned dinner into a circus. His cynical stare as he waited for the joke to sink in made her skin bumpy and when she got the joke, she had to keep from giggling and twittering like a teen-ager. In between glasses of wine, she tried to remember the last time she had laughed so much. He leaned across the table, his round head glistening and he whispered,

You might want to lay off the wine for a spell.

Why? She said. Are you dangerous?

Do I look dangerous?

Let me ask you something, Olive said.

In English?

Have you ever butchered a steer?

Last Sunday, he said.

No, I'm serious. Have you ever butchered a steer?

He finished his wine, refilled the glasses with a careful turn of the bottle at the last moment to catch the last drop before it dribbled down the side and then he held his glass up. In the ruby red light, his skin turned pink and his teeth, as he smiled, seemed to drip red. He said,

You know, in some circles, wine is blood.

Do you believe that?

I'm not a believer in anything I can't measure. But look, Olive. I'm not a wrangler. I don't own a gun. I can't bench press my weight. I'm fat. I'm bald. I'm short. But yes, I have butchered a steer or two.

He laughed then and Olive watched him. He didn't try to be anything but what he was. She liked that.

Tell me about it, she said.

Okay. My family had a place outside of Garden City. There were eight of us. I was the third. The first boy. I had two older sisters who on any given day could beat the tar out of me with one hand tied behind their backs. And they took turns at it.

We raised our own beef, hogs, ran a small herd of dairy cows. Every winter we butchered a steer, two hogs, and sometimes a lamb. I saw my

97

first blood when I was three and my sisters and mother made blood pudding and sausages.

Do you hate your sisters? Olive said.

Is that how you throw guys off guard, by reading their minds?

With an affectionate pat, he tapped on the empty wine bottle. She noticed that his hand was steady. He said,

This is a Corbière. From a little town in the Midi called Minerve. Do you know it?

I don't know what the Midi is.

Southern France. I own a little winery there—wait—I'm part owner of a little winery there. We can now compete with the Burgundies and the Pinot Noirs but our wine isn't as temperamental and it travels better.

This is your wine? Olive said.

Private reserve. I bring back a couple of cases...

To beautiful Wichita.

He stared at her. She watched his eyes and behind the gentleness there was a rigor that made her hesitate. Maybe she was wrong about all this. He said,

I didn't mean to lay it on so thick. I'm not trying to impress you, but not many women know the first thing about butchering a steer. I hope I didn't scare you off.

I don't scare easily.

Most women won't give me the time of day.

Tell me about your sisters.

This is going to be a long dance, he said.

Do you like to dance?

I learned to jitterbug with my sisters. In church but it didn't do any good.

I go out with a woman, she drinks my private reserve then—boom— she has to be somewhere. The last time I had two dates in a row I was fourteen and hadn't gotten this little belly yet.

Is that what this is? Olive said. A date?

What's your favorite fairy tale?

My favorite fairy tale?

Cinderella?

Puzzled, trying to follow him, her mind clouded with wine, she spoke without hesitation,

Rumplestiltskin.

Straw into gold, he said. Mine is Beauty and the Beast.

She fiddled with her wine glass, the glow of the liquor warmed her face and for some reason, she was at ease with him—no pressure, no expectations. She said,

You know I'm separated from my husband.

Yeah, he said.

You know?

Yeah.

You checked me out?

Um huh.

I should be pissed off at you for doing that.

I'm not evil, he said. I'm not stalking you.

So what do you want?

Why did you say yes?

I told my therapist you smell like flowers and I've never been with a man who smells like flowers and she said I was afraid to go out with you because you're short.

You don't like flowers?

My therapist said I should test myself because you're short and my husband, my ex-husband, is a big man.

What do you want?

My therapist says I want what I can't have.

His eyes never left hers but she didn't feel uncomfortable. He was looking at her, not through her, not gazing at her like a specimen, just a soft and gentle watching. There was a kindness there she hadn't seen or felt for a long time. She said.

Where do you think this is going?

You mean what does a beautiful woman such as you get out of hanging out with a guy like me.

Let me ask you something, Olive said.

Have I ever butchered a steer?

He sat back in his chair, but he wasn't defeated. He waited while she watched him, turnabout. She felt his eyes fixed on her eyes, not on her breasts, not on her hands, but on her eyes. She said,

How do you feel walking into a room with a woman who's three inches taller than you are?

Everybody's three inches taller than I am.

What am I supposed to do with you?

Go out with me again.

And then what?

I can take you to the Midi if you'll go.

I don't speak French.

I do.

I'm a working girl. How would I get time off?

You don't belong in that bank. You need a new job, one that'll challenge you

I like my job.

I know people who can help you get situated.

She studied him for a long time but he didn't retreat, didn't flinch, didn't hesitate.

And what does it cost me?

Nothing. Absolutely nothing.

I better go home now, she said.

He stood. She looked at the cut of his suit. She hadn't noticed before that it was tailored from a worsted wool, maybe even cashmere but she resisted the temptation to touch it. She noticed the still crisp white shirt. The elegant tie. He was short. He was bald. He was fat, but he held his place like a block of granite. She had never seen a man with that kind of presence. He said,

So. Tomorrow night then? Dinner?

Why Beauty and the Beast? She said.

Dream Book

In the dream I'm tied to the windmill, my legs spread wide, knees up like I'm on a delivery table and there's blood, rivers of blood and I scream and I wake up shaking and screaming I see you facing me, but now your tiny and you're using a huge scoop shovel that's larger than your body and you dig the steel blade into my head and I wonder how you got in there and you're naked except for a loin cloth and your breasts are erect as you dip the shovel into a wet slimy sticky mess like tar and there's the smell of asphalt coming from between my legs and you hurl the shovel away. I make no effort to cover myself, I kind of enjoy being on display and there are people watching from the corners of the room and then I look down to see a great gooey stream of snot oozing from between my legs and I say excuse me and I wipe at the snot and there's a man standing at the foot of the bed smiling and he's holding something out to me but I can't make out what it is and then I get off the bed and turn to you but you're walking out the door leaving a trail of something that looks like silk thread and I kneel to touch it and then the door closes and you're gone.

Well, Rose said, you certainly shrank me down to size.

What does it mean?

What do you think it means?

It means I'm messed up.

Did you write it down?

It's in my dream book.

Let me see.

Ham and Cheese

Olive answered the phone, Hello. The voice on the other end was mellow and thick.

Who is this?

Clifford.

I didn't expect you to call.

I talked to that friend of mine at the packing company. He wants you to call him and set up an interview.

Olive fell silent, her heart beating fast. She leaned one hand on the table and closed the cap of the mustard jar. She said,

You didn't have to do that…I mean…I didn't expect anything.

I said I'd call.

I didn't think you meant it.

Why wouldn't I mean it?

Well for one, you're a man and men lie about what they mean.

And what do you think I mean?

I know you want something, Olive said.

He laughed. Olive switched hands and closed the bread loaf, twisted the wrapper and turned it over to seal it. She peeled a slice of cheese from the package and laid it on the ham and then folded the second slice of bread on it. No lettuce, no tomato, just ham and cheese and bread with mustard. She said,

Okay. Let me get a pencil.

Why don't I just come up and give it to you? He said.

You want to give me a pencil?

Go to the window.

Olive walked to the window and looked down. Across the street, she saw him standing beside a car holding a cell phone. He wore jeans, a black T-shirt, and running shoes. She laughed. She said,

You're stalking me.

It's broad daylight. I'm standing in the street.

The car was a long, low, sleek machine with bright red paint and a black convertible top. Olive said,

Is that your car?

Let me take you to lunch.

I'm fixing a sandwich.

Ham and cheese?

Yeah, ham and cheese on whole wheat.

I grew up on whole wheat.

No lettuce, no tomato, no pickle, Olive said.

Just the way I like it, he said. What do you say?

She closed the cell phone and laid it on the table. She cut the sandwich in half on the diagonal. She then re-opened the mustard jar and took two paper plates from the package and laid her sandwich on one. She took a deep breath when the knock came on the door. She opened. He smiled at her. She said,

Come in.

She backed away, leery, not knowing what to expect. As he entered he brought with him his floral scent—light but fragrant—and what she saw in the daylight confused her because he seemed to have lost his softness. The roundness of his body now seemed more angular, harder. His head, still bald and shiny, looked bigger while his eyes, still that deep aquamarine, glistened as he watched her.

He glanced around, nodded. He said.

Cute little place.

It's a dump, Olive said, but you already knew that. Did your investigator take photographs?

What do you think I am?

Have a seat, she said. Do you like mustard?

She put together another ham and cheese sandwich—no tomato, no lettuce, no pickle. They ate in silence. She watched him. He didn't shuffle his feet or clear his throat—he was a man eating a ham and cheese sandwich off a paper plate and wiping his mouth with a paper napkin. She liked him sitting at her table, a solid man not pushing her. She said,

How about a glass of milk?

Umm, he said, nodding.

She poured two glasses of milk and watched him sip at his, leaving a small white spot on his upper lip that he licked at. As he sat there, she remembered their dinner, remembered the wine, the steak, the candles, the flowers on the table. But here, it was just him and her at her table eating ham and cheese sandwiches on whole wheat bread and drinking milk. Olive laughed. Looking up at her, he smiled. He said,

What? I've got mustard on my chin?

No. Nothing.

Something's tickling you.

Really, it's nothing.

He finished his sandwich and he pulled a pen from his pants pocket and wrote a phone number on his napkin and he slid it across the table to her. He said,

His name is Bill Watkins. His company has branches in KC, Chicago, St. Louis, LA and Fort Lauderdale.

Why should he talk to me?

Because I asked him to.

This investigation you made of me, Olive said. How deep did it go?

I wouldn't call it an investigation, he said.

What would you call it?

He shrugged and smiled and in the smile she saw again the rock hard features that had escaped her the first night. That night, wearing his suit and tie he looked soft and flabby. Now she saw a solid block of a man in jeans and a T-shirt that hid nothing, a man so willful and confident he seemed electric. He said,

I talked to your boss.

Olive closed the milk carton and folded her napkin on the table in front of her. She looked at him and again felt his eyes on her like hooks biting into her flesh, but she didn't feel trapped. She couldn't understand it. He watched her eyes, he didn't look at her breasts. He took her in with his eyes but didn't touch her. A man who looked right at her, saw right into her yet made her feel comfortable. She said,

Did you find all the skeletons in my closet?

She told me you're smart, honest, and direct. She says you know your stuff.

You really know how to piss a girl off, Olive said.

You got a degree. You work hard. You didn't date. You could have gone into business, but you married a guy named Tim who took you back to the family farm when his dad died and you've been there ever since.

That's it? Don't you have my high school graduation picture? Don't you know what kind of flowers I wore to my senior prom? Surely you know how old I was when I first had sex.

You're a late bloomer—First kiss, sophomore year at Newman. First sex is none of my business.

Olive twisted the cap back on the mustard jar. Picked up the milk glasses and set them in the tiny sink and ran water in them.

Back turned to him, she waited, hands wet but still he didn't say anything and so she dried the glasses and stowed them beside the little range.

Behind her, he moved and in the air she smelled the faintest hint of flowers and she turned to him drying her hands and she said,

So you do know everything about me but still, here you are.

How much do you make at that bank?

None of your business.

My guess is you pull in around thirty-six grand and you're worth three times that.

Are you trying to buy me?

He stood. He reached across the table. Olive pulled away. He scooped up the paper plate with a few crumbs left from her sandwich. She watched his hand, his arm, which was thick and muscular—something she hadn't noticed when he was wearing a suit. He crushed the plates, balled them up and stuck them in a grocery sack beside the sink. His movements were smooth. His back was broad and muscular under the T-shirt. He turned to face her. His eyes on her were gentle. She smelled his scent—carnations? Roses? Calendula? She said,

Bill Watkins works for you, doesn't he?

You got me there. But look—truth is I need a watchdog.

I've been called a lot of things, but never a watchdog.

There's a lot of slippage in this industry.

Slippage?

You know what slippage is, he said. Inventory slips out the door.

Theft? Why don't you call it theft?

Okay. Theft, he said. There's a lot of it. Cuts into the profit.

And what do you want from me?

I want someone who can read a column of numbers and see the mechanics of embezzlement then crack heads and slam fingers in the till.

There must be people who go in for that sort of thing.

I want you, he said.

You'd trust me with your money?

I want you to trust me.

Do you really own a winery in the Midi?

Um huh.

And the car out there? The one you're driving today...

It's an Aston Martin.

Is that an expensive car?

I really like the way your mind works.

How do you know the way my mind works?

I can see your mind working.

So you can read my mind now?

I know that with a mind like yours, you want to know something you start digging. I like that.

Okay. Let me dig a little bit. That Aston Martin, is it worth more than an Audi R-8?

What do you know about Audi R-8s?

I know a man who sells them.

The R-8 is a fine machine, he said, but you can buy a stable of them for the price on the Aston. You fed me lunch, let me take you for a ride on my pony.

Where are you going to take me?

Have you got a passport?

Black and Blue

She knew she'd have to spend money. No more second-hand-two-year-old consignment clothing from LouAnn's No. She'd spend money. She told Eileen she was going for an interview and that she needed new clothes and Eileen told her about Kathleen's where she bought her clothes and Olive told Janey she had the Interview and that they were going to Kathleen's and Janey said,

Where is Kathleen's?

Where you go to look like a million dollars.

Olive recalled the last time she and Janey had gone shopping, how Janey pushed her to wear something that showed a little more skin, something that didn't shout Sunday School, something that didn't whisper Up-Tight-Bitch.

Kathleen's was on a cul-de-sac called Rue de la Paix—just at the edge of the shopping district on a tree-lined street—Paris in Wichita—the pavement was cobblestone, the trees were plane, the sidewalks wide with no parking meters. A French pastry shop called Chez Irene stood at the bottom of the cul-de-sac like a cork in a bottle.

Well, Janey said, I had no idea this place was here.

Olive looped Janey arm in arm and dragged her into Kathleen's where the mannequins in the window looked human down to the eyelashes and the clothes on them were cashmere and silk and the sales clerk spoke with an accent.

Black and brilliant blue—the fall colors, she said. And when Janey backed away and said she couldn't afford the taxes on anything in the store, the clerk walked around Olive inspecting her, eyeing her back and arms and the curve of her shoulders. She said, Ah, oui, and then she left Olive standing alone while Janey sat on a velveteen chair, legs crossed, eyes glazed.

Olive eyed the shop where there were no racks of suits, no cases of purses, nothing except for the mannequins in the window even to suggest the clothing was for sale. The clerk returned and she motioned to Olive and said, Venez-avec moi, s'il vous plait.

Janey followed, whispering in Olive's ear, S'il vous plait. Jeez.

Through a smoke glass door etched with an intertwined floral and leaf twisting of vines and blossoms, the clerk led Olive to a fitting room with six wood panel doors. She held one open and ushered Olive into a bedroom sized fitting room with chairs and a vanity and mirrors and on the floor a sky blue carpet that deadened the sound of footsteps.

Hanging from a wooden rack there were three suits—all black—and three blouses—in deep cobalt.

Please, the clerk said, at your leisure and she backed out, closing the door.

Janey said: I haven't seen a price tag yet.

If you have to ask, you don't belong here.

This is Wichita, Janey said. She sat at the vanity fiddling with rouges and lipsticks and sniffing bottles of perfume while Olive shrugged out of her jacket and blouse and skirt. Half-closing her eyes, as if in a perfume daze, she slid on one of the black suits and then the blouse and when she opened her eyes to look in the wall-length mirror what she saw shocked and amazed her because the woman there looked like she'd been born to wear that outfit—the cobalt blouse with its subtle frills, the skirt that shaped itself over her frame with a gentle kiss, the jacket that seemed to lift her while at the same time saying Watch out.

Olive glanced at Janey now standing behind her in the mirror and Janey said,

Well, it ain't LouAnn's, huh?

Olive took off the suit and with hesitation bordering on reluctance she dressed in her old clothes then and walked back out to face the smiling clerk. She said,

I'll take two of them.

Oui, madame, the clerk said.

She left. Janey said, in her huskiest French mimic,

Oui madame.

The suits came each with its own box embossed with a small K in the lower left hand corner. Olive carried them. They were so light she wanted to check to see if in fact the suits were there.

Thirty-five hundred dollars, Janey said. You just blew thirty-five hundred dollars because of a fake French accent.

We're going places, Olive said. The interview's tomorrow and if I get this job, this will be my new uniform.

And if you don't get it?

Clothes talk, Janey. Maybe that's your problem, you know. You don't speak the language of clothes.

It's funny, Janey said. I don't hear anything.

They say I know who I am. They say I know what I want. They say I know how to get it.

When did you get all fluent in fashion?

About five minutes ago.

What did they say in LouAnn's ?

They said I didn't know what I was. They said I didn't know what I wanted, and they said I was too silly to get it.

Janey opened the door to the Chrysler. Olive laid the twin boxes in the back seat. Janey got in and buckled her seat belt and Olive followed. As she started the car, Janey said,

I'm thirty-five years old and I never know clothes could talk.

Carl

It was 9:30 in a long slow drizzly rain when Olive parked her Chrysler and looked through the windshield at the wet sidewalk. The four story glass and steel building reflected the gray sky making windows look like slick paintings of clouds.

Feeling a momentary quivering in her legs, Olive got out and flipped open the umbrella knowing that the mist would straighten her hair that now hung shoulder length with thick rich extension.

Shaking off the umbrella, she rode the elevator to the third floor. The office was at the end of a long shiny corridor lined with glass doors. A name plaque on the wall said Carl Weathers.

Olive entered.

Inside, the office was mahogany and glass. A man sat at a glass desk that had only a computer monitor and a telephone on it. He stood as she entered.

He was skeletal. What remained of his slicked back hair looked like the ruff of a dead ground squirrel. His face was sunset red with splotchy, whiskey veins webbing the nose. He held out a lily colored cold bony hand. And as he held Olive's hand his wounded pink eyes raked her from hairline to hips with a lingering stopover on her cleavage. He said,

I see you found the place.

Olive said: I know the city. I graduated from Newman.

She sat down and crossed her legs.

DeShawn

It was a cool evening so Olive put on a sweater. She was smoothing her lipstick when she heard the horn honk. At the window, she looked down to see Eileen waving from her car. In the evening light, the pale blue of the sky reflected in the windshield leaving the last of the clouds like a painting on a silver screen.

Olive grabbed her purse, locked the door and stepped out into the hallway that smelled, tonight, of liver and onions and stuffed bell peppers. Down the stairs to the second floor landing where the Wichita State sophomore smoked his joints and played his Rap so loud the doors rattled. Out in the street, in the night air, Olive smelled the city—the scent of car exhaust and asphalt, the sound of airplanes and motorcycles and for a moment, she stopped to take in the symphony, the cacophonic symphony that she liked so much. Each part, part of a life and she remembered her first day at the studio on J Street, how alone she was, but how the sounds around her had reassured her—unlike the monotone flatness of the prairie, the single note melody of the farm, with its dull droning of tractors in the background.

Eileen opened the door, Olive slid in, felt the slickness of leather against her bare skin and she regretted not wearing pantyhose, but the seat was warm. She said,

So you got a new car.

You mean what happened to the Prius?

Yes.

It's in the garage. This is my prowler. It only comes out at night. It's a Beamer. A BMW, the ultimate driving machine.

How can you afford a BMW on a manager's salary?

Eileen laughed, set the car in gear. She said,

I steal a lot. Not really. Remember I told you I wasn't always a bank manager.

Basketball, Olive said. I remember.

Eileen looked at her, eyes trimming Olive from head to thigh.

You look absolutely seditious tonight.

111

Seditious?

Well, with that much skin showing, you could subvert an entire civilization.

The way she said it gave Olive goose bumps. She smoothed at her legs regretting that she had worn just a skirt and blouse because Eileen was dressed in high fashion in a bright red chemise and a pearl necklace that shimmied like bone against her skin.

Eileen drove in silence out to Interstate 135 then east on K 400 where she parked in a lot beside a restaurant with a blue neon sign that said Chez DeShawn.

A friend of mine owns this place, Eileen said.

A basketball buddy? Olive asked.

Um huh. From the old days.

Eileen Norburg got out of the car and waited for Olive who stopped to adjust the strap on her sandal. When she looked up, Eileen again had her fixed in her sights, eyes glistening, mouth open just a shade. From her kneeling position, Olive was reminded of how tall Eileen was, how thin—almost frail, and how long her legs were and how the spiked heels added to her height. Olive said,

Spiked heels.

We're not at GECU, Eileen said, you can be as wicked as you need to be.

Eileen held out a hand to help Olive to her feet. Olive said,

Why didn't you tell me you were going whole hog, I'd have dressed up too.

You could wear a gunny sack and still be queen of the ball.

Well, you look gorgeous.

I am gorgeous, Eileen said.

Gripping Olive's arm, Eileen led her into the restaurant, into soft light and potted Ficus and walnut paneling. Light piano music from a player on a dais cascaded through the room. At the maitre d's stand, a young black woman in a black and white uniform smiled. She wore a black bow tie. Her hair hung in wet ringlets to her shoulders.

Eileen Norburg, Eileen said.

DeShawn reserved your corner table. He's not here but he wants to see you. This way, please.

Olive followed Eileen and the hostess to a table set with white china and yellow napkins. Stem-ware glasses, cut crystal water tumblers, half a dozen forks, knives, and spoons in elegant thin silver. Candles flickered in lavender glass holders.

Wow, Olive said. Do you bring everyone who quits here for a farewell dinner?

Oh, no, Eileen said. Just the special ones I want to keep in touch with.

Are there a lot of those?

One, including you.

She smiled and sat down and Olive watched the precision of her motions—the smoothing of the skirt, the flutter of the cloth as her skirt raked it, the small adjustment to the napkin, the repositioning of the silverware, the attention to detail. Olive admired the long red nails, admired the way Eileen, like an animal checking its lair, made a nest. Olive remembered how impressed she had been with Eileen's couture in the office. Every morning, she arrived looking crisp and sharp, every day in a different ensemble. She seemed like a professional model, a model to respect for her purity. And then unfolding a napkin in her lap, Eileen said,

I'm so glad you could come tonight. You don't know how much it means to me.

You've really helped me, you know. I mean, you've been just a perfect role model. Without you, I'd still be wearing white bras and granny pants.

That's very funny. You in granny panties.

Olive, looked away, touched the water glass not understanding the gratitude when it was she, Olive who owed so much to the woman sitting across from her. She was searching for a reply when a tall black man approached the table. His head was shaven, but he had a thick beard and gold ear rings. He wore a sedate dark suit, crisp lavender shirt, and a cobalt tie. He moved like water on glass and he stooped to kiss Eileen's cheek, he said,

Hello darlin' you're looking like the franchise tonight.

DeShawn, Eileen said, this is my friend Olive.

Yes, he said. The lovely and charmante Olive I've heard so much about.

He took Olive's hand and kissed it. His beard was wiry and hard and a shiver ran up Olive's arm. DeShawn said,

For you, tonight, I ordered up a special seafood mixed grill.

Excellent, Eileen said, you remembered how I dislike steak.

No, beef, guaranteed—a simple salad with a pomegranate-walnut purée dressing, cracked crab with lemon juice, scallops—are you ready? Butter tarragon sauce, followed by lobster tail, French bread, and, if you can still walk—a chocolate mousse with carmelized almonds.

You do know how to spoil a girl, don't you, DeShawn?

And the good lord knows you are one special girl, sugar.

Eileen patted his hand and looked at him and there was a link between them that Olive hadn't seen before. Two tall, beautiful people touching like old friends. The wine steward came with wine. He uncorked the bottle and poured a splash in a glass that DeShawn tasted and smiled and said it was perfect and then he said,

I'll leave you ladies to your dinner. If you need or want anything, and I mean anything, darlin' you call me, you hear?

Oh I'll call you, Eileen said.

He laughed then and left them and Olive said,

What a hunk.

All six feet ten inches of him.

I'm glad the company is paying.

But, Eileen said, the company isn't paying. I'll miss you and maybe this little soireé will help you remember me when you're off touring the country with your Prince Charming.

My Prince? He's my boss.

Clifford Kissner is not just a boss, lady. Do you know how many lackeys stand between him and third tier management? You've landed a whale, Miss Malone, and my only question is—do you know what to do with a whale? God. I remember the day you came to me for your interview. The hayseeds were dropping out of your hair and I knew you were ripe for a change and my goodness have you ever changed.

Eileen laughed and raised her glass in a toast. She said,

So, here's to change. All kinds of change and to all manner of secrets revealed.

Olive sipped her wine. And it was good. It wasn't a Corbière, it wasn't Clifford's private reserve, but it was a crisp white with a nice tang. Setting the glass down, Olive said,

Eileen, there's one thing that's not clear to me.

Just one?

You said DeShawn is, was a basketball friend.

Um huh. We were teammates with the Falcons until he blew out his knee and they traded him.

You were a professional basketball player? I'm confused.

I was confused for a long time, but I'm not confused any more. Look at me. What do you see?

Eileen smiled. She leaned across the table to grasp Olive's hand. She said,

I've given up on men, love.

Olive looked at her and waited while Eileen poured more wine and Olive watched her thin fingers, the hands delicate instruments, nails painted, pointed—but those hands gripping a basketball? It didn't seem possible. Olive felt a strange thing boiling in her chest then and her head was spinning and she felt herself lifting off the chair but then, Eileen picked up her glass and she said,

What do you see, love? When you look at me, what do you see?

I see a beautiful tall graceful confident woman...

Eight years ago I was running up and down a ninety-foot court with nine sweaty men. I haven't always had this body. These breasts? Hormones and silicone. This skin? Hormones and every treatment you can imagine. Facial hair? You understand why I have no facial hair? Every single one removed by electrolysis. This face? Surgical steel and fine sutures. This voice? Hours of coaching, days of projecting. And the rest of me? The thing that made me and DeShawn buddies? Gone. I am woman, love. There is nothing left of Jermaine Norburg except the signing bonus and a bank account from three years of running up and down with those nine bodies.

Eileen stood and she pirouetted, hands out like a dancer, hair wrapping around her face like a model in a breeze and when she faced Olive again, she leaned down, hands on the table, those long nails spread out like red talons. Olive looked up at her, looked at the tops of her breasts in the tight bodice of the dress. Olive understood, in that moment, how much Eileen had changed and how much it had cost her. She had given up her entire past to be who she was, no matter the cost, and Olive felt a new link to her, a deep link not unlike the bond she felt with Clifford. The price of change. Eileen sat down then, and, looking at Olive, she touched the nail of her left index finger to her lips and she raised her eyebrows. She said,

Friends?

Olive smiled but her head was still spinning and her heart beating like a bird's and her throat constricted and she thought she was going to choke, but she caught herself and she said

Oh my god. I am an idiot. Everyone knows but me.

It's not a secret.

I had no idea.

Not even one tiny suspicion?

Eileen...You take my breath away.

I could do that under different circumstances.

Eileen's eyes twinkled and she pressed her hand over Olive's. She said,

I can teach you so much more than you already know, so drink lots of wine, all right? Lots and lots of DeShawn's wine.

Kansas Gothic

It was a big house. An old house. A three story house with a widow's walk and six curved bay windows that reflected the clouds like giant mirrors. Twin sycamore trees framed the entry from the street like a portal into a past she knew, wanted to forget, but which held memories that would not let her go.

Olive stood beside the Chrysler, hand on the door as if making a decision about whether to go or to stay. She imagined Toby in a swing in another sycamore on Tim's farm and he was a little boy with white hair and an impish smile.

Turning, Olive looked at the other houses on the block—all regular frame houses with lawns and fences and concrete driveways. None of them held up beside the Kansas Gothic mansion. None of them would be there in a hundred years.

You sure you got the address right? Janey said.

I was here last week. This is the right place.

Wow, Janey said. It's like something out of a horror movie.

Lots of room for kids, don't you think?

Olive closed the door and walked up the path between the great sycamores and she heard bees and flies buzzing in the warm Spring sun and she smelled fresh dirt and the dusty fringe of pollen wafting in the air. She climbed the steps—eight of them up to the broad wooden porch. The door was open. She went in.

The floors were red oak with the hard wood darkness of age and the stains of a hundred years of living. From the front door, Olive saw twin staircases winding up to the next floor and to each side short corridors leading to closed doors.

You think it's big enough? Jane said. You don't own a vacuum and this place would take an army of little cleaning guys with eight hands and sharp teeth.

I like them big.

Olive trekked up to the second floor landing that led to a string of bedrooms each with its double bay window facing away from the street,

116

each with a view of a small apple orchard. At the back edge of the lot there was a small tool shed and a greenhouse that had lost its glass and stood open as a bombed out church.

That's where they bury the bodies, Janey said. Doesn't that worry you?

Not a bit.

I want to know how you can afford this place.

Olive faced her friend whose eyes were wide and glistening. She said,

It's reasonable.

Let me tell you, I didn't know there were still places like this in Wichita.

It was the home of a cattle baron, Olive said.

All the good stuff's gone. How did this survive?

It's on the historic register.

Great place for a Halloween party.

All the houses around it were built when the family let them subdivide the acreage, Olive said. It was fifteen acres when it was built and it stood here alone.

How do you know this?

I know the guy who owns it.

Does he have a brother?

Five sisters, two brothers, Olive said. But they're not part of this.

Janey grasped Olive's arm. She smiled. She said,

You didn't tell me about this guy.

Nothing to tell.

Are you sleeping with him?

Not yet.

There's no free lunch. And I know. I'm a waitress, remember?

Stop it. It's a business arrangement.

Hoo hoo, Janey said. A business arrangement.

She snapped her fingers and smacked her lips.

I mean it, Olive said. He owns it. I know him. He'll let me rent it.

Rent. Huh.

Olive left her and walked up the next flight of stairs, passing the view windows that lighted the stairwell to the third floor and then up another flight of stairs to the widow's walk. From there, the city lay stretched out flat to the river to the west and to the east straight out to the airport.

First time I ever saw it like this, Janey said.

Umm, Olive said. Let's go.

We still haven't found the bodies.

There are no bodies, Janey.

How are you going to furnish a place like this?

One room at a time, Olive said. Starting with the kitchen.

Let's see it, Janey said.

The kitchen, at the back of the house played out onto a broad screened in porch. Instead of the antiques she expected, Olive saw a gleaming modern stainless steel kitchen big enough for a restaurant.

Holy shit, Janey said. If you can't make the rent, you can take in boarders.

Olive said,. He didn't tell me about this.

Who, I expected an old wood burner or a coal chute, but look at this—brand new stainless steel and big enough for when you open a restaurant.

It is bit, Olive said. And new in the last week.

This guy must really like you, doll. He's forking out a lot of dough just to get in your pants.

It's not like that, Olive said.

It's always like that. I can't even get a guy to open the door for me without he's expecting at least a humjob and you get Better Homes and Gardens just by keeping your legs closed. I tell you life just ain't fair. But you got lots of room for your kids.

I've been thinking about that.

What's there to think about?

I don't think I can bring them here and I can't go back.

You're thinking about letting that jackass you called a husband keep'em?

He's not that bad.

Not that bad? Look, you've been bitching for a year and I can tell you as someone who's been fucked so many times I don't need no roadmap to show me some guy's a turd and from what I've heard your ex is the ace of shits.

I'm beginning to think the kids are better off on the farm.

What're you talking about? How many kids get a chance to play hide and seek with the Addams Family?

The City's no place for kids. Better to keep them pure for as long as I can even if I can't if you know what I mean.

Look at you. They should at least get a chance to see the bright lights.

I think the decision's already made.

Who is this you're giving up your kids for?

I met him at the bank.

A banker.

Not a banker.

Jesus, Olive. Give me something.

He's just a guy. He likes me. I'm going to work for his company... One of his companies.

118

Janey leaned against the stainless steel fridge and then slid to her haunches. Looking up, she said,

What kind of Cinderella story is that, huh? You come to town a virgin...

I guess you weren't listening, Olive said. I have two kids. I've been raped and you took me into your subterranean secret sex den where I got a free education.

And in one year you go from a shit hole to a sixty-four room palace.

It's not a palace.

It's money, Janey said. I know money and I'll bet this guy stuffs his pillows with hundred dollar bills.

I have no idea.

What part of concubine don't you understand, Olive? Good god.

You're trying to make it something it's not.

You've never slept with this guy?

No. Come on. I want to check out the basement.

Sure, let's go check out the basement.

The stairs to the basement were well lit and had been redone in steel so each footstep rang like a bell.

In the basement, parquet floors and wood paneling gave the room a warm feeling. At the far end, there was a pool table, a bar, and Tiffany lamps alongside red velour easy chairs.

This is where he chains them up before he kills them, Janey said. Check for blood and then run like hell.

Olive laughed as Janey faked being chained to a wall.

Don't ravage me, please, don't ravage me, Janey said.

Hmm, Olive said. He's redone this too.

What do you mean he's redone it?

There was no parquet. And there was no pool table.

I'll tell you what I think, Janey said. This guy is up to no good. A dungeon, soundproof walls, all you need is a few whips and chains and you've got yourself a torture chamber.

You should feel right at home, Olive said.

I never do whips or chains on the first date, Janey said. Let's go. I'm hungry. Does your guy own a restaurant?

As a matter of fact he does, Olive said.

Maybe he can give us a cut rate on a Porterhouse.

119

Bridle

In the dream there's a rope around my neck and Tim tries to saddle me and put a bridle on me but I spit it out and he's on my back straddling me. I'm sweating and he slides off but he hangs onto my hair pulling it hard and twisting my neck until I think he's going to break it. And then it stops. I wake up. I hate dreams and I hate to write them down because what good does it do? Rose wrapped the afghan tight around her legs and stuck her pencil behind her ear while she adjusted the rug. It was chilly in the office. Outside the sky hung thick and gray with clouds and the sun was a dull disk behind the clouds. Rose said,

You write them down because they're speaking to you.

Why can't you just tell me what they mean?

Why do you want to take the easy road?

I don't have time for this.

What would you be doing if you weren't here?

Olive sat up, crossed her legs. Rose said,

You look nice. You've changed your hair again. Very stylish. You're not the farm girl who first came to see me. Are you seeing your man who smells like flowers?

Yes.

Are you sleeping with him?

Yes but why do you need to know that?

Change, Rose said. I kneed to know how you're changing and what you do tells me how much you're changing.

Why didn't you tell me that months ago?

Because you wouldn't have heard it. What do you think the rope dream means, Olive?

I know what it means—Tim tied me down. He hung onto me and treated me like an animal.

And now? Do you feel wild, Olive? Really wild? In your dreams, do you feel wild and free?

I'm always floating in my dreams.

Disconnected?

Yes. I've got a new job, I've moved into a big house.

You left one big house and now you're moving into another one.

I need a place for Nan and Toby. I'm bringing them to the City as soon as I get settled.

That's what you said months ago.

And I mean it.

If you meant it, you'd have done it. If they're here, you can't go hunting anymore.

I'm not hunting anymore.

Because of your man of flowers?

Yes.

Olive stood and paced from door to window. She looked out at the gray sky and the wet sidewalks. Across the street, a truck was backed into the Woodland Market unloading crates of vegetables—lettuce, celery, mushrooms. Olive watched the men working. Watched the way they bent their backs as they handled the heavy boxes and crates. Bodies. In the rain. Sweating. Turning, Olive said,

For ten years I never so much as touched myself not even in the shower. Now, sometimes I wake up ready and I do.

Any particular trigger?

I want to tell Sheila I slept with her husband. No, that's not right. I didn't sleep with him, I picked him up in a bar and we had sex and I didn't know who he was until she asked me over and I met him. I should tell her her husband is a cheat. A pervert. A sadist.

How do you feel when you're with your new man?

He's different.

How is he different?

He cares about me. He asks about me. He never pressures me.

Olive resumed her pacing. I'm traveling a lot in this new job.

You travel but you're going to bring your babies to the city.

I know what you're saying—not very smart is it? Should I tell Sheila?

Do you think you should tell Sheila?

What are you saying? That she knows about me?

About you? I have no idea. But about him, she probably knows what he's doing.

Why are men such assholes? Here's Sheila, she's a cancer survivor and living every day afraid she'll die and her asshole husband cheats on her all the time and shares his experiences with his asshole friend Harold. They're like little boys hitting tadpoles with a hammer.

Why? Maybe she's happy the way things are.

She said she's a wife in name only. That means she doesn't have sex with her husband and so he goes on the prowl.

And that's how you ran into him—two hunters on the prowl.

I wasn't on the prowl. I was... I was hungry. I needed someone to want me for what I am not because I'm some valuable work animal who has to earn her keep.

That's how Tim made you feel?

He made me feel dirty. He was so fast and messy. I hated the feel of his slime between my legs.

Ah, Rose said.

Ah Ah Ah. What?

So that's why you ran?

I didn't run. I left. I took my babies and I left and I'm glad I left. I'm not going back. You just don't know how it was being tied down.

The babies? Rose said. Anchors or albatrosses?

Sex

She straddled him, legs clamped to his sides like she had mounted a horse bareback. She looked at his face as his hands trailed down to her waist. Still in her, he was thick, still hard. He went down slowly after they made love, holding himself back until she had stopped screaming, until her breathing slowed. She liked that, like the unhurried way he took her, controlled her before releasing himself.

His hand gripped her waist, lifting her, then settling her again and she looked down at his thick chest, his muscled belly, a surprise still every time she saw him naked—she remembered her first sight of him in the bank—a short fat bald guy who smelled of flowers but now what she saw was a man who made her come until her back ached, until her skin flushed and burned. She raised up on her knees, still enamored of the fullness he gave her, but she, hot and sweaty and exhausted, slumped to her side and he rolled to face her. He said,

That ought to hold you for a while.

She smiled, still too weak to speak. He trailed his fingers over her face, soft pads of fingers that found nerve endings she didn't know she had in her body. She said, her voice reedy,

Every time with you I find nerve endings I didn't know I had.

Did I hurt you?

No. no. You just wear me out.

Where will you be next week?

Chicago.

I can meet you there…if you want.

She raked her nails over his chest, felt the hard flat muscles and the wiry hair. She said,

Some things are bothering me.

Then they're bothering me too.

The house.

What about the house?

I haven't gotten the lease papers yet.

There is no lease, he said.

123

That's not right.

It's my house, he said. I can do what I want with it.

Do you always get your way?

Not always. They elected W and I didn't want that.

We never talk politics, she said.

And we don't talk religion. That's one thing. What's the other thing?

What?

You said some things are bothering you. There's the house. That's taken care of. What else?

Olive snuggled into him, felt his still hot body, the sweat slow to cool. She took a deep breath—took in the scent of flowers. Even after sex, he still smelled of flowers and she liked that fresh clean smell and she didn't know how he did it—making everything seem effortless. She whispered,

I have a problem.

Let my lawyers handle it.

Not that kind of problem.

He laid a thick arm across her waist. She felt the strength in him. He said,

Tell me, I'm a good listener.

Before I met you, I did some crazy things.

Enumerate, he said. We'll compare craziness.

Are you always going to be like this?

Are you always going to be testing me?

One night I met a man in a bar. We had sex. He was rough. I liked it. His name is Daniel and he's the husband of a woman I went to State with. I didn't know who he was until she invited me to dinner. And then he had the guts to come here acting like he owned me. With flowers. He's dangerous. He's a danger to Sheila, he's a danger to every woman he picks up.

Sheila's your friend?

Yes. He's a pig. He's out there right now looking for another victim and who knows what kind of disease he's spreading. Rose thinks I should tell Sheila before he brings something home to her…she's had cancer…

Whoo, he said. You're really pissed at this guy.

What do you think? Should I tell Sheila?

Suppose you do tell her. What do you say?

That's what Rose asks me. I'd tell her he picks up women. I'd tell her he has anal sex with them. I'd tell her he shares his trophies with his pal Harold who put moves on me.

Sounds like those boys have a little club you don't want to join.

You're not surprised or disgusted with me? Do you want to do it that way?

He laughed. He sat up. Plumped his pillow. He said,

Come here.

She leaned into him. He wrapped his arm around her, pulled her closer, kissed her hair. He still smelled fresh and as she lay against him, she felt his breathing, the slow rise and fall of his chest. Nothing seemed to fluster him. Nothing tilted him, or skewed him. He was rock solid. He said,

Olive, your past is yours. Some guys get all worked up if their woman isn't a virgin. Some guys see every man from a woman's past as competition. If you want to tell me all your secrets, that's good. If you don't, that's good too. Just being with you makes me happy. Seeing you makes me happy.

So you don't think I'm a filthy and perverted slut?

The only thing I'd worry about with a guy like that is STDs.

I wouldn't do that to you, Olive said. I got tested. Twice. I was so stupid.

Okay, he said. There's enough stupid out there for all of us. Suppose you told her about this. What would you tell her?

So. Should I tell her?

What I know is that if something eats your gut out, you have to take care of it. You like this woman? Do you want to keep her as a friend?

Depends, doesn't it?

What do you think will come of it?

You mean what will she do?

Um huh. This telling thing, is it for her or for you?

You mean am I telling her just to get even?

Face it, Olive, you're a vengeful little bitch.

Olive lay against him, smelled the flower scent rising from his skin. She felt safe. She felt whole. She said,

Rose thinks I have to tell her.

Do you trust Rose?

She knows everything I ever thought, every dream I have. I've confessed all my sins to her.

So you do believe in sin?

I believe I did some stupid things. And I told her about every one of them. I mean everything.

You got your money's worth.

She knows about you.

Good, Clifford said. I want her to know. I want everyone to know.

He looked down at her, stroked her forehead. She watched his hand as it slid to her breast, to her waist, to her belly and then to open her legs. She closed her eyes. She clasped his hand, held it tight against her. He whispered,

125

Do you want me to go with you?

No. I think this is friend to friend, face to face.

I have an idea, he said. When you get back from Chicago, take her to lunch. Soak up a few carafes of Eau de Chateau Clifford and when you're both tanked have that friend to friend and see how it works out.

Olive twisted around and slid off the bed but Clifford grabbed her hand. He said,

Where are you going?

To call Sheila.

It's two o'clock.

She'll be awake.

He pulled her back onto the bed and flipped the sheet away and he said,

Does it look like I'm finished with you?

Confession

Late afternoon. Shadows lay across the street like weary bodies half-buried.

From the front seat of the Chrysler, Olive watched Sheila enter the coffee shop, watched her quick gait, and she felt a pang of guilt. Getting out of the car, she fumbled with her keys, her hands sweaty. The dipping sunlight glistened on the roof of the car and for a second, Olive wanted to run. She didn't want to face Sheila. She didn't want to drown in the confession she was going to make. Steeling herself, she gripped the keys tight in her hand, squeezing until the edges bit her palm and then she stood straight. She remembered Rose—you have to talk to her, have to tell her what you are...you're like an alcoholic. You have to apologize if you want to be free. Olive tucked the keys into her purse and crossed the street shielding her eyes from the steep angle of the sun.

She entered the shop swamped with the scent of coffee and the smell of chocolate hanging like a veil in the air. She saw Sheila at a table, head bowed, her hair now long, blond and coiffed to a shining perfection. It framed her face. She wore a bright blue blouse that accentuated the whiteness of the wig but also gave Olive the sense of seeing a package wrapped to perfection without a hint of the flaws that lay beneath. Her arms were bare. She looked thinner than before. Olive hesitated.

About to turn, afraid and ashamed, not wanting to feel the heat in her face as she opened up to her friend, she saw Sheila waving, hand in the air she said, Over here.

Trapped then, Olive smiled and strode to the table. Sheila said,

My god you look wonderful. Whatever you're eating agrees with you.

Olive sat, laid her purse on the table. She couldn't bring herself to look Sheila in the eye so she fiddled with her skirt, adjusted the purse to get it square. Sheila said,

Now just what is so important that you couldn't say it over the phone?

I called because I have a confession to make.

Oh good. I love confessions.

I moved, Olive said. I've left the bank and I have a new job and I'm on the road a lot.

Sheila leaned across the table. She said,

Are you meeting any men worth mentioning?

Olive looked up. Dark circles marred the gleam in Sheila's eyes. Thick pancake makeup masked her sallow complexion. In the corners of her mouth, small cracks opened ready to leak out what was left of Sheila's youth. Prickly heat broke out on Olive's chest. Olive said,

Well. Yes. That's what I need to tell you.

Sheila flipped the blond hair that had fallen over her shoulder. She reached across the table and patted Olive's hand. She said,

Is it scandalous? Is it Harold? He said you two went out. Tell me everything.

There are dangerous men out there, Sheila.

Harold? Dangerous?

No. Nothing to do with Harold. He's a problem, but he's not the problem.

Well, what is the problem then? Did you end up skewered in a cheap hotel again? Is that it? Is history repeating itself?

This isn't easy.

Living in the city is never easy, love. I know.

I'm working now. With Clifford Kissner.

Clifford Kissner? You don't mean the Clifford Kissner? Oh my god, Olive. Did Clifford Kissner do something horrible to you?

No. No. No. Sheila...

Olive gripped Sheila's hand. The puzzlement on Sheila's face was sincere. Her forced smile opened more cracks in her pancake makeup. Olive took a deep breath. She said,

Before I ran into you that day at the bank, I did something very stupid. I was with a man. I went to a bar. I picked him up. He took me to a motel. We had sex. It was messy and ugly and he did things to me I can't talk about.

Olive again wanted to let go of Sheila, wanted to get up, walk out, to disappear but instead she clutched Sheila's hand harder, a hand that was not moist and warm, but cold and dry. Sheila said,

You're pregnant?

No. Nothing like that. This is something different. I went to Rose, like you suggested and she's been good for me...She tells me I have to open up. She tells me I have closed myself away for too long. She tells me I have to talk to the people I've hurt.

Sheila drew her hand back then. She stiffened. She said,

And you've hurt me how?

I'm sorry, Olive said. I didn't plan anything. It was a coincidence. I

128

had no idea who he was and things happened that I couldn't control or maybe didn't want to. All I can say is that I'm sorry.

Sheila closed her eyes. Hands now on the table, palms down, she bowed her head and shook it side to side and then she looked up at Olive. She said,

Why are you telling me this? What right do you have to do this to me?

I'm trying to protect you.

I could kill you for this. Do you know how angry this makes me? If we weren't in a public place, I might just claw your eyes out. You have really hurt me, Olive. Really hurt me.

Sheila, please. It was stupid, but I didn't know. How could I? It just happened. I'm just thinking of you.

If you really care about me, you won't say a thing. You will just drink your coffee and eat your stupid pastry. You can't understand what you've just done to me.

It was one night, one time and then at dinner... that night. I didn't know I had betrayed you. How could I know that? One night. One time. Sheila, he's dangerous.

After you left with Harold I talked to Danny. I made him tell me how he knew you. He knew you. I know that. I know everything.

You know?

Of course I know. I knew the minute you walked in the door.

Sheila, listen. I betrayed you but it wasn't on purpose.

Sheila held up a trembling hand. Olive shoved back her chair, ready to stand, ready to leave now that the door had opened but she didn't feel better, she didn't feel light or happy or free. She felt the grinding in her stomach that turned into a knot and her jaw tightened. Sheila fixed a stare on Olive's eyes. She said,

I need a friend, Olive. After what I've been through, I just need a friend. I didn't know you were one of his...victims.

He came to my studio the day after the dinner, Olive said, He didn't want to leave. I had to throw him out, Sheila. I was ashamed of what I'd done but I didn't know. It was all so disconnected and ugly.

Will you stop? Please? Just stop baring your soul for one minute and listen to me.

Sheila. They...Daniel and Harold, they share their conquests like little boys splitting a candy bar. What they're doing is risky and almost criminal.

Do you think you can save me? Do you think I'm a fool? I don't ask what he does, I don't ask where he goes, I don't ask who he sees.

He doesn't use any protection.

And I need a friend. An old friend who understands me.

You can leave him, Olive said.

You're not hearing a word I'm saying to you, Sheila snapped. You are so naïve. You're like a little crusader trying to clean up the world after you've spread you legs. What joy is that? Listen to what I'm saying.

Sheila took off her wig. Olive was startled. Sheila laid the wig on the table. In the overhead light of the café, her head was shiny, bare. With a pained look on her face, Sheila ran her hands over her head. Olive watched the tears bud in the corners of her eyes. Sheila's head skeletal. The ridges under the skin visible like small bony cracks in the skull. Sheila said,

I can't leave him, honey, because I need his god-damned medical insurance. The cancer is back. It's metastasized to my breasts and it'll be just a while till it gets to my spine. Dozens of lymph nodes are involved. I'm beyond surgery so I'm left with chemo. Do you know what the treatments cost? Do you have any idea? Do you have any idea what I'm going through? Without his coverage I'm dead in a month.

Sheila opened her purse and stuffed the wig into it. She looked at Olive, a hurt smile on her lips. Her gaze was clear. She said,

I'm trapped. He's got me and I'm not going anywhere. All I want is a friend. I don't care if he sodomizes his little whores. Did he do that with you? That's his favored style, always has been. Did he? We're sisters then, aren't we? I don't care about that. I just need a friend to talk to. I don't care if he gets a disease that he deserves, I don't care. I do not care. What about me? Who cares about me? I know that I have another treatment on Wednesday. It will cost six thousand dollars. Do you care about that? Leave him? How can I leave him?

Jesus Saves

Olive waited at the big window until he had parked and then she stood straight, took a deep breath and went to the door. Through the glass, she watched his slow deliberate walk up the path between the twin sycamores that arched high into a leafy canopy. He stopped to adjust his belt—a gesture she knew so well—and he touched his Stetson as if practicing a Sunday hello at church. The hat looked new. No sweat stain around the crown. She noticed his boots—new, shiny—and as he climbed the steps to the porch he grew larger until he loomed in front of her—only the glass door panel between them. His presence gave her the shakes. He took off his hat and held it in front of him like a boy scout. He smiled.

Olive opened the door, stepped back. He half-bowed as he entered. He cleared his throat. He said,

Thanks for seeing me, Olive.

How are you, Tim?

Could be better, he said. Didn't get much of a harvest 'cause the rain beat down the wheat.

Can I get you a cup of coffee?

Nah, he said. Can't stay long enough to drink it. Gotta see a banker and as I recall you didn't make such hot coffee.

I've learned a lot, she said.

Well, okay then.

He followed her into the kitchen with its stainless steel appliances laid out in the French Provincial style with its cutting board and counter surfaces.

Tim stood, hat in hand, looking around. She watched him as she poured coffee from the press and handed him a mug. She said,

Have a seat. I guess you have something to tell me and bad news is better taken sitting down.

Aw, it's not bad news, Olive.

He sat down. His enormous body overwhelming the chair. His face was ruddy from sun but he had just shaved—she remembered what a chore it was for him to shave a thick beard that ate blades. She remembered buying him an electric razor for his birthday, but it didn't last because his wiry beard chewed up the cutters, forcing him back to the safety razor. He smelled like Old Spice—his favorite cologne, his dad's favorite cologne, his grandfather's too. He said,

This here's a pretty big place you've got.

It belonged to the Campau clan.

The cattle people?

The same.

I tell ya, Ollie, you sure wormed your way outa that prairie dog hole you fell into back there in town. What did you sell to get this place?

What do you want to tell me, Tim?

He set his cup on the table, hands steady. He looked at her, his green eyes flecked with gold and he said,

Well, it's about the kids.

What about the kids?

Things are getting a little bit complicated.

I have this place because I'm ready to bring them here—now.

Well, that's what I want to talk about, Olive. I don't think that's going to happen.

What have you done, Tim?

Well, tell the truth? I met a woman—a widow gal—lives in town. You know her, Kate Younger.

I know of her.

You know she's got two kids just about Nan and Toby's age.

Tim. Just say it.

Well, she's moving out to the place to live with me.

I see, Olive said. And this affects me how?

I want a divorce, Olive, and I'm going to keep the kids.

No you aren't.

Tim reached into his hip pocket and drew out an envelope that he handed to her. He said,

Open that envelope and read it.

As she read, heat rose in her face and she was floating again, swirling, spinning down into the water from the top of the windmill, diving into a black hole. Tim said,

The lawyer says that's a temporary writ all legal and everything and he says it gives me sole custody. Law's pretty clear, Olive. You abandoned your babies and you ain't seen 'em in a year. That's what that line 'willful abandonment' means. See it there?

Olive's eyes burned but she didn't break. She folded the paper and laid it in the middle of the table. He was watching her, his eyes narrowed, his mouth a hard line in his sun-burned face. He said,

Lawyer says I can give you a lump sum for the equity you got in the farm and if you take this deal and if we don't go into court with that unfit mother stuff, you do all right. It's a good offer.

An offer?

We never signed a prenup and so any judge's gonna see this as right so long as you don't get all huffy and you don't go to court on it 'cause you'll get hurt, Olive. Hurt bad.

Who is this woman?

I told you.

They're my kids.

My kids too, Tim said. And it's clear, Olive. You left them same as if you'd dumped them on a street corner. Kate is a good woman and a good mother and she'll be good to the kids.

A good stepmother.

Better than no mother the way they been for the last year.

You're not going to do this, Olive said.

Tim picked up the envelope, folded it and tucked it into his shirt pocket. He said,

It's done. You can cash out or not. If you want to fight it, I'll drag you through it like you ain't been drug before so that's it.

Olive got up. She rattled the coffee mug in the stainless steel sink and in her gut there was a knot that made her sick and she looked out the window into the big yard—a hundred feet deep—and she tasted the vomit in her throat. She gripped the sink ledge until her hands cramped and then she took a deep breath. She watched Tim thrust a pen at her. She took the pen, looked at Tim and then at the paper.

Sign it, he said.

I'm not signing anything.

You just god damn sign it, woman.

How much, Tim?

Two-hundred twenty-five thousand. And you sign away the mineral rights.

What mineral rights?

The gas company's done some test holes and there's likely a little reservoir of natural gas under the North Section. But they're not a hundred percent sure.

Olive glared at him. He still sat at the table, hat on his lap, cup in front of him. He looked at her for a long time. He said,

You hurt me real bad, Olive. I had a crop to get in and you didn't just walk out on the kids, you walked out on me, you walked out on Mom and Dad, you cut and ran and you gotta pay for all that hurt. Times I thought my heart was going to fall out of my body. I'd come in there were some nights

I figured I might as well take a twelve gauge to my head. But Reverend Howard sat me down and helped me clear my head. Then I met Kate 'cause she was grieving after her man died on her. We shared a lot of hurt before we found Jesus Christ together. He's in our hearts now Olive. He's showing us the way. I wanted the lawyers to deliver this but Jesus told me I had to look you in the eye 'cause you're poison.

And Jesus told you to take my babies to get even, is that it, Tim?

Like I say, it's done. Now if you'll just sign that piece of paper, I'll get outa your hair.

I don't want your money, Tim.

Your choice, he said. I'm just trying to somehow make sense out of ten years of being married to you.

And two hundred twenty-five thousand dollars is what you come up with?

You never used to wear short skirts. And your hair. What happened to that long blond hair of yours? You look peeled like one of those…what do they call them…lesbians. So, be a good girl and sign that paper.

She watched him get up, rising to his full height. He was huge. She said,

You want me to sign this, Tim? I'm not signing anything till I have somebody take a look at it.

She folded the papers up and laid them on the table and then she fixed her eyes on Tim and she said,

You'll be hearing from me when I make up my mind.

He finished his coffee and set the cup on the table. He said,

You're right about the coffee. You did learn something.

He turned on his heel and headed for the door. His hat grazed the door frame as he walked out. She heard the door slam. Heard his footsteps on the porch. She looked at the folded papers on the table and she closed her eyes and felt herself floating again. Adrift. Swirling in a spinning black hole with no where to hold on. This time, she was sure, she would hit the water and keep going and it was very deep. She had never hit bottom before

.

Grace

Olive stopped at the gate where the sycamore tree stood, its leaves, once thick and green, falling. Its mottled gray bark looked like skin peeling from its trunk. Sitting in the Chrysler, Olive looked at the house, looked at the curtained windows. She shut off the engine and got out.

The September air was hot. Still muggy. To her left the windmill creaked, its blades twisting in a slow churn as the prairie wind held steady—the hard hot wind that carried off your sweat without cooling you down. Olive felt a chill as she glanced up at the windmill. In the light it didn't look dangerous. For a moment, she wondered if she had in fact been up there that night, in the dark. She closed the door of the Chrysler just as a chicken hawk flapped out of the sycamore, screeching and spiraling up into the sky. Olive shielded her eyes, listening for more, but heard only the long slow beat of the windmill blades.

She opened the gate. The grate of metal on metal. Ten years that gate had squawked every time it opened and every time it grated on her nerves. But Tim, always wrapped up in plowing or planting or harvesting or running animals to auction, never had time to oil it. A tiny thing.

She walked up the narrow concrete path to the house. In a year, the paint on the shutters had blistered, the clapboard siding had turned chalky, the screen door hung ajar as if the closer spring had broken. Olive searched for the house key on top of the door frame but it wasn't there. And then, startled, she stepped back to the edge of the porch as the door opened and Grace, wearing a strawberry frock and a white apron stood at the threshold, her hands dusted with flour. Olive said,

Mom? What are you doing here?

I heard you drive in.

Where are the kids?

They're with Dad, Grace said. He took them into town for lemon custard ice cream.

I came out to talk to Tim and the woman.

Kate, Grace said, her name is Kate Younger.

What's going on, Mom?

I'm baking bread, Grace said.

But why are you here?

Dad and I brought the babies out. Tim and the woman had to talk to the lawyers because he's adopting. You might as well come in.

Grace held the screen open, a dish towel in her floured hands. Olive entered. The living room smelled of baking bread and air freshener. Inside, the house was changed.

New furniture.

New carpet.

New pictures on the walls.

It's all hers, Grace said. They moved the old things out to the barn and they brought her things from town.

Olive felt a hardness in the pit of her stomach. The brocade sofa, so feminine, the brocade arm chairs, so comfortable, the glass and wood coffee table like uninvited guests. All of it changed the room. It was no longer hers.

You're too late, you know, Grace said.

Why am I too late?

It's all over already. They're gone.

You didn't have to let them go.

Tim had papers, Olive. All legal. I can't say I blame him for doing what he did.

They're my babies, Mom.

Not anymore, daughter. Not in the law they're not.

You knew I'd come for them.

We waited. You know we waited. You knew I wouldn't give my grandchildren to a stranger but now you've got the law involved.

What's she like?

She's a nice woman. A church woman. Prays to Jesus. She's a good mother to her babies. They're the same age as Nan and Toby. They get along, the four of them and for what it's worth, she seems to make Tim happy. She's a woman who knows how to make a family.

Grace wiped at her hands with the dish towel. There was a small dusting of flour on her left temple. Olive choked because she had seen that flare of white so many times but now her mother smelled like an old woman. She smelled of liniment and powder and raw hand soap.

Didn't you ever need to get away, Mom?

What you did's not right.

You're judging me without knowing everything.

Here's what I know—you left your babies and you left your husband and you missed my birthday and me and Dad's anniversary and you didn't write or call on Danny's....

Grace sniffled. She turned her back. Olive wanted to touch her and she raised a hand but her mother drew away. She said,

Eight years he's been dead and you...you never think about what you're doing to folks. Sometimes if I didn't know, I'd wonder if you were mine.

I'm sorry about Danny, Mom, and I'm sorry I missed your birthday.

And I'm glad Dad isn't here to see what you've become.

What have I become, Mom?

Tim told us about how you live in town.

I have a good job, Mom. I live in a big house. There's a yard and trees and sheds where Nan and Toby can play. I'll make them happy.

Oh, it's too late, Olive. It's way too late to make amends. To answer your question. Yes. I sometimes thought about getting away—I told you that the day you brought the babies to me. But I love your Dad and he loves me and he might have loved you once, but we can't put up with all this, Olive—you gave up your place. Someone else is here.

She's changed everything, Olive said.

Some things on a farm you need to change, some thiings you can't.

Olive opened her purse, took out the folded papers and laid them on the kitchen table.

What's this? Grace said.

Using a fountain pen, Olive signed the papers. She looked at Grace. She said,

When Tim comes back, tell him I made up my mind.

Olive then stormed out of the house. The screen door exploded behind her. Stopping at the Chrysler, she looked up at the windmill and there, hanging from its wire, the way it had hung for fifty years, the metal dipper twisted in a dull clanking against the water tank. She got in the car and as she started the engine, she saw her mother standing in the doorway, the kitchen towel in her hands. In the shadow, her skin looked coppery. Her lips creased with age, dark freckles on her hands looked like holes burned in her skin. She squinted at Olive, her eyes hard and unforgiving. Olive breathed a sigh. That woman in the doorway, that woman with flour on her face, in twenty years that woman could have been Olive.

Olive dropped the Chrysler in gear and drove away and this time she did not look in the rear view mirror.

137

Elevens

Every time he touched her, she felt less guilty.
Every time he touched her, she closed her eyes.
Every time he looked at her, she felt electricity.
Every time he opened a door for her, she felt like a flower blooming.
Every time.
And he wanted nothing in return.
She talked, he listened.
She cried, he handed her a handkerchief.
She laughed, he smiled with her.
And he wanted nothing in return.

He watched her eat and she felt like a glutton, but he insisted—more, he said, you have to keep up your strength.

He watched her shower, and she didn't feel naked.

He watched her step out of the shower and he held out a towel to her and dabbed at the beads of water on her skin and she shivered.

And he wanted nothing.

When she traveled, he took her to the airport and met her when she returned.

He never asked what she did when she was alone, and she didn't tell him that when she was alone she thought of him. Thought of him as she ate alone, thought of him in the elevator to her room, alone, thought of him at the end of each business meeting.

At the end of each day he called her to ask how she was and always, no matter where she was, as she talked to him there would be a knock at the hotel door and when she opened it there was always a bouquet of flowers. Sometimes white carnations, sometimes yellow mums, sometimes blue bearded tulips so rare they came from a private breeder in Oregon, and, sometimes when she was having her period, the flowers were red roses and the card was always addressed to Carmencita.

And he asked nothing in return and so she was free to give him everything she had because with him she was never empty.

With him, she opened up and she gave and always found more to give. He replenished her just by taking everything she had, every time he held her and she was glad to let him into her without question.

He asked for nothing but like a poor man on a street corner he was happy with whatever fell at his feet.

It was late. The big house was quiet. Against the windows, behind the thick curtains, rain danced with short, hard clicks. He lay beside her, facing her, watching her. She raised a hand to his face and closed his eyes and she said,

Stop.

No, he said.

You make me nervous when you stare at me. So stop.

All right, he said.

Why are you so agreeable?

I have everything I want, he said. When you have everything you want, you tend to be agreeable.

Are you tired of me?

No.

Are you fed up with my neuroses?

I thought Rose cured all that.

She says you can't cure a neurosis, Olive said. You learn to live with it.

Okay, he said. I'm not fed up with your neuroses. Keep them. It's like seeing you in high heels.

What?

High heels. You look like a gazelle when you wear high heels.

I'm not a gazelle. I'm a farm girl. I'm supposed to have both feet on the ground and be able to cut through all the bullshit in the world because I'm the salt of the earth and no one can pull the wool over my eyes.

American myths die hard, Olive. Like cowboys and the goodness and sweetness of the heartland—crap. And the purity of the American GI? Who believes that anymore? No one. And the myth that Thomas Jefferson was an enlightened man who didn't own slaves when we know…what do we know about that? And I'm living proof that the myth of the self-made man is pure trash—I didn't build the highways that truck my meat to your house, and I don't grow the corn that feeds my beef either. That's just more garbage. And there's the myth that we live in a democracy when we all know it's a plutocracy with privileges for the rich that the poor can't imagine. You're tainted now, Olive. You're a painted lady with a fine ass and a taste for city life so live with it.

You like my ass?

It's a sweet ass. I also like your belly and your breasts and your elevens.

My elevens?

Those little tendons there just where the collar bones connect to the sternum.

The elevens? Why do you call that the elevens?

Looks like two ones. Turn your head to the side.

He traced her throat, the tip of his finger running up and down. He said,

See? That's your elevens. I like your neck, I like your belly button, your ankles, your feet, your hair, your ears, the little fuzz where your hair shades down to your cheek.

She said: Stop. Does anyone but you call that the elevens?

I have my own anatomical terminology, he said. Your nipple? That's your daisy.

She said: My daisy?

Looks like a black eyed susan.

You nut, she said.

And your belly button? Where it puckers? That's your yo yo.

She said: My yo yo?

Looks like a yo yo, doesn't it? The way it curls around.

You're making all of this up right here, right now.

Um huh. And something's bothering you, he said.

She said: I'm going to change my name.

All right. Good idea. How about changing it to Mrs. Clifford Kissner?

Olive sat up and she glared at him until he reached over and touched the tip of her nose. He said,

Did I tell you I like the way your nose tilts up just enough to keep it from being perfect? If you were all perfect, I don't think I could live with you.

What did you just say?

You can change it to anything you want so long as there is no intent to defraud. Do you intend to defraud?

Tell me what you just said.

And your eyes. I look at your eyes and I get all tense inside because I have no idea in the world what you're thinking.

Cliff? She said.

Every time I see you without your clothes on I want to burn every stitch of clothing you own because any one as beautiful as you shouldn't cover it up, but then it wouldn't be just for me.

Stop, Clifford.

He closed his eyes. He said,

Okay, I'm not staring now.

What did you say?

You heard me.

Eyes closed, he groped for her, his hand coming to rest on her hip and then sliding down to her thigh before reversing its way and gliding up to her waist. She shuddered. She said,

My life is such a mess, you'd be sorry.

I lied, he said.

What?

I don't have everything I want.

What part of me haven't you had?

I'm missing one thing.

Olive leaned close to him and pried his eyes open with two fingers and he rolled onto his back and surrendered. He said.

I'm awake, I'm awake, did I miss the plane?

You're so nice, Olive said.

Not nice, just patient, he said. We can do it.

She said: I went to see Tim.

He took a deep breath and he sat up and curled into lotus position like a phallic Buddha and he reached for her hand and she knelt like a supplicant in front of him and he said,

Was that wise?

He's got my babies, Olive said. He's got a Christian woman named Kate Younger and she's living with him on the farm and she's going to adopt my babies.

Olive felt a flood rush over her, then an emptiness and she cried and still he sat watching her and then when nothing more coursed from her eyes, he wiped at her cheeks and tasted his finger and he said,

Now you're in me.

Did you hear me?

Yes.

She's going to be the mother to my babies.

What does that do to you?

It makes me feel like my heart has stopped.

I pay a KC law firm a big retainer, he said. If you want your babies, we can get them.

I did something stupid, she said.

In ink?

Yes.

Well, that just makes it harder, but if one lawyer did it, another one can undo it.

You'd do that for me?

He smiled then and he circled her waist and picked her up as though she weighed no more than a bouquet of flowers. She had forgotten how

141

strong he was, how graceful he was, how powerful and in his hands she felt the strength she'd seen the first time in her studio on J Street and he sat her on him and he entered her and he was thick and hard and he filled her and she held onto him, felt him moving inside her and he whispered,

It would be a whole lot easier if your name were Kissner.

Oh my god, she said.

She clutched at him, her breath heaving, her whole body in spasms and she couldn't stop the quivering in her shoulders, the quaking of her belly, the trembling of her thighs and she felt him expand and contract in her and she fell onto him and he said,

I'll do what you need to do for as long as it takes.

Her voice guttural, she said: How do you do that to me? It's not fair.

What do you say, Olive?

Do I have to say yes right now? I'd say yes to anything right now.

And then he gripped her waist and forced her down on him and she came so hard her head snapped forward and her teeth cracked and she collapsed over him, flowed over him and he said,

I love that about you, that wetness, your own little river.

And then he rose up and bit her ear lobe and he said, Say yes.

Fountain Pen

Olive looked out the window into the shimmering heat of the Wheatland Market parking lot where the woman got out of her black SUV. She wore red shorts, white sandals. Her hair was up in a ballet twist that let twin curls dangle over her ears. She wore a white sleeveless blouse. Her arms, tanned and toned looking, like an athlete. Olive waited for her to open the door, to pull her kids out, but she shifted her shoulder bag and locked the SUV. Then she looked around. She put on a pair of dark glasses. She walked to a red car—Olive didn't know what make, and she got in the passenger seat and she leaned in and kissed the man at the wheel.

And then the beer truck arrived and the driver rolled up the door and stacked cases of beer onto a dolly that he hauled into the store.

Olive turned to Rose who shifted sending the afghan off her knees to the floor revealing her bare legs. Legs as lithe and tan as the legs of the woman in the red car. Olive said,

I think I know why I'm here. It doesn't have anything to do with waking up in a hotel or finding a hundred dollars and it has nothing to do with Daniel. I just want to start my life over. I want to rewind the tape to the beginning and start over.

You are in rebellion, Rose said. The way you've changed, the things you want.

I know it's too late for some things but until I get the sex problem under control I can't get where I need to go. There are two babies in the mix now. At first I just wanted to leave them, but now, with Clifford, I'm not so sure. He's says that if I want them, he has people who can work on it.

He has the resources to do that?

He has the resources to do what he wants.

Is that what you want?

How do you start over? Olive said.

You learn from your mistakes, Rose told her. But like all rebellious adolescents you never think your actions through. And you, Olive, you let your narcissism lead you around by the nose.

At last I have a name for it.

We're all a little bit tainted, Rose said, but narcissism always finds new victims.

I had a dream two nights ago, Olive said. I was up on the windmill looking out over the fields and the entire wheat crop had turned black. There was an irrigation wheel spewing red water over the wheat, but it didn't do any good. And off in the distance, the horizon was a rusty orange. The air looked like it was on fire and I had trouble breathing. It was all very disturbing. When I woke up, I was paralyzed.

Where do you feel the dream? Rose asked. In your throat? Your neck?

My chest, Olive said. Even now it's like there's someone standing on me and I can't breathe.

Does the weight have a name? Rose said.

You mean does he have a name?

Does he? One of your conquests?

I'm past that, Olive said. What does it mean if I want to change my name?

How would you feel about that?

Olive looked at Rose who was holding her notebook in her lap with a fountain pen poised over the page. The fountain pen, bright yellow with a red clip on the cap, was new. Rose said,

Why do you want to change your name?

Olive is a farm girl's name.

It's a solid name, Rose said.

The woman in the black SUV doesn't bring her children to the market anymore. Something's changed her.

Does she bother you? The woman in the SUV?

She has a lover, Olive said. A man in a red car. They meet in the parking lot of the grocery store. Maybe she needed to start over just like I needed to start over. I don't understand marriage. Never. And I don't think I ever will.

If Clifford wants to fight for your babies. I think you should let him.

And if I get to keep them? What then? Do I give up my job? Become a stay at home mom? I don't want to be a mother, you know that, but it won't go away, will it?

I'm afraid not, Rose said. Let's go back to the dream for a moment. What do you think it means?

Before I would have said it was a dream about black wheat and red water, but then I met you and I know it means something else. I'm not sure what, but everything in it is dead so I suppose it means all my dreams are dead. It's nothing new. I've known that for a long time.

But you're starting over with Clifford, Rose said. And you're living a

Cinderella dream complete with the castle and the prince.

Rose made a note in her book using her fountain pen. Olive liked the change. The permanence of ink. She was ink now, no longer pencil that could be erased. It made her feel good. Rose looked up from her notebook, her eyes riveted on Olive. It was a strange look, an open look, one Olive had never seen in her before as if Rose was showing her a side she had always kept hidden. The office was cool, as usual, the usual afghan, Rose's dress was the usual gray—a gray mask that hid who she was the way the flat unremarkable feathers of a female sage grouse made her unremarkable, but Rose was shining from the inside now, and her face was alight in a way Olive had never seen. There was an easy grace to her now, as seductive and open as any of the tattooed women Olive had seen in the sexual underworld. Olive felt a shiver move up her spine. Rose had let her inside for a peek at who she was. Rose crossed her legs, the first time she had crossed her legs in months. Olive turned away, paced back to the window where she knew she could stand for the remainder of the hour without another word from Rose if she chose to keep silent.

The black SUV was still parked in the sun.

The driver of the beer truck had finished his work and now leaned against the truck on the shady side smoking a cigarette. He opened a can of beer, foam shot out of the can, a shower of white that the man sipped leaning over while the spill dripped to the ground. Olive had never seen that before—the drinking. And then he crushed the cigarette on the ground and squished the beer can in his fist and tossed the can into the cab of his truck and then got back on the road. Olive waited for the meat delivery truck to appear, but it was running late. The heat was changing everything. She turned to Rose who, still very much the enigma, now sat in silence, no longer hidden in gray. Rose did have a secret life. Who did she see? Who did she make love to? Olive said,

You have a lover, don't you, Rose?

At my age?

Are you ever too old for sex?

Never too old to think about it, Rose said.

Do you have someone who makes you happy? Someone you don't wear gray for? Did he buy you some sexy underwear? Do you make love naked?

Rose looked away and for a moment as if she were no longer in the chair, no longer in the cold room, no longer the psychiatrist with all the answers. She closed her notebook and capped her fountain pen. She smiled.

Olive left the office. Outside, the heat hit hard, the humidity cramped in her chest. The Chrysler was hot, the steering wheel burning. Olive started the car and as she backed out of the parking lot, she saw the black SUV at Wheatland Market. She hesitated and then, decision made, drove across the street where she parked beside the black SUV. Getting out of her Chrysler, she looked inside the SUV for a sign, a name, an address, something to tell her who this woman was because she wanted to talk to her, to know her. She wrote down the license number and then she got into her Chrysler and waited, engine running, air conditioner cooling, until the red car returned and the woman got out. Her twin curls were now tucked up into the ballet twist and she looked disheveled—a look Olive knew well, the look of a woman who had just orgasmed, the color of sex still painted on her cheeks and on her throat, the residue of passion showing in the feline narrowing of her eyes.

She glanced in Olive's direction but dismissed her with the automatic smile reserved for strangers and then she leaned into the red car and this time Olive saw the man. He was young, black hair, lean face. The woman didn't want to leave him. She held onto his hand and kissed him again and stroked his face before letting go. He drove away. The woman walked toward the market entrance. Olive got out of her car and called to her,

Excuse me.

The woman turned. She had just put on her dark glasses, but Olive saw the glow around her eyes, saw the flushed skin, the half-open lips. Olive strode up to her and she said,

Can I talk to you for a minute?

What? Who are you?

I have an appointment with my therapist every week, just across the street and I see you here, shopping…and I just thought.

So you're one of the crazies?

I guess I am, Olive said.

That whole building is full of shrinks, the woman said, but you don't have horns growing out of your head so I guess you're not a danger.

May I walk with you? Olive said. I need to pick up some things.

The woman facing her changed as she spoke—the glorious fire of sex faded a little with each word and for a moment Olive felt sad and ashamed that she had broken into that private space. As they walked toward the market entrance, Olive glanced down at the woman's sun-tanned legs glowing like molten gold in the hot Kansas sun. Olive said,

I used to see you here with your children, but lately you're alone.

Um huh, the woman said. My kids are away.

Away? Olive said. For the summer?

With their father.

Together they entered the store what smelled of fresh cut flowers and the pungent odor of fruits and vegetables laid out in neat stacks—the grapes in piles, the apples and oranges in sharp pyramids, the melons green and gold mountains some with their sides split open showing red interiors lined with rows of dark seeds.

.The woman chose a cluster red grapes, half a split watermelon. Two Gala apples. She said,

The apples are from New Zealand at this time of year.

Are your children with their father here? In Wichita?

The woman stopped, turned to face Olive. She lowered her dark glasses and let her eyes flicker over Olive's face. She was easy now, relaxed, clear, unafraid. She said,

Do you have children?

I'm divorced. My babies are with my ex.

Oh, the woman said. Then we won't be setting any playdates...

The woman glanced at a stack of oranges, picked up a plump fruit, then she turned her eyes back on Olive. She said,

What do you really want?

I just want to talk to you, Olive said, that's all. The man in the red car, is he your lover?

The woman set down the orange. She looked down the aisle where a produce manager was finishing an arrangement of Anjou pears garnished with splashes of red plums arrayed like ornaments. She said,

I don't think that's any of your business.

Your babies are with your husband. Have you left him for the man in the red car?

Maybe you are a nut case, the woman said. Look, I have to finish my shopping so if you don't mind.

You're starting over, aren't you? Olive said. You're starting a new life with the man in the red car.

The half melon the woman was holding slipped from her hand and shattered on the floor. With the sudden splurge of bursting flesh, the sweet smell of ripe fruit swept over Olive—the meat on the floor was bright red, the seeds black in the pulp and juice. The produce manager snapped alert and sped to the spill on his floor and with a scoop but without a word of reproach cleaned up the sweet smelling and broken melon. Juice dotted the woman's legs—bright red splashes against the golden tan of her skin.

Backing away from the red mess at her feet, the woman hunched her shoulders, her face clouded and the impatience boiling out of her turned her skin as red as the plums plunked among the Anjou pears. But then, she laughed, the ruddiness running out of her, and she smiled and she said,

Does that shrink give you mind reading lessons, too?

I'm sorry, Olive said, I didn't mean to upset you, but we seem to have a lot in common...

Yes, the woman said. He's my lover. He's younger than I am, and he's a mess of man but he makes me feel so alive sometimes I think I'm going to crack open. I don't know why I'm telling you this—did my husband send you to spy on me?

Have you lost your babies?

There you go, the woman said. Reading my mind.

But you're not living with the man...the red car?

He has a girl friend, the woman said. It's not the usual kind of thing.

Are you thinking...do you want to get married again?

Married? If I get married, I lose my income...

Alimony?

Um huh. Have you had lunch?

No, I just finished my session with the doctor.

Do you want to have lunch with me? The woman said. I think we have a lot to talk about.

Nan and Toby

Olive got out of the taxi in front of the house, paid the driver without speaking as he opened the trunk and set the suitcase on the ground. Olive, tired from the flight from Phoenix, pulled the suitcase up the steps and into the foyer.

The house was dark. The air conditioner was running, the rooms were cool. She flipped on the lights and tossed her keys on the low boy beside the door just as her cell phone chirped. She answered. Clifford said,

How did it go?

Hi. I just got in.

I tracked your flight, and I wanted to meet you but I got held up. You forgive me?

Is something wrong?

Just business. Still up for dinner?

Um huh, Olive said.

See you in an hour, he said.

After he hung up, Olive held onto the phone like an anchor. Then she set it on the lowboy with the keys and went up stairs where she undressed and got into the shower, letting the soothing hot water pour over her. She shampooed, rinsed and, getting out, dried off and checked her short cropped hair in the steamy mirror. She decided not to blow dry it. In her bedroom, she opened the closet.

It smelled of cedar. It smelled of pent up perfume, She ran her fingers over the dresses, the suits, the pant suits, the coats and jackets, skirts and blouses all arranged by color and style. She remembered her first visit to LouAnn's with Janey and how she chose with an eye on her pocketbook— only two dresses, only one skirt and only one blouse. It had seemed outrageous then spending so much on herself. She pulled an electric blue pant suit and a chrome yellow blouse from the rack and tossed them on the bed.

In the smaller closet, she looked at the twin rows of shoes—all arranged by style and by color within style—high heels, spiked heels, flats, strapped sandals, strapped high heels, strapped spiked heels, sneakers, flip-flops, and, her favorites, the strapped black spiked heels that made her feel wicked and impure—a feeling she no longer ran away from. Thank you Rose.

She selected a pair of yellow spiked heels, and she remembered asking Clifford how he felt going into a room with a woman three inches taller than he was. And he had said, Everybody is three inches taller than I am, so wear the heels, you look good in heels. As she slid on her underwear, she remembered LouAnn saying—You can't bring back the undies, they're yours for keeps. Um huh. Okay. And Olive looked at herself in the floor length mirror before she put on the pant suit. Her pubic hair was now shaped into a small V. The butterfly tattoo on her belly seemed to perch on the V.

She ran her fingers over its wings, remembered the bite of the needle and Clifford's hand tight on her as she lay down for the artist who said not to worry, he'd seen half of Wichita naked. She smoothed at her belly. Still flat. She'd lost a few pounds during the week. She had the look of a hungry lion, Clifford told her the first time he saw her in red—she liked that. A hungry lion.

Electric blue made her skin glow. She liked that. Chrome yellow silk at her throat gave her face more light. She liked that. Using the vanity mirror, she stroked on just the faintest touch of blue eye shadow, just the thinnest line of eyebrow pencil to darken the blond brows. Standing, she was ready.

Turning, she saw the two photos on the wall beside the vanity and she stopped.

Three days in Fort Lauderdale, two days in Phoenix and she hadn't thought about her babies—not once. She went to the pictures in their silver frames—you have to frame them, Clifford told her, look at the pin holes—they'll be ruined.

Olive lifted the pictures down and set them on the vanity and she studied them. Nan's photo was from her fifth birthday, Toby's from his third. In the photos they both had her blond hair and her features—They're definitely your kids, Clifford said the first time he saw them. Olive propped the pictures side by side against the vanity mirror and looked at herself in the glass and then at the children and she ran her fingertips over her lips and over the faces of her babies and then, her fingers, moving as if they were disconnected from her hands, unlatched the tabs at the backs of the frames and pulled the photos out.

She set them on the vanity.

Moving like a woman with absolute purpose, she went to the bed and drew out the battered leather suitcase and tossed it on the bed, opened it. It smelled hot and moldy. It smelled of saddle soap and perfume. It smelled of the dirt from Tim's farm and the little studio on J Street and it smelled of old shoes and it still carried the odor of sweat and fried onions and bacon and the faint scent of shampoo from a long time ago when, once, the cap of a bottle had leaked into the leather. She gritted her teeth. Held on to fight the swirling, floating feeling just at the edge of her mind. And then, it stopped, the floating, and she let go.

Her chest relaxed as she breathed in the smells, each one hooked to something or someone in the past and then she returned to the vanity and the pictures and she took them like an offering and laid them to rest in the suitcase along with their silver frames. She closed them up. Closed off the smells and the odors of her past and she hefted the suitcase, now so heavy it hurt her arms, and slid it back under the bed and she left the room.

Downstairs she picked up her phone and keys and put them into a blue silk purse she chose from a half dozen that hung on hooks and she shut off the lights and stepped outside into the warm air of an autumn evening, into the smells of the city and the odor of sycamores dropping their dusty leaves.

Clifford, right on time, stood beside his Aston Martin. He wore a blue suit and black shoes. As always his shirt and tie looked crisp, the tie a startling yellow—had she chosen the yellow blouse knowing she would match him like flowers in a vase? The shirt glistened in the light, chrome white, pure white, clean and pure and white. He smiled at her. He opened the door. She got in.

The car smelled of flowers. It was either lavender, which he loved, or freesia which he adored. She remembered asking him about the floral scents once as they lay in bed still warm from sex, the scent of flowers rising like the perfume of a spring morning, and he said that they were attars he had distilled in France. A man who cared about himself enough to have a private cologne. She liked that.

You smell good tonight, Olive said.

He stopped, hand on the key. She turned to face him. She smiled. He looked worried. She caressed his neck. And she said every thing was okay and he started the car. It throbbed with a pleasant power. Olive leaned back in the leather seat. She was very much at ease with her hand resting on his muscled shoulder. He said,

You look tired.

I'm all right. I bought new school clothes for the kids.

They'll love you for that.

And I was thinking we could get new portraits.

I'll set it up, Clifford said. Get the photographer out here.

What would you say to a family portrait?

You and me?

151

All of us. You, me, Nan and Toby.

Well, the lawyers say we'll have them for our first visit next Friday. We can do it then.

What if they've forgotten me? Olive said.

They can't forget you, you're their mother.

Lemon Custard
From Short Story to Screenplay

I wrote Lemon Custard as a short story for Throwback and Other Stories, my second collection of short fiction. I used the short story as the basis for the novella and the novella then turned into a screenplay.

Why a novella?

The novella isn't a short story that got long, it isn't a novel that got short. A novella has a single story line, few subplots—one at most—and a limited number of characters. These traits make the novella a good starting place for a screenplay. The challenge of adapting a three hundred page novel with three subplots and a hundred characters is this—what do you leave out? Adapting a novella is straightforward. One protagonist, one story line, one set of characters.

Lemon Custard, the novella, isn't Lemon Custard the short story made long but a new creation that spins out of a circumstance—Olive Keller, the Missing Mom. The novella is her story. The kernel of the novella lies in this exchange between the Grandpa and Nan from the short story:

Eat faster, Butch, Nancy said.
No, I said. I'm not gonna.
I'll tell Mama, she said.
She won't do anything, I said.
Butch, don't argue with your sister now.
Nancy licked her Lemon Custard for a while and then she said,
Grandpa, when is Mama coming back?
Umm, Grandpa said. I don't know, Nance.
Why did she go away?
Well, baby, sometimes people have to go do that to get square with themselves.
What does that mean, Grandpa? Get square?

Once the novella was in place and Olive had learned what it meant to get square with herself, I adapted it as a screenplay. I'd been working with

Bob Ray, Stewart Stern, and Ryan Winfield—all high order writers—and with their help, the screenplay took shape fast.

The logical next step was to attach a few pages of the screenplay to this volume so readers could see how the story developed and how the process of adaptation to screenplay changes not just the structure of the story, but the characters and, above all, the dialogue.

I learned from the screenwriters that each line of dialogue has two layers to it. First and foremost dialogue reveals character traits and personality while riding on a bed of subtext. The second role of dialogue is to lay pipe, as the screenwriters call it. Laying pipe means that the characters drop hints about the future, reveal elements of backstory, and plug in any red herrings while layering in symbols.

There are other differences between the story and the novelal and between the novella and the screenplay concerning Point of View or POV. The narrator in the short story speaks in the First Person. It's his story. He speaks in the present tense. In the shift from short story to novella, the Point of View shifts to Third Person Limited—it's Olive's story. She's in every scene but the story is in the past tense. The adaptation to screenplay loses both the First Person of the story and the Third Person of the novella. In the screenplay, the Camera becomes the I. The camera moves in all directions, in and out of character POV with much more freedom. So you write for the camera. The camera sees only actions and images. This little detail can be one of the major differences between the novella and the screenplay.

Adaptation is both a challenge and a joy as you discover how to handle the problems in each genre. The way I see it, movies have rewired our brains. As writers, we have to learn to think in action and image. But it's a two way street—Writing a screenplay can make you a better novelist. Writing a screenplay sharpens your sense of impulse, forces you to write tighter, drives you to ride the mythic wave.

Here is Lemon Custard.

Lemon Custard
A Screenplay
By
Jack Remick
Based on the novella
By
Jack Remick

FADE IN:

To black. We HEAR the SOUND of wind blowing and the METALLIC CLANK of a chain rattling against steel. The SOUND of a heavy tractor engine approaches then fades. Silence except for the sound of the wind and the clanking of metal on metal.

EXT. A FARM IN KANSAS. NIGHT

OLIVE KELLER (29) stands on the platform of a windmill looking over the railing. 30 feet below there's a big HORSE TANK full of water. She's holding a red Chinese silk FAN.

In the distance, Olive SEES the headlights of the tractor coming toward her. The tractor turns, the headlights disappear. Olive climbs up on the railing. The wind whips her long blond pony tail and rips the fan from her hand. We HEAR the tractor. Olive WATCHES the fan pinwheel and float and in the spinning, she SEES NAN (8) and TOBY (5) arms flailing and the fan flits into the horse tank and Olive falls off the rail, arms outstretched. She slams back into the steel frame of the windmill.

Fade to black.

INT. A FARM HOUSE BEDROOM. NIGHT.

On top of an old leather SUITCASE with straps and steel buckles there are photographs of NAN (8) and TOBY (5) the children in Olive's suicide vision. Olive is jamming kids' clothing into two other suitcases. She kneels between two beds where Nan and Toby are sleeping. She caresses their heads then she closes the suitcases.

EXT. A FARM HOUSE. NIGHT.

Olive loads suitcases into the trunk of a green CHRYSLER 300 and slams the trunk. Nan and Toby in their pajamas sleep on the back seat.

The SOUND of the tractor gets louder, then it bores straight for the Chrysler. Olive, looking angry, gets in the car. She leans her forehead into the steering wheel, then she closes the door, starts the car and hurtles away from the house just as the tractor stops, lights pinning the Chrysler.

In the rear view mirror Olive sees TIM (41)her HUSBAND in the headlights of the tractor holding out his hands as if to question what's going on.

INT. LIVING ROOM. PAUL MALONE'S FARM. DAY

The kids' suitcases stand by the front door. Olive sits at a table with Grace (60) and Paul (65) her mother and father. Olive looks haggard as if she's been up all night. Nan and Toby, looking cute, sit side by side on a sofa holding hands. Nan is scratching a scab on her knee.

> OLIVE
> It'll just be till I get things under control.

> PAUL
> Whatever's going on between you and Tim is none of my business, Olive, but we've got two babies here.

> OLIVE
> I wouldn't ask this of you, Dad but I need to leave Nan and Toby while I get some things worked out.

> GRACE
> Where are you going, Olive?

> OLIVE
> Wichita.
> (to Nan)
> Sweetheart, don't pick at the scab.

> NAN
> It itches, Mommy.

OLIVE
I know, baby, but scratching will make it worse.

GRACE
I have something for that. Come with me, sugar.

Grace leads Nan from the room. Toby tucks his hands between his knees.

OLIVE
It won't be for long,Dad.

PAUL
Have you talked to your brother about this?

OLIVE
Dean? No one can talk to Dean anymore. He's off somewhere in another world with that woman he married.

PAUL
They're coming this weekend to finish up the plowing and he'll want to know why your babies are here.

TOBY
Mommy.

OLIVE
Just a second sweetie.
(to Paul)
Tell him what you like.

Grace and Nan return with a plate of cookies and two glasses of milk. Nan now has a Dora The Explorer band-aid on her knee. Toby's face lights up.

TOBY
Cookies.

Nan folds a napkin across Toby's lap and hands him a chocolate chip cookie then a glass of milk and then she sits beside him, cookie and milk in hand.

TOBY
Thank you.

GRACE
Now, Missie, do you mind telling me, just what business you've got in Wichita?

OLIVE
I'm going to find a job.

PAUL
Do you need money?

GRACE
She's got a husband, Dad, why would she need money?

OLIVE
Oh Dad, I don't know what I need.

GRACE
You need some common sense, that's what you need.

PAUL
Why don't you stay here, sweetheart? You can have your old room, right Mother? She can move her sewing machine out and I'll call Tim, tell him what's cooking and you two can fix it up when he's done working his ground.

OLIVE
(sharply)
He's never done working his ground, Dad. That's the problem.

GRACE
You listen to me, child. Tim's got a right to know what you're up to.

OLIVE
Mom. Please. You can't make it better.

Nan and Toby finish their cookies and their milk.

NAN
Grandma, Toby got some crumbs on your couch.

TOBY
I'm sorry, Grandma.

Grace goes to Toby, folds up the napkin with his cookie crumbs in it and then sits between the two children, an arm around each one's shoulder.

GRACE
Just you don't worry yourself about a few crumbs pumpkin. This old couch has seen so many cookie crumbs...

Grace tickles Toby and pulls his ear. Olive glances at Nan and Toby and SHE'S BACK ON THE WINDMILL leaning over the railing and the WIND plucks the fan from her hand again and she's floating then SPIRALING as she follows the red FAN into the water.

Nan and Toby snuggle against Grace.

Olive is CLIMBING BACK DOWN OFF THE WINDMILL HANDS SHAKING. She looks at Paul and there's panic in her face.

Olive grips her hands together so they don't shake. Paul reaches for her, just about to touch but he holds up.

OLIVE

Tim's suffocating me, Dad. Last night I climbed the windmill and I
really was going to jump and the only thing was the babies.
(pause)
I can't take being out there anymore alone. One more day and I go
crazy.

Paul screws up his face as he listens to Olive. We SEE the weathering in
his skin, the sun spots. His eyes are watery, the eyelashes burned off by the
sun. He seems to age ten years as Olive talks.

PAUL
What have you told the...
(in a low voice)
Babies?

OLIVE
I told them you'd take good care of them and that you'd take them
into town for lemon custard ice cream every Sunday.

GRACE
And you think lemon custard ice cream will make everything just
hunky dory.

OLIVE
Nan can get Toby dressed and help him brush his teeth.
(Olive's eyes tear up)
I brought clean clothes. It's a month till school starts and I think I
forgot their pajamas but I'll have things under control by then.

Long silence.

PAUL
How will we reach you?

OLIVE
I'll call. I'll get the kids when I'm settled in town.

PAUL
Settled. That sounds like you made a pretty big decision.

OLIVE
I guess I have.

Grace leaves the kids on the sofa, goes to the table, picks up the cookie plate and milk glasses. She looks at Paul and then she leans over Olive. There's pain in her face, mouth turned down at the corners.

GRACE
(in a whisper)
You just never stop disappointing me, Olive.

PAUL
There's no call for that, Mother.

INT. OLIVE'S APT. IN WICHITA. DAY

From an open window, Olive looks at the street where a trash can overflows with garbage. Newspapers crumpled on the sidewalk. Cars. The SOUND of a motorcycle ripping past. Olive closes the window. The LANDLORD stands in the doorway beside Olive's old leather suitcase.

LANDLORD
Well?

OLIVE
I'll take it.

LANDLORD
You don't know what I'm askin' yet.

OLIVE
It's just a place to stay.

LANDLORD

Two hundred then. First and last and a hundred deposit. You can cook in the room long as you don't stink it up so the others complain.

Olive pulls her money clip from her Levis pocket and counts out five hundred in fifties.

LANDLORD
A woman like you, carrying that much cash in this city someone'll knock you in the head.

OLIVE
I don't have a checking account.

LANDLORD
You a student? You look kinda old for a student.

OLIVE
I went to Xavier a long time ago.

LANDLORD
Xavier? That's Catholic huh? I hear it's not much of a school.

Olive offers him the five hundred. The landlord hands over the key and, pocketing his money, turns to leave but hesitates.

LANDLORD
No air conditioning, but there's a hardware store over on 11th. You can pick up a fan there.

OLIVE
I'm used to the heat, thanks.

The landlord exits.

Olive surveys her apartment. It's a single room painted yellow. A twin bed, no closet. A tiny refrigerator under the sink. A chrome-legged table. Two straight chairs--green enamel. She goes to the bathroom. It's tiny, no sink just a stool and a shower stall with a clear plastic curtain on a shower ring.

Olive sets her suitcase on the bed, opens it and lays out the two photos of Nan and Toby on the table. She closes the suitcase, slides it under the bed then leaves the apartment.

INT. KIOWA CAFE. DAY

Olive reads the Herald Want Ads. A coffee cup on the table in front of her.

JANEY(28) a waitress, approaches with a pot of coffee. Janey wears a short skirt, scooped blouse. A red, blue and yellow flower tattoo marks her right shoulder. Janey touches Olive's arm the way friendly waitresses do.

        JANEY
        Can I warm that up for you?

        OLIVE
        Oh thanks. I'm not used to more than two cups a day and I haven't
        touched the last one yet.

        JANEY
        Did you find what you're looking for in the Herald?

        OLIVE
        Well, there's an opening at KECU but it's not full time.

        JANEY
        KECU...that's the credit union just a couple of blocks over. Are
        you any good with numbers?

        OLIVE
        Um huh. Yeah.

        JANEY
        If I was good with numbers I wouldn't be slinging Adam and Eve

on a raft.

OLIVE
(laughing)
Adam and Eve on a raft?

JANEY
Scrambled eggs and toast? You know something, you've got gorgeous hair. I noticed it when you first came in. Musta taken ten years to grow it that long.

OLIVE
I always wear it in a pony tail.

JANEY
(touching Olive's arm)
Boy, I'll tell you--if I had hair like that I'd never cut it.

Janey takes her coffee pot away when two customers enter and sit at the counter.

JANEY
What can I get you folks?

VOICE 1
Are you Janey?

JANEY
That's right.

VOICE 2
A friend of ours said you can get us into the Tomb.

JANEY
The Tomb?

VOICE 1

Our friend said it's a leather club.

JANEY
What's your friend's name?

Olive circles the ad from KECU, drops a dollar on the table and exits.

INT. KECU A CREDIT UNION. THE NEXT DAY

KECU is a glass, steel and plastic one story modern building. Olive enters.
She wears a denim skirt, a sleeveless blouse so thin it shows her bra straps,
flats, no stockings. Hair in a pony tail.

Olive approaches a desk where EILEEN NORBURG (35)a black woman
wearing SWOOPY glasses with bright red frames sits working. Olive
stands in front of the desk holding her little CLUTCH PURSE under her
arm.

EILEEN
(looking up)
Yes?

OLIVE
I'm Olive Keller. I called about the interview.

EILEEN
Miss Keller. Please have a seat.

Eileen stands. She's tall, around six feet, very chic, dressed in a blue
tailored suit, red blouse, pearls. Long red polished FINGERNAILS. Her
EYES are made up with a light purple shadow, her LIPSTICK is purplish
umber. She shakes hands with Olive.

EILEEN
Well, Miss Keller, what can you do?

OLIVE

I have a degree in accounting from Xavier.

EILEEN
Do you have a résumé?

OLIVE
Résumé? Uh...I didn't think of that.

EILEEN
(looks amused)
Well then, tell me something about yourself.

OLIVE
(very eager)
Well, for three years I kept books for the Faculty Club at Xavier
and then I graduated and I got married and I've been doing the
books for the farm for eight years.

EILEEN
(glances up, smiling)
So it's not Miss Keller?

OLIVE
No. Two children. A boy and a girl. The girl came first..Nan and
Toby, he's five...

EILEEN
Okay. Why do you want to work at KECU?

OLIVE
(nervous)
I need a job and I'm good with numbers. It's a huge farm--twelve
hundred acres.

EILEEN
Oh my. That is...

OLIVE
We ran cattle, we had pigs, dairy cows and the wheat land. I know the farm business.

EILEEN
You say *had* pigs...*ran* cattle. Ummm.

Eileen pulls off her chic lenses and studies Olive like a doctor examining a specimen. Olive fidgets and fondles her purse trying to hide her hands.

OLIVE
Well...I...

EILEEN
I see that you've taken off your ring. You must be in transition?

OLIVE
Transition? You can tell?
(relieved)
Everything is changing so fast right now.

Eileen puts her swoopy glasses back on, opens a desk drawer. Olive stands clutching her purse.

OLIVE
Okay, well, thanks. I hope I didn't take up too much of your time.

EILEEN
Can you start Monday?

OLIVE
Monday?

EILEEN
It's part-time as you know. You won't be at the window, so if you're looking for face to face with clients, you'll have to wait until something opens up later.

OLIVE
(ecstatic)
I got the job? I got the job?
(pause)
Really? Oh thank you. Thank you, thank you. Thank you.

Eileen stands, holds out a slender, polished hand that if you could smell it would be perfumed and soft. She holds a BUSINESS CARD in her RED FINGERNAILS. Olive smiles like her face is about to crack.

EILEEN
KECU has a dress code, Olive. No bare shoulders, no tattoos showing, no skirts cut above the knee, pants are all right, but no spiked heels.

OLIVE
Spiked heels? I've never owned a pair of spiked heels in my life.

EILEEN
And no tattoos?

OLIVE
Oh no. No. No.

EILEEN
Everyone seems to have them these days. All right. Monday morning eight o'clock.

Olive almost runs out of the office.

Eileen watches her, an enigmatic smile on her face. She shakes her head.
EXT. THE STREET OUTSIDE KECU. MOMENTS LATER

Olive stands with her hands over her mouth breathing hard. She looks at the card in her hand. She SEES her shattered fingernails. She glances down at her feet. Her broken toenails look like saw-edges. REFLECTED IN

THE PLATE GLASS WINDOW SHE SEES EILEEN NORBURG IN
HER CHIC SUIT HAND HER THE CARD, HER LONG RED
FINGERNAILS FLASHING.

A MOTORCYCLE buzzing past BRINGS Olive back and in the window
she sees herself in her frumpy denim skirt and her chintzy blouse.

INT. A DRUG STORE. WICHITA. LATER

Olive pushes a shopping cart down the COSMETICS aisle. She stops at
NAIL POLISH, selects a color. We SEE EILEEN'S red nails, the color
doesn't match. Olive selects another bottle, same routine. Satisfied, she
drops the polish in the cart. She studies NAIL FILES, NAIL CLIPPERS,
EMERY BOARDS, then she finds a PEDI-EGG. We SEE the CALLUSES
on Olive's palms. As she reads the label we SEE how to use a pedi-egg.
Olive drops the pedi-egg in the cart. She FINDS a bottle of lotion, cracks it
open, sniffs it, Olive closes the bottle, sets it back on the shelf, selects
another, same routine several times until she finds one that satisfies her.
Olive at the LIPSTICK DISPLAY case chooses a sample--UMBER. She
holds it up to her mouth, in the mirror we SEE EILEEN'S purplish umber
lips. Olive sets that one down then chooses a BRILLIANT CHINESE RED
that she drops in the cart.

Olive stops at a display of scarves. She selects a red one. In the MIRROR,
she holds it up and we SEE EILEEN'S RED BLOUSE. The shopping cart
is loaded with cosmetics as Olive heads to the cashier. She stops when she
SEES gilded picture frames on a rack. She drops two of them in the cart.

The cashier, an Asian woman (35) with ink black hair and pale powdered
skin, eyes made up like a fashion model, has nails as long as scythes. She
scans the items.

     CASHIER
     Would you like to buy a Milky Way today?

     OLIVE
     Milky Way?

CASHIER
Manager's special. Buy one, get one free. Half-price. It's a good deal really. Better to eat junk when you're hungry--empty calories, no fat.

The cashier glances at Olive. Smiles.

CASHIER
Where do *you* work out? God, you look *terrific*. Is it that place over on 11th? God, you have just *beautiful* skin. Did you find everything you need?

OLIVE
Yes. I think so. I just got a job.

CASHIER
Thirty-seven fifty. Cash or charge?

Olive pulls her money clip from her clutch purse, hands a fifty dollar bill to the cashier who makes change but her long nails give her trouble with the bills. Olive watches the cashier's hands. The nails are long, but the skin is perfect. Olive rubs her right palm on her skirt then holds it behind her back.

INT. KIOWA CAFE. EVENING

On the table in front of Olive there's a pile of ground-off skin and the nail polish, clippers, emery boards, lipstick are lined up like instruments on an operating room tray. Olive scrapes away at the calluses on the palm of her left hand with the PEDI-EGG, then switches to the right palm adding to the pile of sand-like skin. She rubs her palms together and then with nail file and emery board sands at her nails until their cracks and snags are smooth.

Waving her polished left hand, Olive blows on it, then, polish still moist, she tries to paint the nails of her right hand but she knocks over the bottle of polish, looks up at Janey who's smiling.

JANEY
You're not very good at this, are you?

OLIVE
I got the job.

JANEY
Hooray. Now you're one of the working poor. You better let me help you with that or you'll be here all night.

Janey wipes up the spilled polish with a wad of napkins.

OLIVE
I'm sorry, I didn't mean to make such a mess.

JANEY
'Sokay. Something about this place makes people messy, you know? And that makes me the mess cleaner upper. So you got the job.

Janey sits beside Olive and polishes Olive's nails.

OLIVE
I can't remember the last time I wore nail polish.

JANEY
You're running from something, aren't you? I can tell by that free-at-last look in your eyes. You didn't have it yesterday. And the minute I saw you yesterday I knew you were like a little lost lamb right off the farm.

OLIVE
How do you know that?

JANEY
I seen it a bazillion times. Bright and shiny eyed girls, first time in

the big city and that long blond pony tail is a dead give-away. And so you got hired at KECU and you're going to need some new clothes.

Janey finishes the nails, blows on them, looks at Olive.

JANEY
There. Let that dry and you're a new woman. You know, your hands are kinda rough and...you don't have any make up on but you still've got that glow.

OLIVE
You know a place? For new clothes?

JANEY
Just about every girl who ever got hired there at KECU came in here after Eileen cut her down to size.

OLIVE
She seemed nice to me. I didn't even bring a résumé.

JANEY
She ain't what she seems, sugar. You have a place?

OLIVE
On J Street and you're right I do need some clothes. Eileen said.

JANEY
Eileen hit you with that dress code, didn't she? She means it too. If they smart off and get inked she cans'em.

Janey shows her tattoo. She laughs

JANEY
No tats, right? No short skirts, right? No spiked heels, right?

OLIVE
Wow. She's...I have never seen anyone that...elegant. She's like...I don't know.

JANEY
I'll tell you what. I'm off tomorrow. We can run over to LouAnn's Consignment. She's got a good eye for last year's fashions and when you walk outta there you won't recognize yourself. I'm Janey, by the way.

OLIVE
Olive. Olive...Malone.

JANEY
Okay, Olive Malone, I'll see you around ten, right here?

INT. OLIVE'S APT. MORNING

Olive lies awake looking at the photos of Nan and Toby now pinned to the wall by her bed.

SHE'S IN BED ON THE FARM AND NAN AND TOBY FLOAT OVER HER JUST BEYOND HER GRASP AS SHE REACHES FOR THEM, BUT THE KIDS FADE.
Olive rolls over, gets up. She wears a FRUMPY COTTON NIGHTGOWN. She checks the alarm clock. 4:00. She turns on the light, runs a glass of water then walks to the window to shut off the window fan.

She LOOKS out on the street. She SEES--the overflowing litter can on the corner. Blown newspapers jammed against the tires of her Chrysler. A man parking a MOTORCYCLE glances up at her. He wears LEATHER and BOOTS. He puts on his HELMET, BUTTONING his jacket he lights a cigarette and keeps watching until Olive backs away from the window. She turns off the light, then peeks out the window to see the motorcycle tear down the street.

Olive SHOWERS. Gets dressed in 501s, chambray shirt, and sandals. She sits at the table, hands folded in front of her. She checks the clock--5:00.

INT. LOU-ANN'S CONSIGNMENT SHOP. DAY

Olive and Janey in a dressing room. Olive models a blue silk dress.
EILEEN NORBURG IN THE MIRROR TURNS AS OLIVE TURNS,
HER LONG RED NAILS SWEEPING OVER THE BODICE OF THE
DRESS.

> OLIVE
> Tonight?

> JANEY
> It's Saturday. What else are you going to do?

> OLIVE
> I've never been to a night club.

> JANEY
> It's not exactly a night club...it's more like a...hunting ground.

> OLIVE
> (modeling the dress)
> What do you think?

> JANEY
> Honey, with your shape, you could wear a gunny sack and make it
> look good.

> OLIVE
> Should I take them all?

Olive steps out of the dress. She's wearing her WHITE BRA, WHITE
GRANNY PANTIES. She pulls on her 501s, chambray shirt, and sandals.

Janey shakes her head.

OLIVE
What?

JANEY
We're still in Kansas.

INT. LOUANN'S CONSIGNMENT SHOP. MOMENTS LATER.

LOUANN (40)finishes stacking Olive's purchases--two skirts, two blouses, two dresses, bras, panty hose, panties on the counter by the cash register.

LOUANN
That comes to three hundred.

JANEY
Ooooh, is that going to bankrupt you?

Olive takes her money clip from the hip pocket of her 501s and counts out three hundred in fifties.

LOUANN
A money clip. I haven't seen a money clip since they closed the air base.

OLIVE
It's very practical.

LouAnn stuffs everything in two bags.

LOUANN
You can trade up anytime except for underwear. That's yours.

OLIVE
There are seven days, why do the panties come in packs of three?

JANEY
That's how they get us, idden it?

Olive and Janey exit the shop. On the sidewalk, Janey grabs Olive's arm.

> JANEY
> So, you're okay with tonight?

> OLIVE
> I said I'd go with you.

> JANEY
> I'll come over to your place around eleven.

> OLIVE
> Eleven? At night?

> JANEY
> Nothing worth doing starts until midnight, love. Ta-ta.

INT. OLIVE'S APT. LATER

Olive stands in front of the bathroom mirror wearing a black bra and black panties. Her pubic hair runs wild under the elastic. She covers her delta with her hands and closes her eyes.

INT. OLIVE'S APT. LATER THAT NIGHT

Janey sits on a chair, legs crossed. Her THIGH TATTOO shows. She's holding the pictures of Nan and Toby that are now in gold frames. Olive is in the bathroom.

> JANEY
> So these your kids?

> OLIVE
> Um huh. Nan and Toby. Nan's eight, Toby's five. They're with my Mom and Dad. Toby starts school in September.

JANEY
Cute. They look like you. You divorced or something?

OLIVE
Something. Tim, their Dad? He's. Well, kind of hard to live with.

JANEY
He's a man. All men are hard to live with. You know, that black outfit you bought today...you ought to wear that.

OLIVE
What's wrong with this skirt?

JANEY
Well, for one, it's denim, two it covers too much, and three, well, when you're hunting skin is bait.

OLIVE
That skirt is for work.

JANEY
Oh yeah, Eileen will love that.

JANEY/OLIVE
(together)
Nothing cut above the knee.

Olive emerges from the bathroom wearing a short denim skirt. She's hemmed it so it strikes her at mid-thigh. She wears a low cut sheer blouse.

JANEY
Well, gag me with a spoon...the woman has thighs. I like it, I like it. Lots of skin. You've got such beautiful skin but I don't know if they'll let you into The Tomb wearing sandals,

EXT. THE CHRYSLER, INDUSTRIAL SECTION. NIGHT

Olive driving, turns onto a dark street.

> JANEY
> Just up there, at the end by that warehouse.

Olive parks. The only mark for the night club is a small NEON SIGN of a GRAVESTONE over the door. In front of the warehouse there is an impressive array of MOTORCYCLES, MERCS, BEAMERS, CHEVIE PICKUPS.

EXT. OUTSIDE THE TOMB NIGHT CLUB. NIGHT

Olive stands beside the car. Hesitating. Janey is headed for the door. She stops, turns, hands on hips cocks her head and holds out her hands like 'what are you waiting for?'

> OLIVE
> I don't know about this, Janey.

Janey comes back for her, puts her arm around her shoulder.

> JANEY
> Are you a virgin?

> OLIVE
> No. I've just never done this before.

> JANEY
> Do I have to say it?

> OLIVE
> Say what?

> JANEY
> There's a first time for everything. Look at you. My god, you're so tight your head's gonna pop. Come on.

The door of the Tomb opens, a couple in black leather staggers out, laughing. Chains flash. Black leather as they run to a pickup where, leaning against the door, they kiss.

Olive hesitates.

OLIVE
I don't think I can do this.

Grabbing Olive's arm, Janey drags her to the door, raps on the door, it opens on BEEF (TOO UGLY TO HAVE BEEN BORN HENCE NO AGE) a HUGE MAN in black leather sleeveless vest, head shaven, tattooed from shoulder to the backs of his hands.

BEEF
Janey, honey. Where you been?

JANEY
Hi Beef. Are those new tats?

Beef sticks out his tongue. He has two silver tongue studs. He wiggles his tongue with a gleam in his eye.

BEEF
Give you ten bucks Janey if you and your cute little friend sit on my studs.

JANEY
No freebies, Beef. It's her first time.

BEEF
I dint know there's any virgins left.

JANEY
She has no idea what she's getting into.

BEEF
Still costs ten to play, Janey.

JANEY
Give him ten, honey.

Olive pulls ten dollars from the money clip in the pocket of her Levis skirt.
The ten disappears in Beef's Technicolor paw.

OLIVE
You didn't tell me it would cost ten dollars.

INT. TOMB NIGHT CLUB. MOMENTS LATER

The TOMB is noisy, crammed with tattooed women and black leather
men. No room to breathe. Chains every where. Tall women in black leather
boots and leather garter belts. Men wearing sunglasses. Olive watches
open-mouthed as a bare-breasted woman kneels in front of a tall black man
and caresses him. No one pays any attention.
Olive follows Janey to the bar where she's ordered two drinks from the
bartender, a tall scrawny woman with ink black hair down to her waist,
nose studs and ear plugs.

JANEY
Pay the girl, honey.

OLIVE
I only have nine dollars left.

JANEY
What happened to that wad I saw?

OLIVE
I left it at home.

JANEY
Okay. I'm good for it.

Holding two cocktail glasses Janey knees Olive in the butt and forces her to a table where they sit.

> OLIVE
> They all have things stuck in them.

> JANEY
> (shouting)
> Piercings. It's that kind of club.

> OLIVE
> What kind of club?

Janey takes Olive's hand and slides it between her legs. Olive freezes. Janey smiles.

> JANEY
> They're called clit rings.

> OLIVE
> Why down there?

Janey touches her breasts.

> JANEY
> Here too.

> OLIVE
> Two?

Janey unbuttons her blouse to show GOLD NIPPLE RINGS.

> JANEY
> Three down, two up. Double your pleasure.

> OLIVE

You don't have any underwear on.

JANEY
Don't need it. I'm gonna get laid, just gets in the way. Let's dance.

Janey knocks back her drink and pulls Olive to the dance floor but they're separated when MR. DARK slides between them. He's sweaty in a leather vest, tight leather pants with a bulge at the crotch. His nipples are pierced with thick chrome rings. He pulls Olive to him, she resists as he slides his hands around her waist and down over her butt. She tries to draw back. He leans into her.

MR. DARK
Third floor on J St, right?

OLIVE
What?

MR. DARK
Third floor. You didn't wave to me. Bike? On the street? You're the green Chrysler.

MR. Dark is tugging on Olive's arm, Janey pulling on the other. Janey wins, drags Olive back to the table.

INT. A TABLE. MOMENTS LATER

Olive at the table with Janey who's talking to a WOMAN with PURPLE HAIR. Her midriff is bare, she has two jeweled rings in her navel.

JANEY
Her first time, she doesn't know what she wants.

WOMAN
Jesus, Janey. A virgin? Lucky you!

JANEY

I don't think so.

Janey makes a ditzy swirl with her fingers at her head.

OLIVE
I have to pee.

Janey points to a hallway. The woman backs away and licks her lips.

WOMAN
Watch out, you never know who you'll find in there.

Olive in the hallway SEES two doors--TOPS and BOTTOMS. She chooses BOTTOMS.

INT. TOILET. MOMENTS LATER.

Olive stands looking at herself in the mirror. She leans on the sink, but CAN'T LOOK AT HERSELF as she slides her hand under her skirt. She's excited, trembling, but then the door opens and two women enter. Olive yanks her hand away. Paying no attention to Olive, one of the women plants the other on the counter and buries her face in her crotch. Olive exits.

INT. TABLE. MOMENTS LATER

Janey's seated at the table with a man. He's thick, bulging arms. Bald head slick with sweat. His hand with a ring on each finger rests on Janey's leg. She's smoking, head back, as she looks at him through tight squinted eyes.

OLIVE
I have to go, Janey. I'm not ready for this.

JANEY
(coming down)
What? Ready for what? This is Kit, sweetheart. He says he can make me happy. He says he can make everybody happy and he'd

like to make you happy too but that'd be three of us to make happy and I don't know if a threesome'll make you as happy as it'll make me 'cause you're kind of so uptight you can't pee, right?

> OLIVE
> A threesome?

Janey strokes Kit's bald head, leans into him and kisses him between the eyes.

> JANEY
> God, I love that head. She's a virgin, baby, never been under the whip.

Janey waves her hand with the cigarette in it.

> JANEY
> (to Olive)
> Go on then. Kit'll make me happy and then...who the fuck knows who he'll make happy after he makes me happy. Right, baby?

INT. VICKY'S HAIR SALON. DAY

> VICKY
> You're sure you want to do this?

> OLIVE
> Shoulder length and dyed black.

As VICKY works on Olive's tresses, DISSOLVE MATCH TO EILEEN NORBURG IN THE SALON CHAIR.

INT. KIOWA CAFE. A WEEK LATER. NIGHT

Olive enters, walks to the counter where Janey is brewing a pot of coffee. Janey WATCHES Olive in the mirror as she sits. Janey finishes her work, wipes her hands.

JANEY
Good gravy, girl, did you sell your hair?

OLIVE
Do you like it?

JANEY
I kinda miss the pony tail, but yeah. The new you won't be able to walk down the street 'cause every guy sees you'll want a piece of you. Look, I'm sorry about the other night. I was high and...well...can we still be friends?

OLIVE
Did he make you happy?

JANEY
(intimate smile)
I couldn't sit down for two days and I have a yeast infection what does that tell you?

OLIVE
What do you mean?

JANEY
Oh god. *You* have got to get out more. Yes, he made me happy. Men are here so we can use them. You tell'em what you need or they just walk all over you. Like a lot of hot women, you don't know what you've got. That skin, that body...work your equipment, honey. Really work it and you can get anything you want.

OLIVE
You know, you're a bad influence on me.

JANEY
Bad me, bad me can't help telling the little country girl what she

really wants. Say, Max whipped up one hell of a pecan pie, you want?

> OLIVE
> Good choice of words.

Janey smiles and flutters her eye lashes.

INT. LOU-ANN'S CONSIGNMENT SHOP. DAY

Olive in the fitting room has on a pair of emerald tap panties. She stuffs herself into an emerald push up bra then admires what she sees as she adjusts the bra.

> LOUANN
> C cup, too tight, honey?

> OLIVE
> I look like a cow.

> LOUANN
> C cup is just the ticket then.

Olive slips on a short blue skirt, puts on a low cut CHINESE RED BLOUSE. She stands looking at her image in the mirror for a long time then she sits on the chair and steps into a pair of three inch RED HIGH HEELS. She's now close to six feet tall.

INT. KECU. DAY

Olive at KECU working. She wears a cobalt blue dress. Eileen Norburg leans over her desk. Eileen in lavender--suit, stockings, high heels. She's holding her lavender framed glasses in her teeth as she points to the computer screen. Twirling the glasses, she steps away.

> EILEEN

That's a good catch, Olive. Not bad for a country girl.

OLIVE
Thank you.

EILEEN
I mean it. The woman you replaced couldn't spell. You're making yourself indispensable.

INT. OLIVE'S APT. EVENING.

Olive stands eating a SUBWAY SANDWICH at the window watching the street. The photos of Nan and Toby hang on the wall over the bed. Olive turns, still holding her sandwich, she goes to the door.

LANDLORD
Sorry for all the hassle. I got a plumber coming to work on that shower drain but he can't get to it till morning.

OLIVE
I'll manage.

LANDLORD
If you wanna, my wife says you can shower at our place.

OLIVE
I'll be fine. Question...who pays for the plumber?

LANDLORD
The man.

INT. KECU. DAY

Olive looks up from her work. She SEES SHEILA (30)studying her, dark glasses hooked on her finger. Olive stands.

SHEILA

Olive? Oh my god. I thought that was you, but your hair? Oh my god. You cut your hair. And black?

Olive goes to her, warm embrace, then, at arm's length.

OLIVE
You look wonderful.

SHEILA
You haven't added one year to that face. How do you do it? Tim? Where are you hiding that hunk of man?

OLIVE
I just moved back to town.

SHEILA
Good thing because I'd be mad if you've been here a while and didn't call me. You're working here?

OLIVE
It's just part time.

SHEILA
Well, let's get together. We can catch up. I can hardly wait to hear what you've been up to, but you're working...Look there's that French pastry shop out by the college. Do you remember?

OLIVE
The Eclair.

SHEILA
The Éclair. It's still there and the éclairs are just as fattening as they were, but now they've added espresso--it seems to be the next phase.

OLIVE
Sure, I'd love to get together.

SHEILA

I'm going to Houston for two weeks, but when I get back...you can count on it. Bye-bye.

Sheila smooches Olive, then backs away and exits. Olive watches her through the window as she gets into a bright red Audi convertible. Olive returns to her desk.

Eileen Norburg approaches her, papers in hand.

EILEEN

Is Mrs. Masterson a friend of yours?

OLIVE

Masterson? That's Sheila Anderson. We were roommates at Xavier for two years.

EILEEN

Her husband finances a lot of his cars through us. He runs a car dealership. Several, actually.

OLIVE

So you didn't mind if I talk to friends on the job?

EILEEN

As long as you don't make a habit of it. It's good for business to work with people you know. I believe there's more to you, Olive Keller, than you let on.

OLIVE

You mean you think I have a secret life?

EILEEN

I'd be surprised if you didn't.
(considered long pause)
We'll have to go to lunch one of these days. Are you up for that?

INT. OLIVE'S APT. NIGHT

Olive sits at her table eating her sandwich and a container of potato salad. She's facing the photos of Nan and Toby on the wall. Finished eating, she goes to the wall, removes the photos and turns them face down on the bed.

Pulling the old suitcase from under the bed, she sets out the push-up bra, short blue skirt, the CHINESE RED BLOUSE, and a blue silk purse. From under the bed, she drags the red high heels.

EXT. OLIVE'S CHRYSLER. NIGHT

Olive driving, stopping now and then in front of a bar, a tavern, but nothing looks good until she spots a club with a lot full of BMWs, Mercs, Escalades. Parking, she checks her face in the mirror. She strolls into the bar, every curve in motion.

INT. AN UPSCALE BAR. NIGHT

No tattoos here, no leather. Quiet blue-light bar, soft music just loud enough to cover a whisper, a dozen tables, booths, about as sedate as it gets. Olive slides onto a stool at the bar. The bartender LENNY (24) gets to her right away.

> LENNY
> What can I get you?

> OLIVE
> What can you give a lonely woman?

Lenny looks at her. He's sloe-eyed, pink cheeked, too innocent to be behind the bar.

LENNY
Picador.

OLIVE
Picador.

LENNY
Rum, crème de menthe.

OLIVE
I've never had crème de menthe.

Lenny pours her the Picador, she sips it.

OLIVE
Mmmm.

LENNY
Without the rum it's a Stinger. New York special.

OLIVE
Well, I better have half a dozen then.

LENNY
Half a dozen, they'll carry you out of here.

Olive sips the drink, then looks in the mirror behind the bar. She sees a man, DANIEL (37) watching her from two stools down. She turns to face him, crosses her legs. He moves next to her. He's blocky, muscled, wavy black hair, very white teeth. He wears BLACK SLACKS, A RED SHIRT open at the neck, a GOLD MEDALLION flashes in the opening.

DANIEL
We're twins.

OLIVE
I'm sorry?

DANIEL
Red shirts. Twins. Can I buy you a drink?

OLIVE
I have a drink. It's a Picador. The bartender said it's a woman's drink.

DANIEL
(to the bartender)
A couple more of the same, Lenny.

OLIVE
What's that cologne you're wearing?

DANIEL
You like it?

OLIVE
It's very strong.

Olive and Daniel drink together in silence. He watches her, she watches him in the mirror. She finishes a third Picador, then slides off the stool.

OLIVE
(glassy-eyed)
I better be going.

She stumbles. Daniel catches her. They're face to face. She's as tall as he is.

DANIEL
You're too drunk to drive. Let me call you a cab.

Daniel's hand circles her waist and he shuffles her out of the bar.

EXT. AN UPSCALE BAR. SECONDS LATER.

Daniel leans Olive against a black Audi and kisses her, a light kiss, a test kiss. Olive trembles like a mare under the brush.

> OLIVE
> My car is here somewhere.

> DANIEL
> Mine's right here. There's a place just down the street.

> OLIVE
> I just want to be happy.

> DANIEL
> Happy's my middle name.

INT. A MOTEL ROOM. NIGHT

Daniel presses Olive against the wall, his hand under her skirt. She drives into him, she's hungry. Olive thrashes as his hand finds her.

> OLIVE
> Oh god.

> DANIEL
> You're one wet mama, aren't you?

Olive fumbles with his belt, his zipper, but he makes it easy. He pushes her back on the bed, strips naked and kneeling on the bed, unbuttons her blouse, hikes up her skirt and spreading her legs, enters her. She orgasms and she's grabbing at him, eyes closed but then he pulls away and rolls her over. Spreading her again, he rapes her anally. The gold chain whips against her back as he thrusts into her and she whimpers.

> OLIVE
> Don't...don't...You're hurting.

DANIEL
Why do you think I do it, you sick bitch.

INT. A MOTEL ROOM. LATER.

Olive in the shower. Blood dripping down her legs. LOOKING AT THE
SWIRLING BLOOD SHE'S SPINNING, FLOATING. REACHING FOR
THE WALL SHE SLIPS TO THE SHOWER FLOOR AND IN THE RED
SHE SEES THE CHINESE RED FAN TWIRLING DOWN THE DRAIN.

EXT. A STREET OUTSIDE OLIVE'S APT. AN HOUR LATER

Olive parks on the street. She gets out, leans her head against the door for a
moment. Looking up she SEES TIM getting out of his PICKUP TRUCK.
He's huge. She locks her car then dashes to the doorway.

TIM
(shouting)
Woman! Don't you run away from me!

Olive jerks to a stop like she's on a chain. She turns. She SEES TIM
walking toward her. He wears--a cowboy hat, cowboy boots with pink
rosettes cut in them, jeans and an elaborate cowboy shirt with pearl colored
snaps.

TIM
People are starting to wonder.

OLIVE
What do you want, Tim?

TIM
I wanna know when you're coming home to me and your kids.

Olive pushes on toward the building hunting for the key. Tim follows. He
tries to grab her arm, but she shakes loose, hurries inside.

INT. OLIVE'S APT. NIGHT

Tim follows her into the apartment. He looks around. Olive isn't there.

TIM
Where'd you go?

We HEAR the toilet FLUSHING. Olive comes out of the bathroom straightening her skirt. She SEES Tim PICK up the photos of Nan and Toby from the bed.

TIM
Not much of a place you got here.

OLIVE
It's all I can swing right now.

Tim holds up the photos in one hand. It's a huge hand.

TIM
What'd I do? Just tell me that.

OLIVE
Tim, I'm not feeling too well right now.

TIM
Where've you been dressed like that at three o'clock in the morning?

OLIVE
Did Mom and Dad tell you where to find me?

TIM
You don't call for three weeks, yeah. Christ, Olive. I just finished plowing and now I've got to swing over to Colorado for a load of hay.

OLIVE
Are the babies okay?

Tim sets the photos of Nan and Toby on the table and takes off his hat that he sets on top of the photographs.

TIM
School starts in a week, Olive. Are you drunk? And what did you do to your hair?

OLIVE
I'm working now.

TIM
Well, 'cause you're not there I gotta hire a couple hands to help me get the hogs to auction.

OLIVE
Why are you *here*, Tim?

TIM
I can't farm and raise two kids by myself.

OLIVE
They'll be all right with Mom and Dad until I get settled.

TIM
Settled? I haven't been settled since you ran off.

OLIVE
And I haven't been settled since Toby was born.

TIM
Well don't get too settled 'cause one way or the other I'm taking what belongs to me.

OLIVE
I belong to you? That's what's wrong, Tim.

TIM
I don't want you smelling like a French whore. You're my wife. You've got duties. There's work to be done. I've got ground to work. I've got seed to plant. I've got cattle to run.

OLIVE
Don't herd me, Tim. I'm not one of your cows.

TIM
This isn't fair to me, you know that. Hell's fire, woman, I need you.

Olive goes to the window. She LOOKS down at the Chrysler and the pickup. She SEES the garbage can still overflowing with trash. Mr. Dark's motorcycle is backed into place by the fire hydrant. Olive turns.

OLIVE
I'm not coming back with you, Tim.

TIM
What do I have to do, Olive? Hog tie you? Rope you down? Haul you back to where you belong and put you on a tether?

OLIVE
You're not putting your leash on me. Here I wear a dress every day. I wear high-heeled shoes. Ten years with you and the only time I ever wore a dress was to church.

TIM
All that can change. Just come back.

OLIVE
It won't change, Tim. You can't change. Tomorrow, back there, I'd get up at four-thirty to milk your cows. Look at my hands.

Olive holds out her hands. We SEE her red fingernails.

OLIVE
I have fingernails. Woman have fingernails, Tim. I didn't know I
had fingernails and my calluses are gone.

TIM
And I don't see no wedding ring.

OLIVE
I'm not coming back.

TIM
But it's honest work. Real hard honest work and it's dirty, but
wheat don't grow on hardtop. You go nothing here.

OLIVE
You better go now.

TIM
I drove five hours to get here.

OLIVE
I'm not feeling well. You can't stay.

TIM
You think that's why I'm here?

OLIVE
You said I had duties. Isn't that what you want?

Olive goes to the door, holds it open. Tim looms over her, stern faced, grim
lipped. He's holding his hat. He exits to the corridor.

OLIVE
I'll call Mom and Dad tomorrow. We'll work out something with
the babies.

TIM
I don't know what I did to make you hate me, woman, but this isn't over.

OLIVE
I don't care, Tim. I just don't care.

Olive closes the door, stands with her back to it and she sees herself reflected in the window glass and SHE'S FLOATING ABOVE THE FLOOR AND SHE LOOKS DOWN AT HER FEET AND THERE'S A POOL OF BLOOD BENEATH HER, A GOLD MEDALLION SWIRLS INTO IT. Olive runs to the bathroom.

INT. KECU. DAY

Olive SEES Eileen with LARRY (45) A TELLER. Eileen--hands on hips-- is not happy. She stands like a vulture over Larry. His FACE is red, his hands tremble. Olive goes back to work. Eileen approaches Olive.

EILEEN
Let's get some lunch.

OLIVE
Sure.

EXT. EILEEN'S CAR. DAY

EILEEN
You're too good to be part time at KECU. Completely wasted. You should be in a corporation somewhere.

OLIVE
If only.

EILEEN
Sometimes I want to bite peoples' heads off. I'll have to fire Larry

because he fouled up Mr. Kissner's personal account by over thirty thousand.

OLIVE
Mr. Kissner. He's the short, fat, bald little man?

Eileen smiles and looks at Olive and nods.

EILEEN
Short, fat, bald and very rich.

TWO MEN in a pick up draw to Eileen's side, window down. MAN ONE whistles.

MAN ONE
Hey beautiful, how do I get to your apartment?

Eileen glances at Olive.

MAN ONE
Come on. At least give me your number.

As the pickup turns off we HEAR the men laughing.

OLIVE
You must get that a lot.

EILEEN
More than I used to.

OLIVE
He's right, you are--really beautiful.

Eileen glances at Olive as she pulls into a parking lot of a small restaurant.

EILEEN

The idiots. They think that's cute. They wouldn't know what to do with me if they ever got a chance.

INT. A FERN BAR AND CAFÉ. DAY

Eileen and Olive sit in the window of an elegant café playing canned music.

EILEEN
Have you been here before?

OLIVE
No, I just grab a sandwich from Subway.

EILEEN
I noticed that. Eating at your desk. You're ambitious, aren't you?

OLIVE
I don't know.

EILEEN
A lot of women meet here. Are you looking?

OLIVE
Looking? For what?

EILEEN
A new job.

OLIVE
There doesn't seem to be much right now. I should be looking for a bigger place but that'll have to wait until I land something that pays a little more.

EILEEN
Bigger for your children, right?

OLIVE
Nan and Toby.

EILEEN
What else are you looking for? Did I ever tell you I played ball at Wichita State?

OLIVE
Ball. You mean basketball?

EILEEN
We went to the regionals every year I was a starter.

OLIVE
You're sure tall enough.

The waitress KATHY (28) brings water and a menu.

EILEEN
The usual, Kathy. And for my friend here...

OLIVE
Whatever you're having.

Kathy leaves. Eileen spreads her napkin and gives Olive a serious looking over.

EILEEN
I get together with friends on game night to watch. Sometimes we go to the games, but that's not been happening much lately. So are you close to working it out with your ex?

OLIVE
My ex? Well. It's kind of in a mess right now.

EILEEN

Let me rephrase--are you seeing someone?

OLIVE
I've been out a couple of times with my friend Janey. She works at the Kiowa Café. We...uh..went to the Tomb once.

EILEEN
The Tomb? Now there's a place not many find on their own. We'll have to get together sometime with Janey.

OLIVE
Can you do that?

EILEEN
You mean because I'm you're boss? I can show you another side of things sometime if you'd like. Ah, lunch.

Eileen picks at her salad. Olive follows suit and as she chews, she notices that Eileen's eyes are fixed on a point that can only be the center of her cleavage.

INT. KECU. LATER

DEAN (31) Olive's YOUNGER BROTHER, enters the bank. He's tall, blond. He marches straight to Olive's desk.

OLIVE
(worried)
Dean. What's wrong?

DEAN
We need to talk, Sis.

OLIVE
(shushing him)
Not here. There's a Starbux on the next block. Five minutes.

Dean exits. Olive checks around but everyone is busy. She gets up, goes to Eileen who's wrapped up in her own work. She looks up. She's wearing black today. Her makeup is mauve blush, chocolate eyeliner, purple lipstick.

> OLIVE
> I need a few minutes.

> EILEEN
> Are you caught up?

> OLIVE
> Um huh.

> EILEEN
> Problems?

> OLIVE
> Family.

Eileen makes a go-on gesture with her long index finger.

INT. STARBUX. MOMENTS LATER

> DEAN
> Three-fifty for a cup of coffee.

> OLIVE
> Why are you here, Dean?

> DEAN
> Because Mom and Dad are too pissed off to say anything, but I sure as hell will. What you're doing is criminal.

> OLIVE
> You don't understand.

DEAN

What don't I understand? You cut off your hair, you look like a tramp in those shoes. What the fuck are you thinking?

OLIVE

Is that all you have to say?

DEAN

If you stay here, you'll rot from the inside out. You don't belong in this filthy city, you belong on the farm.

OLIVE

You and Tim sing the same song, Dean. What do you want me to do?

DEAN

Be a mother, for Christ's sake. Get your ass back to Tim and take the load off Mom and Dad.

OLIVE

I'm not going to do that.

DEAN

And I'm not going to let you fuck up those babies. You don't belong here, they don't belong here. On the farm, if you get dirt in your teeth, it tastes like dirt. Up here it tastes like dog shit. You want your babies to eat that?

OLIVE

Are you finished?

DEAN

You can't just cut them off like you butchered your hair, Sis. What happened to the woman who got up early, who grew her own food? You were living a good Christian life so where did that woman get to? You owe it to Tim.

OLIVE
I don't owe Tim Keller anything.

DEAN
You owe your babies and you owe Mom and Dad. They're already thinking they've got'em for the long haul.

OLIVE
You don't care about them, Dean. You don't care about my kids, you really don't care about me. All you care about is how your big sister looks to the world.

DEAN
Mom said you hadn't called in a month. They're blood, Sis. Your blood and your flesh the way god intended it and you don't just write off blood.

OLIVE
I'm going back to work now, Dean.

DEAN
You go ahead and do that, Sis. You just go right ahead and do that. But if you cut yourself off, you're gonna end up on your face in the filth.

INT. KECU. DAY

Olive at her desk is talking to Eileen. She GLANCES up as Sheila enters. She looks very thin. Her skin is wan and sallow. She wears a black short skirt, black voile blouse over a black bra. Black high heels and sunglasses. Her hair is platinum blonde. She approaches Eileen and Olive.

EILEEN
Mrs. Masterson.

SHEILA
May I borrow Olive for a moment.

EILEEN
(to Olive)
Let me see that spread sheet when you get caught up.

Eileen leaves.

SHEILA
She is just about the most stunning woman I've ever see.

OLIVE
How was Houston?

SHEILA
Tiring. Have you had lunch?

OLIVE
Not yet, but I can go any time.

SHEILA
Let's go to the Éclair, just like old times.

OLIVE
Let me check with Eileen.

Sheila's POV:

Olive walks to Eileen's desk. Eileen glances at Sheila then nods and waves.

INT. ÉCLAIR PASTRY SHOP. LATER

Olive and Sheila at a table in noonday sun. On the table we SEE two éclairs, a cup of coffee and a glass of milk. Sheila's hands on the table brush Olive's. Their hands are very much alike with long painted nails.

Sheila WEARS a big DIAMOND RING.

SHEILA
Before you ask, it's a wig. I have a dozen of them because it's my
one absolute necessity...and you, you've done something crazy to
your hair, too.

OLIVE
I do remember you as raven-haired.

SHEILA
Raven-haired, you sound like that art history professor, what was
her name? You know...

OLIVE
Meredith, I think, Meredith Clausen.

SHEILA
At least you still have a memory. The chemo has ruined my...

OLIVE
Chemo?

SHEILA
I have cancer, sweetheart.

OLIVE
Oh Sheila.

SHEILA
The radiation killed every follicle on my head and the chemo killed
my pubic hair.

OLIVE
I had no idea you had cancer.

SHEILA

Have, you sweet thing. Have. It's uterine and operable, thank god.

OLIVE
Oh Sheila. I'm so sorry.

SHEILA
That's why I was in Houston. I went to the tumor review and saw the uterus. It looked like mother of pearl.

Sheila tears a chunk from her éclair. She licks the filling from her lips, sips at the milk. Olive WATCHES her but doesn't eat.

SHEILA
(wiping her mouth)
Now suppose you tell me what you're doing working at that bank.

OLIVE
I left Tim.

SHEILA
Oh my. Did he cheat on you?

OLIVE
Why do you say that?

SHEILA
They all cheat, don't they? Men?

OLIVE
Nothing like that. I used to have dreams, I guess and one day I woke up and found myself ten years older on a farm with two kids and a husband who stinks of diesel oil at night. I might as well be one of his cows the way he treats me. So I had to get away and Wichita seemed like a good place to start over.

SHEILA
How does the big hunk handle that?

OLIVE
I'm not going back. Oh, Sheila. I feel awful talking about my little problems after what you're going through.

SHEILA
You look worried, darling, tell me what's wrong.

OLIVE
You mean besides the fact that I left my husband and abandoned my two kids and I'm living alone.

SHEILA
Are you seeing someone?

OLIVE
No, not really.

SHEILA
What does that mean? Not really?

OLIVE
Well, I have been to bed with a couple of guys.

Sheila clutches Olive's hand. Leans toward her, eager.

SHEILA
Oh, really! Well tell me about the sex. In detail.

OLIVE
Sheila.

SHEILA
Listening to my friends is as close as I get to sex now. I don't remember the last time Danny touched me. I think he's afraid of hurting me or ashamed of me because, after all, I am a disease. Now tell me...what did you do and who did you do it with? Tell

me everything.

OLIVE
Well, last Saturday night I went out hunting...

SHEILA
Hunting? That sounds delicious...

FLASHBACK

INT. A CHEAP ROOM HOTEL. EARLY MORNING

Olive lies FACE DOWN NAKED on a gray bed. Her CLOTHES are piled on the floor. On TOP of her BLACK SKIRT there is a HUNDRED DOLLAR BILL. A pair of black panties hangs from a chair. Rising, she looks around, sits up, stands. She looks down when her feet hit the floor. She SEES worn out linoleum with black patches cut through like paths. As she steps, she kicks her RED HIGH HEELS across the room.

In the BATHROOM she sits on the toilet and then she SEES HERSELF in the mirror but the silvering is gone in patches and her REFLECTION is spotty, PARTS OF HER ARE MISSING--her neck is half there, her right shoulder gone.

She RUNS water in the sink--a slow dribble of grayish fluid that she SPLASHES ON HER FACE. Returning to the bed she sorts out her clothes--panties, blouse, skirt and gets dressed. She SEARCHES for her PURSE. Squatting, she reaches under the bed, draws out the purse and then, startled, she IMAGINES THE IMAGE OF A MAN'S FACE, NO EYES, NO EARS, NO NOSE JUST HAIR AND A MOUTHFUL OF ORANGE TEETH. She STANDS, wobbling, shaky, holding her high heels, EXITS to a DARK HALLWAY.

INT. HOTEL LOBBY. MOMENTS LATER.

A STRAWBERRY HAIRED WOMAN smoking a big cigar STANDS

behind the DESK READING a NEWSPAPER. She LOOKS at Olive.

WOMAN
See ya, sweetheart.

OLIVE
Where am I?

WOMAN
Well, sweetheart, if you don't know, who the fuck does?

OLIVE
How did I get here? Was I alone?

WOMAN
No, sweetheart, you wasn't flyin' solo.

OLIVE
Did you see who I was with? Do you know him?

WOMAN
Everybody comes in here is named Smith. Are you okay? You look kind of peaked.

OLIVE
I don't know.

WOMAN
You better get some help, sweetheart. You get this lost every time you get laid, you might not find your way back.

OLIVE
What time is it?

WOMAN
Five o'clock Sunday morning, sweetheart.

Olive exits the hotel.

EXT. STREET. MOMENTS LATER

The street is dirty gray. She REALIZES that she's still holding her high heels. She LOOKS up and down the street, opens her PURSE, takes her car keys and punches the LOCK BUTTON, LISTENING for the CHIRP. She TURNS a CORNER. The Chrysler is angled into the curb, window down. Olive tosses her shoes through the window, gets in, leans her head against the steering wheel and SOBS.

END FLASHBACK

BACK TO SCENE

       SHEILA
       Oh my god. I hope you're on the pill. Did he use a condom?

       OLIVE
       I don't think so. I remember the smell...you know what I mean.

       SHEILA
       You were raped. You have to get tested.

       OLIVE
       Tested for what?

       SHEILA
       AIDS. And he has to get tested too. You're playing with fire,
       Olive. There are diseases that can kill you.

       OLIVE
       I don't...I didn't...have any idea.

       SHEILA
       Don't you read? Watch TV? Oh, you really have to get to a clinic. I

know a therapist who can help you.

OLIVE
First a clinic now a therapist?

SHEILA
You were raped and drugged with one of those date rape drugs.
Roh something. It totally blacks you out.

OLIVE
I don't want to remember it.

SHEILA
Do you remember Rose Jorgensen? She taught psychology when
we were in school. She's wonderful and she's in private practice.

OLIVE
You think I need a psychologist?

SHEILA
You have some issues, Olive, whether you believe it not. You were
raped. You left your children and you ran away from your
husband. Let me give Rose your number. I'll set up a meeting. I
know a clinic--you can use my doctor, and then you're coming to
dinner with Danny and me.

OLIVE
Sheila, I can take care of myself.

SHEILA
Oh god, when you talk like that I really start to worry.

Sheila digs in her purse, finds a fountain pen and a note pad. She jots down
Olive's number.

SHEILA
I'll call Rose.

OLIVE
Sheila. Stop. That's not something I want to do.

SHEILA
It doesn't matter. You have to.

EXT. OFFICE COMPLEX. WHEATLAND AVE. DAY

Olive parks her Chrysler. She LOOKS at the building through the windshield. She REACHES for the ignition but STOPS.

FLASHBACK

WOMAN
You get this lost every time you get laid, you might not find your way back.

END FLASHBACK

Olive pulls the key from the ignition.

INT. OFFICE BUILDING. DAY

Olive HESITATES in waiting room of Suite 301. An inner door opens on ROSE (54).

ROSE
Olive? I'm Rose. Come in. Please.

INT. ROSE'S OFFICE. DAY

ROSE
Please, sit down.

Rose takes one of the ARM CHAIRS. A YELLOW PENCIL is tucked in her hair. She WEARS a LONG GRAY DRESS, BLACK FLATS. As she sits, she pulls an AFGHAN from the table beside her and wraps it around her legs.

> ROSE
> I keep the room cold. If you get chilly, there's an afghan beside you under that end table. Please sit.

> OLIVE
> I don't know why I'm here.

> ROSE
> Your friend Sheila mentioned that you have a problem.

Olive walks to the window, looks out. She SEES the PARKING LOT of the WHEATLAND MARKET. A WOMAN gets out of a BLACK SUV with TWO CHILDREN, a BOY and a GIRL. They enter the market.

> ROSE
> I'm over here.

TURNING, Olive SEES FOUR BLACK AND WHITE ABSTRACT PAINTINGS on the wall behind Rose. On the wall she SEES THREE DIPLOMAS IN HEAVY WOODEN FRAMES.

> OLIVE
> I'm sorry.

> ROSE
> What is the problem?

> OLIVE
> (still standing)
> I was out drinking. I woke up in a hotel room naked.

Olive studies the DIPLOMAS.

OLIVE
I don't know how I got there, I don't know who took me there.

ROSE
Ah.

Rose retrieves a notebook from the table and pulls the pencil from her hair.

ROSE
And you have no memory of anything?

OLIVE
Nothing. Someone left a hundred dollars.

ROSE
Ah.

OLIVE
Is that all you say?

ROSE
Tell me about yourself and your family.

OLIVE
My family?

ROSE
Are you married? Children? Where do you work?

OLIVE
I was raped. That's why I'm here.

ROSE
Let's talk about that then.

Rose adjusts the afghan, closes the notebook. She's been here before with the reluctant client.

ROSE
(soothing voice)
I have a son. He's a mathematician. I have one granddaughter who
is half-Chinese--her mother is also a mathematician. I have an MD,
a PhD and I'm a licensed psychiatrist. My husband of thirty-five
years died in April of lung cancer.

Olive, relieved, SITS in the ARM CHAIR facing Rose.

OLIVE
(starts slowly then faster)
I have two babies. Five and eight.
(beat)
I'm married to a man ten years older than me and I've left him and
I don't really know why, but I was drugged and raped and I can't
remember even going there.

ROSE
Probably Rohypnol. It's the preferred drug. There are others. But
tell me about your family. Your mother and father.

OLIVE
They're Catholic but they haven't been to confession in twenty-five
years and
(beat)
They'd fall into a meat grinder before they'd ever admit to a
stranger that they had a problem and they would both die if they
knew why I'm here.

ROSE
Strict?

OLIVE
My mother is--kind of.

ROSE

And your husband? Where is he?

OLIVE
I'm leaving him because he makes me sick.

Olive clears her throat. She's BREATHING HARD.

OLIVE
(choking)
That just slipped out. Sorry.

Rose lays down her notebook. Standing, she HANDS Olive a box of
TISSUES then sits back down.

ROSE
How does he make you sick?

OLIVE
He kept me on a tether for ten years. For ten years I've either been
pregnant, cooking, or cleaning out chicken coops. He married me
so he'd have a cow to give him children and he just smothered me.
I don't know...

ROSE
Tethered. That's an interesting word.

OLIVE
That's the way I feel with Tim.

ROSE
Tim is your husband?

OLIVE
Yes.

ROSE
He's a farmer?

OLIVE
Um huh. He works the ground, but I do everything else. I milk cows, feed chickens, do laundry and I keep the books because he doesn't trust anyone with his money. And I was going crazy. One night a few months ago, I climbed the windmill and I was going to jump because I was going to get away one way or the other.

ROSE
Ah.

Olive GLARES at Rose. Rose SMILES.

ROSE
Had you gone up before? On the windmill?

OLIVE
Sometimes when the babies were asleep. It's kind of a secret place only I can get to.

ROSE
But that time it was different?

Olive makes swirling, eddying motions with her hands as she looks at Rose.

OLIVE
I got dizzy. I...wanted...I don't know what I wanted.

ROSE
Do you go out drinking often?

OLIVE
Does it matter?

ROSE
Well, we can talk about that next time. One last thing. Are you

221

worried that you're pregnant.

OLIVE
I'm not pregnant. Next time? You think I have to come back? I thought...

ROSE
(Rose smiles)
Don't decide right now. Call me in a couple of days. If you feel that you need to come back, I'll keep this hour open.

Olive STANDS. She REELS against the back of the chair, almost FALLING. Rose RISES to her feet.

ROSE
Have you had morning sickness?

OLIVE
I'm not pregnant. I know when I'm pregnant. I don't know why I get dizzy when I talk about it but I'm spinning right now. I don't want to talk about it.

ROSE
You were drugged and raped, Olive. You woke up naked in a hotel bed with a hundred dollars. That doesn't happen every day to every woman who goes out for the evening.

OLIVE
That's what Sheila said.

Rose HANDS Olive a business card.

ROSE
My numbers are there. When you're ready.

Rose GUIDES Olive to the door. In the waiting room, Olive SEES a FRIZZY HAIRED WOMAN in a very short skirt, low cut blouse. HEAVY

MAKE UP. Dangly EARRINGS. She TOSSES a magazine on the table. A RED FLOWER TATTOO shows on the swell of her left breast.

                    TATTOOED WOMAN
          Hey doc, I know I'm early, is it okay?

Olive rushes from the office and into the hallway, the SOUND of her heels rings in the stairwell.

                    ROSE
          Teresa. Please. Come in.

INT. KECU. DAY

OLIVE POV: she WATCHES

CLIFFORD KISSNER (40)at Eileen's desk. Larry, the teller, stands like a toy soldier at attention, hands clasped behind his back while Eileen talks. Larry nods then turns, leaves, walks out the door. Clifford shakes hands with Eileen. She's six inches taller than he is. Clifford leaves.

INT. OLIVE'S APT. NIGHT

OLIVE'S DREAM--

SHEILA stands in the Éclair Pastry Shop. She looks down at her feet as a long pink worm crawls from between her legs. Helpless and horrified Olive tracks the worm as it snakes across the floor then wraps itself around Olive's thigh and slides up into her. Olive tries to push it away but she's paralyzed. Her belly swells to the size of a basketball then explodes into a pink shower of worms.

Olive lies on her bed. She's SWEATING. She flips back the sheet and presses her hands into her belly. Then she gets up, runs a glass of water. She LOOKS out the window on the street. She SEES Mr. Dark's motorcycle under the street light.

Olive searches in her PURSE for ROSE'S BUSINESS CARD. Holding the card, Olive lies down pressing the card to her belly.

EXT. OFFICE COMPLEX. WHEATLAND AVE. DAY

Olive parks her Chrysler just as the WOMAN in the BLACK SUV pulls into the Market parking lot. The two children are in their child seats.

INT. ROSE'S OFFICE. DAY

Olive in the stairwell to Rose's office SEES INSECT WINGS stuck to the wall. She touches the wings, they fall, spinning, to the floor and Olive grabs the hand rail and leans against the wall breathing hard. Olive IMAGINES the RED CHINESE FAN FLUTTERING into the WATER TANK.

We HEAR: Doors slamming. Olive runs up the stairs.

INT. ROSE'S OFFICE. DAY

As she enters, Olive SEES the black and white paintings only now they're TREES bending in a heavy wind.

As Olive talks to Rose, she keeps flashing images of her "hunting trips".

> OLIVE
> Tim inherited the farm from his father who was a friend of my Dad's. When Tim's dad died, Tim came to Wichita and asked me to marry him. I was twenty and I was still a virgin.

Image: Olive on her belly, the Gold Medallion beating her back.

> ROSE
> After four years of college?

OLIVE
You were at Xavier. You know. Tim was older, and he's so big, it was hard to say no. The first night we had sex, I got sick because his semen smells so strong it gags me.

Image: Tim rolling off of Olive in bed. She turns her head to avoid looking at him.

OLIVE
He'd come in me and for days I smelled him every time I peed or squatted, or sometimes just driving to town I'd smell it and have to pull over and vomit. After Toby I started taking the pill.

Image: Olive squatting in the seedy hotel to retrieve her purse. ON her FACE as she blanches, about to gag.

Nervous, Olive stands, walks to the WINDOW. She SEES the WOMAN and her TWO CHILDREN getting into the black SUV, driving away.

ON ROSE taking notes.

OLIVE
I grew flowers on the farm. All kinds of flowers. You plant seeds and they grow. What can you grow here?

ROSE
But you left the country, Olive you come to the city and you go hunting. How do you feel coming back from your expeditions?

ON Olive's FACE as she TRACKS the SUV out of the lot.

Images in rapid succession: Two women in the toilet of the Tomb. The gold medallion. The red shirt.

OLIVE
You mean do I think sex is dirty?

ROSE
Is it?

OLIVE
What about you?

ROSE
My hunting days are over.

OLIVE
I went out one night, to a bar. I wanted to get out of the leather
world that Janey lives in.

ROSE
By leather you mean S and M?

OLIVE
Whips. That sort of thing. So I found a place and I picked up a
man, maybe he picked me up and we went to a motel. He raped me
in my bottom. I didn't know people did that.

ROSE
In your bottom? You mean anal sex?

OLIVE
Yes.

ROSE
Are you ashamed of that?

OLIVE
The thing I remember most is his bright red shirt and his gold
medallion beating on my back. .
(pause. Olive turns)
I have to go. I'm having dinner at Sheila's tonight.

EXT. SHEILA'S HOUSE. NIGHT.

Olive parks her Chrysler behind a midnight blue AUDI TT. She gets out. She WEARS a red dress with a scoop neck, high heels.

INT. SHEILA'S HOUSE. NIGHT.

Sheila opens with a squeal and hugs Olive.

> SHEILA
> (whispering)
> You look absolutely edible, my dear.

Sheila ushers Olive into the living room where HAROLD (35) sits on a white sofa while DANIEL (37) fixes drinks. The living room is white everything except for twin splashes of blue--a huge monochrome painting in cobalt and the plush carpet of the same color.

> SHEILA
> This is my husband, Danny, and this is Harold the friend I mentioned at the Éclair. Feast your eyes, you two, on Olive, my dear dear friend from Xavier when we were still innocent.

> DANIEL
> (his back to the women)
> And you two're still feasting on chocolate at the Éclair.

Daniel turns, martini glasses in hand. Daniel wears a RED SHIRT half unbuttoned, black SLACKS, black PENNY LOAFERS. A GOLD MEDALLION ON A CHAIN dangles in the V of the shirt.

Daniel glances at Olive's breasts then fixes on her eyes. He OFFERS her a martini.

Olive LOOKS at the medallion, then at Daniel.

227

DANIEL
You don't like martinis?

Olive takes the glass.

OLIVE
I've never had a martini but I did have a Picador once.

DANIEL
I pour a mean martini but I can whip up a Picador for Olive.
(he laughs)

SHEILA
She's a country girl, Danny. Maybe she doesn't share your
eccentric tastes.

Harold uncoils from his white sofa.

HAROLD
I'm Harold. Shel's told me you're from Plains.

Olive nods and sips at the martini.

SHEILA
Harold designs things...exactly what do you design, Harold?

Sheila flutters to a pair of easy chairs where she sits looking like a flower
in the cup of the white chair.

HAROLD
No shop talk, okay?

SHEILA
Harold's company is hiring, Olive. Oh, my, I smell meat. Come
with me, love, I need some help in the kitchen.

INT. KITCHEN -- LATER

Sheila drags a roast from the oven.

> SHEILA
> He didn't lose everything in the divorce.

> OLIVE
> Who?

> SHEILA
> Harold. It's his blue car out front, a TT something. His ex had her own. Oil or gas I can't remember which...my memory. Carry the potatoes, will you, love?

> OLIVE
> Is this your way of telling me he has money?

> SHEILA
> Why do you think I asked you here?

INT. DINING ROOM -- LATER

Olive SITS across from Harold. Daniel CARVES the roast.

> DANIEL
> You like it rare, Olive?

> OLIVE
> Medium.

> DANIEL
> End piece then? Honey?

> SHEILA

You know I like it rare.

Harold is so busy staring at Olive's cleavage his roast beef has congealed on his plate.

> OLIVE
> (to Harold)
> Sheila told me you drive the TT?

> HAROLD
> That's right. What kind of wheels are you in, Olive?

> OLIVE
> A Chrysler 300. It's a year old.

> HAROLD
> You oughta talk to Danny, get him to cut you a deal on an Audi.

> OLIVE
> I'm always looking. I might be in the market for a TT. Does it have a big back seat?

Daniel coughs, spits out a hunk of rare beef.

> HAROLD
> Back seat? No. Not the TT.

> SHEILA
> Are you all right, Danny?

> HAROLD
> Careful man, you'll choke on that Kansas City beef.

> DANIEL
> Bit off more than I could chew.

Daniel clears his throat, sets his fork down then gets up and pours wine all around. Stands beside Olive.

Olive looks at his hand, SEES the wedding ring.

> DANIEL
> TT's a muscle car. You think you can handle a muscle car.

> OLIVE
> If it's expensive and exciting, I can.

> SHEILA
> What does one of those things cost, Danny?

> DANIEL
> Raw, they come in at thirty-five.

> SHEILA
> Raw?

> DANIEL
> Stripped. With all the extras, they'll go upwards of forty-five.

Daniel is looking right down at Olive's breasts.

Olive drops her fork and leans forward.

> SHEILA
> Are you okay, Olive?

> OLIVE
> I'm not feeling well.

> SHEILA
> Can I get you anything?

> OLIVE
> I think I should go. I'm getting dizzy.

SHEILA
I hope it wasn't the meat. Danny?

OLIVE
My head is splitting.

SHEILA
Let me get you some tylenol.

OLIVE
I better go before I get sick all over your table. I'm sorry.

Olive gets up. She's UNSTEADY, grips the back of the chair.

HAROLD
I'll see her out. Okay?

Olive gathers her purse and heads for the door. Harold right beside her being attentive.

Sheila watches her guests at the door.

SHEILA
I hope she's all right. I really wanted her and Harold to hit it off.

DANIEL
She'll eat him alive.

SHEILA
What?

DANIEL
Nothing. What's for dessert?

EXT. STREET. MOMENTS LATER

Harold holds the door to the Chrysler open. Leans in.

> HAROLD
> Are you gonna make it?

> OLIVE
> I'm fine. I get this way sometimes. It's vertigo.

> HAROLD
> I've had that. Say...I know...this isn't the best time, but Shel's really high on you. Look, there's this great barbecue place out by the airport if you like ribs and burnt ends.

> OLIVE
> I have two children.

> HAROLD
> It's just dinner.

Olive inserts the KEY into the ignition. LOOKS at Harold. He steps back

> HAROLD
> (shouting)
> I'll get your number from Shel.

INT. OLIVE'S APT.-- LATER

Olive lying on her bed, talks on the phone to Sheila.

> OLIVE
> No, I'm not pregnant.

> SHEILA
> Is it the flu? The way you ran out and Harold said you looked pale.

> OLIVE
> Harold.

SHEILA
He thinks you're the best thing since whipped cream.

OLIVE
It's like he'd never seen breasts.

SHEILA
You were spectacular. That rosy skin is enough to make any man stare. When are you going out with him?

OLIVE
I'm tired, Sheila. I'll call you.

SHEILA
No, I'll call you. Danny really liked you by the way.

Olive hangs up, looks at the table where the PHOTOS of Nan and Toby stand. Outside, A MOTORCYCLE rips past. Olive closes her eyes.

OLIVE'S DREAM--Horror dream of babies with dirty faces, she washes them, skin falls off. She's floating off the windmill SPIRALING down toward the water. When she hits the tank, she tries to get out, but Tim's BIG HAND comes out of nowhere and SHOVES her back down.

Olive WAKES up gasping for air.

INT. A WATERFRONT RESTAURANT. NIGHT

Olive across from Harold. Between them there's a PILE of BARBECUED RIB BONES.

HAROLD
I have a little place just down river from here. Isolated so no one can hear you scream.

OLIVE

What?

HAROLD
You know? Like in outer space--no one can hear you scream?

OLIVE
Oh.

HAROLD
I like to kayak.

OLIVE
Have you ever butchered a steer?

HAROLD
What?

OLIVE
Have you ever smelled a washtub full of blood? Or watched the guts of a pig fall into a vat?

HAROLD
You know, you've got me pretty worked up, Olive. All that talk about butchering a steer. I've been out with half a dozen of Shel's friends and no one's ever said anything about butchering. Look, we both know why you're here so let's get to it--Danny and I share everything.

Olive looks at Harold.

HAROLD
I know all about it. He picks you up at Lenny's, gets you to that dungeon of a motel--we like the same things, so--come on. My place or we can get a motel if that's the only way you swing.

Olive picks up a steak knife. Harold draws back.

OLIVE
(playing with the knife)
Tell me something. Does Sheila know about this little boy's club of yours?

HAROLD
Sheila doesn't live on this planet. Her idea of sex is reading a Harlequin romance.

Olive stands, drops the knife then reaches across the table and rakes his face with her fingernails. He doesn't grunt or groan.

He SMILES.

HAROLD
Is that all I get? I can take whatever you've got. Come on.

Olive snatches up her purse, digs out a twenty dollar bill and drops it on the table.

OLIVE
Buy yourself a Hershey bar, you can share that with Danny.

INT. ROSE'S OFFICE. DAY

Olive stands with her back to Rose at the window watching THE WOMAN get out of her BLACK SUV alone. No children. She goes into the market.

ROSE
What do you want, Olive?

OLIVE
I want to be happy and I want to feel good.

ROSE
And hunting, as you call it, makes you happy?

OLIVE
I don't want to be bored. Tim was boring. I hate being bored. Do you know how dark it is out there?

ROSE
Is that what you want from the city? To keep from being bored?

Olive turns to Rose. She SEES the black and white paintings where the brush strokes have turned into lightning flashes linking the paintings together.

OLIVE
I had sex with Sheila's husband.

Rose lays her notebook in her lap. Olive kneels in front of her. Rose plants a hand on her shoulder.

OLIVE
I went to dinner with them.

ROSE
Sheila and her husband?

OLIVE
(disjointed confession)
And another man named Harold and Danny, Daniel, Sheila's husband is the man with the red shirt and the gold medallion that I picked up who picked me up and he's the one...anal sex...in a uh...and he does it all the time, drags women to motels to have them that way and I walked into Sheila's and I smelled his cologne and I got sick 'cause I was right back there in that motel and he kept staring at me and I have to tell Sheila or I won't ever be able to look at her again because she doesn't know about this stupid thing that her husband does with this guy Harold...

ROSE
Pull yourself together. You know--

(smiling)
This is a first--I don't think I've ever touched--a client during a session.

OLIVE
I have to tell her.

ROSE
(Rose comforts Olive)
Here it is the twenty-first century and you're as naïve as some nineteenth century immigrant in a flour sack dress expecting people to care about you, but that's not the way the world works anymore.

INT. KECU. DAY

Clifford Kissner enters. He NODS at Eileen, then beelines to Olive's desk.

Eileen shuffling papers watches this transaction. Clifford shakes Olive's hand, then leaves with another nod to Eileen.

INT. KECU. MOMENTS LATER.

Eileen standing by Olive's desk.

EILEEN
Well that was unexpected.

OLIVE
Wow.

EILEEN
What did Mr. Kissner say to you?

OLIVE
He asked me out to dinner.

EILEEN
Olive! What did you say?

OLIVE
I said yes. Saturday. Actually--what do I do? He's kind of short.

EILEEN
The Vertically challenged Mr. Kissner. Well, Olive, what some men lack in stature, they make up for with pizazz. We have definitely got to have lunch again soon and I'll tell you all about Clifford Kissner.

INT. KIOWA CAFE. EVENING

Olive reads the WANT ADS. We SEE half a dozen jobs circled in red ink. Janey SITS at the table.

JANEY
What's wrong with the bank?

OLIVE
It's never going to be full time.

JANEY
And why do *you* need full time?

OLIVE
My kids, remember?

JANEY
Sure *I remember.*

OLIVE
Why do you stay here?

JANEY
It's a job. What else am I gonna do?

239

OLIVE
You're smart, you're beautiful, you've got tons of personality.

JANEY
And I got a high school diploma loaded with straight C's.

OLIVE
Don't you want something more?

JANEY
Look. You've got yunguns. You're a brain. You look like a movie star. The way I see it I grow up, I get wrinkles, I die. I'm sure as hell not going back to the farm.

Olive fiddles with the newspaper.

OLIVE
You could go back to school.

JANEY
And live on what? Max just baked a couple of lemon meringue pies. If I cut you a piece will you get off my back?

Janey gets up. Returns with a piece of lemon pie.

JANEY
Did you ever get tested after your creepy thing with that sick fuck?

Olive cuts a bite of the pie. Eats it. Janey WATCHES her then licks her lips.

OLIVE
Turns out that sick fuck is married to my friend Sheila.

JANEY
Holy shit. You're kidding? Is this a crazy world or what?

(beat)
You want to go to a biker rally with me this weekend?

OLIVE
No.

JANEY
You remember Kit? He wants me to move in with him.

OLIVE
And so you're going to a biker rally?

JANEY
Those guys are very cool. Free pot. They give their bikes names,
you know.

OLIVE
Tell Max he bakes A-1 pie.

JANEY
He knows. He's a biker. He and his old lady go to all the rallies.
So. Yes or no?

OLIVE
I'll stick to his lemon pie. Besides, I have a date Saturday.

JANEY
You're no fun anymore. Who with?

OLIVE
What?

JANEY
The date? Don't tell me it's the same sick fuck who screwed you in
that motel? At least the guys at the Tomb have the decency to eat
you out in public.

OLIVE
Janey! You don't go around spouting stuff like that. No. It's with Clifford Kissner. And he's probably never been in the Tomb. The problem is--he's kind of short, chubby, and--you know--bald. The thing is, when I got home after work, there was a bouquet of orchids outside my door from him.

JANEY
Orchids? You idiot. He's like every other man--he just wants to get in your box.

OLIVE
My box?

JANEY
Come on. What do you think? Sex.

OLIVE
Well, I'm not interested but I kind of have to do it because Eileen's got her eye on me.

JANEY
So? You sleep with him she gets you on full time?

INT. OLIVE'S APT. NIGHT

Olive is DRESSING for her RENDEZ-VOUS WITH CLIFFORD. She's just putting on her make up. The vase of WHITE ORCHIDS from Clifford sits in the middle of the table.

There is a SHARP KNOCK on the door. Olive opens.

Daniel thrusts a bunch of DAFFODILS in YELLOW FOIL at Olive. The price tag from the local drug store still on them. He wears his hunting uniform--that RED SHIRT, BLACK SLACKS.

Olive SEES the GOLD MEDALLION. She grabs the daffs and tosses them out into the hallway then tries to slam the door. Daniel pushes it back.

DANIEL
Shall we try it again?

OLIVE
Are you out of your mind?

DANIEL
How'm I gonna know you're pals with Shel?
He kicks the door closed.

DANIEL
Yeah, I know. I shoulda called first. But here I am and you're all dolled up so you must be heading for Lenny's, right? But what the hell, we don' hafta go through all that rigmarole. What'dya got on under that blue dress?

Daniel advances on her. She holds out a hand to stop him.

DANIEL
My God, when you walked through that door at home, I about came in my pants and you acted like...a TT? Big back seat? You really said that?

OLIVE
Leave.

DANIEL
Sure. When I get what I came for.

OLIVE
Did you tell your wife you were coming here for a repeat visit to my bottom?

DANIEL

You got it all wrong.

OLIVE
Wife with cancer. You're a pig. Get out.

DANIEL
You come on like a fucking virgin but you weren't sayin' no at Lenny's.

OLIVE
Your smell makes me sick. You had it on at dinner and you're wearing it now.

DANIEL
You got a shower? I'll wash it off.

OLIVE
That smell won't wash off and Harold told me all about your game.

DANIEL
Okay. So we have a thing. Look. This place? What'dya pay?

OLIVE
You're offering me money?

DANIEL
You're in the driver's seat. What's it gonna take?

OLIVE
Let me see your wallet.

No hesitation as Daniel tugs his WALLET from his pocket and hands it to Olive. She pulls all the cash from it.

OLIVE
Paper boy money. You think you can buy *me* with paper boy money?

DANIEL
Hell, I'll write you a check. What? A thousand a month?

OLIVE
Five thousand. I'll need a new apartment and a TT.

DANIEL
A TT? Are you outa your gourd?

OLIVE
A TT. And five thousand.

DANIEL
Okay. Okay but just a lease on the car. Okay?

He REACHES for her. He tries to kiss her. She TWISTS away holding his cash and his wallet.

Olive walks to the door, holds it open. Daniel chases her. Olive TOSSES his wallet and cash into the hallway. Planting a hand on his chest, she shoves him over the THRESHOLD.

OLIVE
And pick up your stinking daffodils.

Olive slams the door. She SEES Clifford's bouquet of orchids.

DANIEL
(through the door)
You can't see Shel. You hear me? You try to see her and it's all over. You cunt.

INT. A FANCY RESTAURANT. TWO HOURS LATER

Empty CHOCOLATE MOUSSE glasses on the table. A BOTTLE OF

WINE. Olive DABS at her mouth, sets her spoon down.

> OLIVE
> You still haven't answered my question--have you ever butchered a steer?

> CLIFFORD
> You might want to lay off the wine for a bit.

> OLIVE
> You bring your own wine. Amazing.

Clifford refills Olive's glass with a careful turn of the bottle.

> CLIFFORD
> You know, in some circles wine is blood.

> OLIVE
> Are you a believer?

> CLIFFORD
> I believe in anything I can measure. Look, Missus Keller.

> OLIVE
> Olive. Malone. I changed my name.

> CLIFFORD
> Olive Malone, I don't own a gun, I can't bench press my weight. I'm fat. I'm bald. And I'm short. But yeah, I've butchered a steer or two.

Olive laughs.

> OLIVE
> And you bring wine to a place that must have plenty of it's own.

Olive leans forward, her décolletage glistens in the low light, but Clifford's eyes never move from Olive's eyes.

CLIFFORD
My family had a place outside of Garden City. There were eight of us. I was the third--the first boy. I had two older sisters who on any given day would beat the tar out of me and take turns at it.

Clifford refills his own glass then resumes his position--never letting got of Olive's eyes. Sincerity here. This is a PROPOSAL.

CLIFFORD
Every winter we butchered a steer, two hogs, and a lamb and this wine goes with lamb because it's a Corbière from a little town in the Midi called Minerve.

He toasts Olive. She sips her wine.

CLIFFORD
Do you know the Midi?

OLIVE
I have no idea what you're talking about or why you're telling me this.

CLIFFORD
Because I want you to know. I own a little winery in Southern France. Actually I'm part owner. This is our wine. We can compete with the Burgundies and the Bordeaux but ours isn't temperamental and it travels better.

OLIVE
All the way to Wichita.

CLIFFORD
I hope I didn't scare you off with that rap.

OLIVE

I don't scare easily any more.

CLIFFORD
I learned to talk fast to keep my sisters from whomping me. I'm short 'cause they used to take turns pounding on my head and I suppose that's what happened to my hair. I know why I'm fat-- because all the men in my family are built like bales of hay.

Olive laughs, rocks back enjoying this.

OLIVE
I don't think you're fat.

CLIFFORD
Do you think I'm bald?

OLIVE
I won't lie to you.

CLIFFORD
Most women won't give me the time of day.

OLIVE
You know I'm separated from my husband and I have two children.

CLIFFORD
Uh huh. I know.

OLIVE
How do you know?

CLIFFORD
I had a guy ask a few questions.

OLIVE
You had a guy ask a few questions?

CLIFFORD
That's right.

OLIVE
So why did you ask me out?

CLIFFORD
Why did you say yes?

OLIVE
Because--
(pause as she measures him)
You smell like flowers.

CLIFFORD
It's an attar of freesia. They press it in France for me.

OLIVE
It's a nice scent. Your own wine, your own cologne. How do you
feel being with a woman three inches taller than you?

CLIFFORD
Everybody's three inches taller than me.

Olive laughs again. She studies her wine, turns it in the light then looks at
Clifford who's got his eyes still locked on hers.

She SMILES.

Clifford sits back in his chair. He's comfortable and ready for anything that
comes.

EXT. A COVERED WALKWAY--A SHORT TIME LATER

Olive and Clifford wait for a valet to bring Olive's Chrysler. Clifford holds
the door for her until she's situated and the window rolled down.

OLIVE
What am I supposed to do with you?

CLIFFORD
I'll call you.

OLIVE
And then what?

CLIFFORD
Maybe I'll take you to the Midi.

OLIVE
Eileen won't give me time off.

CLIFFORD
She will if I ask her to.

OLIVE
What does it cost me?

CLIFFORD
Absolutely nothing. What's your favorite fairy tale?

OLIVE
Rumpelstiltskin.

CLIFFORD
Straw into gold. Mine is Beauty and the Beast.

OLIVE
You move very fast, Mr. Kissner.

CLIFFORD
Short fat bald guys don't get many second chances.

INT. ROSE'S OFFICE. DAY

Olive STANDS at the window WATCHING the parking lot of the
WHEATLAND MARKET where TWO MEN unload boxes from a MEAT
TRUCK. Olive GLANCES at her watch. The men lean against the side of
the truck smoking cigarettes. They are solid, assured working men. One of
them crushes his smoke on the ground, gets into the truck and drives away.

> OLIVE
> I had an interesting dream two nights ago.

> ROSE
> Are you writing the dreams in your book?

The other man carries a box of meat to a van before re-entering the back
door of the market.

> OLIVE
> Always. Now. In the dream I'm tied to the windmill, knees up like
> I'm on a delivery table. Blood is gushing from between my legs so
> I wake up--very calm about the blood--and I see you facing me,
> but you're tiny and you're using a scoop shovel to dig into my head
> and I don't seem to mind what you're doing and there's a pile of
> black stuff with things in it, but I can't tell what it is, it might be
> worms but it has a chemical smell like the fertilizer Tim uses and
> when I look for you you're walking out the door and there's an
> umbilical cord stringing out of you and I'm attached to the other
> end, but I'm not a baby, I'm me. Just the way I am now.

Rose closes her notebook, sticks the pencil in her hair. She LOOKS
admiringly at Olive who's still looking out the window.

> ROSE
> Well, you certainly shrank me down to size.

> OLIVE

251

It doesn't mean anything.

ROSE
It means you won't need me much longer.

Long pause. Olive CHECKS her WATCH. The BLACK SUV rolls into the lot. She SMILES.

OLIVE
Daniel, Sheila's husband showed up at my apartment. He's a real shit. He offered me money and a car and of course I have to tell Sheila.

The Woman GETS INTO A RED SPORTSCAR that's parked beside her SUV. They drive off leaving the SUV.

OLIVE
(beat)
Last Saturday I had dinner with Clifford Kissner.

ROSE
The man from the bank?

OLIVE
Credit Union. Yes. I like him. He made me laugh and he sent me flowers. Orchids. Ten years with Tim and he never gave me flowers. Grow'em if you want'em, he said.
(pause)
He brings his own wine to restaurants, and he smells nice.
(beat)
We were together for three hours and he didn't stare at my breasts.

Olive turns to face Rose.

OLIVE
She got into another car with a man.

252

ROSE
The woman in the SUV?

OLIVE
She doesn't have her children with her.

ROSE
Are you worried about her or the children?

INT. OLIVE'S APT. NIGHT

Olive's dream:

A rope cinched around her neck bites hard and Tim throws a saddle on her, tightens a bridle in her mouth, but she spits it out and then a naked Tim straddles her bare back and Olive breaks out in a sweat until it drains off her like pouring rain and Tim slides off but hangs onto her hair twisting her neck.

Olive wakes up, she's soaking wet, she's lying on top of the sheet. She gets up, goes to the table, writes the dream in a notebook.

EXT. OLIVE'S APT. SATURDAY NOON

Olive stands at her table spreading mustard on white bread. She peels a slice of ham from a package, a slice of cheese and folds the sandwich. Her CELL PHONE rings. She looks at it, lets it ring, takes a bite of her sandwich. The phone stops.

The phone rings again.

OLIVE
Hello.

CLIFFORD
This is Clifford. How ya doin'?

Olive wipes a streak of mustard off her mouth. Long pause.

    OLIVE
    I'm okay. It's Saturday.

    CLIFFORD
    Look, a friend of mine wants you to call him to set up an
    interview.

Olive takes another bite of her sandwich.

    OLIVE
    What kind of an interview?

    CLIFFORD
    You gotta get outa that credit union. I'll give you the number.

Olive closes the loaf of bread, twists the wrapper. Screws the lid on the
mustard jar.

    OLIVE
    Let me get a pencil.

    CLIFFORD
    Why don't I just come up and give it to you?

Olive walks to the window. Across the street she SEES Clifford standing
beside a bright red sports car, top down. He wears jeans, a black t-shirt and
running shoes.

She laughs.

    OLIVE
    You're stalking me?

    CLIFFORD
    Let me take you to lunch.

> OLIVE
> I'm eating a sandwich.

> CLIFFORD
> Ham and cheese?

> OLIVE
> Ham and cheese on gunky white bread. Mustard. No lettuce, no tomato, no pickle.

> CLIFFORD
> Just the way I like it. What do you say?

Olive closes the phone. Lays out two slices of bread, spreads mustard , slaps a slice of ham and a slice of cheese together to make a sandwich then takes two paper plates from a package and lays the rest of her sandwich on one. She answers the KNOCK on the door.

Clifford is at ease as he enters.

> CLIFFORD
> Cute little place.

> OLIVE
> It's a dump. Do you like mustard?

Olive halves the sandwich on the paper plate. Clifford sits. Olive WATCHES him eat the sandwich.

> OLIVE
> I don't have any wine.

> CLIFFORD
> You got a glass of milk?

Olive pours two glasses of milk. Clifford, at the table, is like a little boy at lunch. A mustache of white on his lip. He licks it off. Olive laughs.

CLIFFORD
What? I got mustard on my chin?

OLIVE
No. Nothing.

CLIFFORD
Something's tickling you.

Clifford finishes his sandwich, pulls a card from his pants pocket and slides it to Olive.

CLIFFORD
His name is Bill Watkins. His company has branches in KC, Chicago, St. Louis, LA, and Fort Lauderdale.

OLIVE
Why should he talk to me?

CLIFFORD
Because I asked him to. I also talked to Eileen. She told me you're smart, you work hard, you married a guy named Tim who took you back to the family farm and you've been there ever since.

OLIVE
Did she give you my high school graduation picture too?

CLIFFORD
How much do you make at that bank?

OLIVE
None of your business.

CLIFFORD
My guess is you pull in around thirty-six grand and you're worth

three times that. You've got two kids to think about.

Clifford stands. He scoops up the plates and glasses. Olive WATCHES his hand. His arm is thick and muscular. In the T-shirt, he doesn't look fat, but solid. He moves with grace as he goes to the sink, rinses the glasses and crushes the paper plates into a ball that he drops in the trash.

>   OLIVE
>   Bill Watkins works for you doesn't he?

Clifford does a slow turn to face her. Leans against the sink, crosses his arms.

>   CLIFFORD
>   Why do you say that?

>   OLIVE
>   CK Industries. That's Clifford Kissner Industries, isn't it?

>   CLIFFORD
>   (smiling)
>   You got me there.

>   OLIVE
>   What do you want from me?

>   CLIFFORD
>   I need a watchdog.

>   OLIVE
>   That's just what every girls likes--to be called a dog.

>   CLIFFORD
>   (laughs)
>   There's a lot of slippage in this industry.

>   OLIVE

Slippage?

CLIFFORD
Inventory slips out the door.

OLIVE
Theft. Why don't you call it theft?

CLIFFORD
Okay. Theft. There's a lot of it. Cuts into profits.

OLIVE
And what do you want from me?

CLIFFORD
I liked the way you handled my account after Larry screwed it up.

OLIVE
Someone else would have if I didn't.

CLIFFORD
You caught it. I need those expert eyes on bigger things.

OLIVE
What kinds of things?

CLIFFORD
The bigger Larrys. Really big. I want someone my people don't
know. I want someone who can read a column of numbers and see
the mechanics of embezzlement then crack heads and slam fingers
in the till.

OLIVE
Embezzlement? You want someone who can sneak in and spy on
people. There must be professionals who do that sort of thing.

CLIFFORD

I want *you*.

Olive LOOKS STARTLED. She RISES, goes to the window.

A long silence.

> OLIVE
> Do you really own a winery in France?

> CLIFFORD
> Um huh.

> OLIVE
> And you press your own cologne?

> CLIFFORD
> Attar, but yeah.

> OLIVE
> And the car out there? That's not the car you drove to the
> restaurant last week.

> CLIFFORD
> This is the Aston Martin.

> OLIVE
> Is it an expensive car?

> CLIFFORD
> I like the way your mind works.

> OLIVE
> How do you know the way my mind works?

> CLIFFORD
> Suppose you spot a manager driving an Aston Martin and he only
> drags down say ninety grand a year?

OLIVE
I'd find out how much an Aston Martin costs and if it costs more than an Audi TT, I'd want to know how he can afford it.

CLIFFORD
The TT is a fine machine, but you can buy a stable of them for the price on that Aston. You fed me lunch, let me take you for a ride on my pony.

OLIVE
Where are you going to take me?

CLIFFORD
I suppose it's too late in the day for a run to Minerve--unless... You got your passport on you?

INT. A FANCY DRESS SHOP. DAY

Olive and Janey enter Kathleen's on Rue de la Paix. Black and brilliant blue suits on coal black mannequins. A CLERK approaches. Janey shakes her head, points to Olive. The CLERK inspects Olive, nods, then disappears. Olive and Janey sit on velveteen chairs. The clerk returns, leads them through a smoke glass door into a fitting room.

INT. FITTING ROOM. MOMENTS LATER.

The room is bigger than Olive's apartment. Mirrors all around. An array of suits, blouses, dresses on clothes horses.

Olive undresses, chic underwear, thigh high stockings. She tries on half a dozen pieces posing each time for Janey who gives thumbs up or thumbs down.

Olive in the tailored suits, black hair, high heels, looks like a fashion model posing for a shoot.

The clerk re-enters. Olive points to two suits--one black, the other cobalt blue. Two blouses.
Olive gets dressed.

INT. FANCY DRESS SHOP. MOMENTS LATER

Olive carries boxes embossed with small floral Ks.

EXT. RUE DE LA PAIX. MOMENTS LATER

> JANEY
> You just blew thirty-five hundred bucks 'cause she had a cute little accent.

> OLIVE
> The interview's tomorrow and if I get this job, I just bought my new uniform.

> JANEY
> And if you don't?

> OLIVE
> Clothes talk, Janey.

> JANEY
> Funny, but I don't hear anything.

> OLIVE
> They say I know who I am. They say I know what I want. They say I know how to get it.

> JANEY
> When did you get all fluent in haute cutter?

> OLIVE
> I learned it all from you.

JANEY
Yeah right. Eileen had nothing to do with it.

Janey opens the door to Olive's Chrysler. Speaks over the top to her.

JANEY
A year ago, you didn't know panty hose from a vibrator.

OLIVE
Vibrator?

Janey giggles, gets in the car.

EXT. AN OFFICE BUILDING. DAY

A misty, rainy day. Olive parks. Through the windshield she SEES a four story glass and steel building.

INT. THIRD FLOOR OFFICE. LATER

CARL WEATHERS stands as Olive enters. He's skeletal. Slicked back hair. Face sunset red. Holds out a bony hand.

CARL
I see you found the place.

OLIVE
I know the city. I graduated from Xavier.

Olive sits down, crosses her legs, leans forward and slides a yellow manila folder at Carl Weathers. He slides it back.

CARL
You come highly recommended, Miss Malone.

INT. OLIVE'S APARTMENT. EVENING

Olive looks out the window to see Eileen waving from her car.

INT. EILEEN'S CAR. LATER

OLIVE
You got a new car?

EILEEN
The Prius is in the garage. This is my prowler. It only comes out at night.

OLIVE
How can you afford a BMW on a manager's salary?

EILEEN
I told you I wasn't always a bank manager.

OLIVE
Basketball, I remember.

EILEEN
I'm sorry you're leaving. I've really liked working with you and, by the way, you look absolutely seditious tonight.

OLIVE
Seditious?

EILEEN
With that much skin showing, you could subvert an entire civilization.

EXT. CHEZ DESHAWN, A RESTAURANT. LATER

A valet drives the BMW away, leaving Eileen and Olive under the marquee.

EILEEN
A friend of mine owns this place.

OLIVE
A basketball friend?

EILEEN
Um huh. From the old days.

Eileen stops to adjust her high heels.

OLIVE
Spiked heels. My my.

EILEEN
There's no dress code at DeShawn's. You're only as wicked as you
need to be.

INT. CHEZ DESHAWN FOYER. LATER

Arm in arm, the two women enter. Both dressed to the hilt. Both tall, black
shoulder length hair, high heels. At the maitre d's podium an elegant
African-American woman greets them.

EILEEN
Reservation for Eileen Norburg.

YOUNG WOMAN
DeShawn's stepped out for a bit, Miss Norburg, but he wants to see
you. This way please.

INT. DINING ROOM -- LATER

Elegance in white china, yellow napkins, stem ware. Arrays of silverware.
Candles in lavender glass.

OLIVE
Do you bring everyone who quits here for a farewell dinner?

EILEEN
Oh no. Just the special ones I want to stay in touch with.

OLIVE
Are there a lot of those?

EILEEN
One including you.

Eileen sits. She's like an animal making its nest in a flurry of purple and long nails.

EILEEN
I'm so glad you could come tonight.

OLIVE
I have to tell you--without you...I mean...You're...the perfect role model.

EILEEN
Oh no.

OLIVE
Without you I'd still be wearing white bras and granny panties.

EILEEN
That's very funny. Granny panties.

DeShawn, a tall African-American man approaches the table. He has a thick beard and gold ear rings. He moves like water on glass. He kisses Eileen's cheek.

DESHAWN
Hello darlin', you're looking like the franchise tonight.

EILEEN
DeShawn, this is my friend Olive.

DESHAWN
The lovely and charmante Olive I've heard so much about.
(to Eileen)
I ordered your favorite seafood mixed grill for you and your friend.

EILEEN
(to Olive)
He knows how much I dislike steak.

DESHAWN
No beef, guaranteed.

EILEEN
You do know how to spoil a girl, don't you, DeShawn?

DESHAWN
Lord knows you are one special girl, sugar.

A wine steward comes with wine, pours. DeShawn leaves after kissing Eileen's hand and bowing to Olive.

OLIVE
What a hunk.

EILEEN
All six feet ten inches of him.

OLIVE
I'm glad the company is paying.

EILEEN
The company isn't paying. I'll miss you and maybe this little soirée will help you remember me when you're off touring the country for

your Prince Charming.

OLIVE
My Prince? He's my boss.

EILEEN
Clifford Kissner isn't just a boss. Do you know how many lackeys stand between him and third tier management? You've landed a whale. God, I remember the day you came for your interview.

OLIVE
Don't remind me.

EILEEN
The hayseeds were just dropping out of your hair. But I knew you were ripe for a change and my goodness, have you ever changed.

Eileen raises her glass.

EILEEN
Here's to change. All kinds of change and to all manner of secrets revealed.

Olive sips her wine.

OLIVE
Eileen, there's one thing that's not clear to me.

EILEEN
Just one?

OLIVE
You said DeShawn is, was a basketball friend.

EILEEN
Um huh. I was a point guard with the Falcons, DeShawn was the power forward but then he blew out his knee.

OLIVE
You were a professional basketball player? I'm confused

EILEEN
I was confused for long time too, but I'm not confused any more. Look at me. What do you see?

OLIVE
I see a beautiful, graceful, confident woman. Tall woman. Very tall.

EILEEN
Eight years ago I was running up and down a ninety-foot court with nine sweaty men.

Olive picks up her wine glass.

EILEEN
There's nothing left of Jermaine Norburg except the signing bonus and a great big bank account. The thing that made me and DeShawn buddies is pickled in my plastic surgeon's lab.

Eileen stands. She pirouettes, hands out like a dancer.

OLIVE
Oh my god. I am an idiot. Everyone knows but me?

EILEEN
It's not a secret.

OLIVE
I don't know what to say. You just take my breath away.

EILEEN
I'd like to do that more often.

Eileen sits down, presses her hand over Olive's.

EILEEN
I can teach you a lot about basketball and some other things too so drink DeShawn's wine and we'll see what happens.

EXT. A GOTHIC MANSION. DAY

Olive parks her Chrysler on a tree lined street in front of a three story ginger-bread house with a widow's walk and bay windows. A row of mature sycamores lines the drive from the street to the house. A tire swing on a rope hangs from a low limb of one sycamore. There's not another house for half a block in any direction.

Olive gets out, Janey stands on the sidewalk.

JANEY
You sure you got the right address?

OLIVE
This is the right address.

Olive walks up the drive under the huge sycamores, Janey follows wide-eyed like a kid on a trip to Oz. Olive climbs the steps to the house--eight steps to a broad wooden porch.

INT. A GOTHIC MANSION. DAY

JANEY
You think it's big enough? You don't own a vacuum and this place needs an army of little cleaning guys with eight hands and sharp teeth.

Janey follows Olive up stairs to the second floor landing where a string of bedrooms each with its double bay window faces away from the street with a view of a small apple orchard and a small tool shed and greenhouse.

JANEY
That's where they bury the bodies.

OLIVE
It was the home of a cattle baron.

JANEY
I didn't know they still had places like this in Wichita.

OLIVE
It was fifteen acres when they built it and it stood alone. All the rest is subdivision.

JANEY
And you know this how?

OLIVE
I know the guy who owns it.

JANEY
Are you sleeping with him?

OLIVE
It's a business arrangement.

JANEY
Great place for a Halloween party.

Olive leads Janey downstairs to a spectacular modern French Provincial kitchen--wooden cabinets, a cooking island, granite counter tops, a tiled back splash, copper pots and pans hanging from a brass ceiling bar.

JANEY
Whoa! I expected an old wood burner, or a coal chute but look at this--this guy didn't hold back.

OLIVE

Hmm. He did it. He told me he was going to do it and he did it.

JANEY
This guy must really like you 'cause he's forking out a lot of dough just to get into your pants.

OLIVE
It's not like that.

JANEY
It's always like that. I can't get a guy to open the door for me without he's expecting at least a humjob and you get Architectural Digest keeping your legs crossed. Jeez, I tell you life just ain't fair. Lots of room for kids though.

Olive leans against a wall.

JANEY
What?

OLIVE
I've been thinking about that.

JANEY
What's there to think about?

OLIVE
I don't think I can bring them here and I can't go back.

JANEY
You're thinking about letting that jackass you call a husband keep'em?

OLIVE
He's not that bad.

JANEY

Not that bad? You've been bitching for a year and I can tell you as someone who's been fucked so many times I don't need a road map to show me--this guy you call your ex is the ace of shits.

OLIVE
Still, I'm beginning to think they're better off on the farm.

JANEY
What're you talking about? How many kids get a chance to play hide and seek with the Adams Family?

OLIVE
It's not that. It's just the city's no place for kids. Don't you think it's better to keep them pure for as long as I can even if I can't if you know what I mean.

JANEY
Look at you. They should at least get a chance to see the bright lights.

OLIVE
I think the decision's already made.

JANEY
Who's making it?

OLIVE
I'll be traveling all over in this new job. I won't have time to be a mom.

JANEY
And I'll still be slinging hash for Max so I don't know crap that's for sure--but I think you're nuts.

INT. OLIVE'S APT. NIGHT

She straddles him, clamping her legs to his sides like she's mounting a horse. His hands grip her hips, pulling her down onto him until she muffles a scream then falls forward face to his chest.

> CLIFFORD
> (whispering)
> That ought to hold you for a while.

She lies on him for a long time before sitting up, looking down at him.

> OLIVE
> Every time with you I find nerve endings I didn't know I had.

> CLIFFORD
> Did I hurt you?

> OLIVE
> Oh. No. No. You just wear me out.
> (pause)
> You smell nice. Even after all that you still smell nice.

Olive rakes her nails over his chest.

> OLIVE
> Some things are bothering me. Like the house. I haven't gotten the lease papers yet.

> CLIFFORD
> There is no lease.

> OLIVE
> That's not right. And you didn't tell me you had the kitchen redone.

> CLIFFORD
> I told you I'd give you the Midi.

> OLIVE
> It's too much. You can't do that.

CLIFFORD
You won't go to the South of France, I'll bring you a kitchen.
That's one thing. What else?

OLIVE
Before I met you, I did some crazy things.

CLIFFORD
Enumerate, we'll compare craziness.

Olive sits on her knees hands on his thighs.

OLIVE
One night I met a man in a bar. His name is Daniel and he's
married to Sheila, a girl I roomed with at Xavier. I didn't know
who he was until she invited me to dinner. Then he had the guts to
come here acting like he owned me. With flowers. He's a danger to
Sheila and to every woman he picks up.

CLIFFORD
You're really pissed at this guy.

OLIVE
Should I tell her? I told Rose but she won't let on what to do so I
need your advice. Do I tell Sheila?

CLIFFORD
Suppose you tell her. What do you say?

OLIVE
I'd tell her he picks up women. I'd tell her he shares his trophies
with his pal Harold. You don't think I'm a filthy, perverted slut?

CLIFFORD
Some guys see every man from a woman's past as competition. If
you want to tell me, that's good. If you don't, that's okay too. Just

being with you makes me happy. Seeing you makes me happy. Not just happy, but doing pretty good for a guy who can't get two dates in row.

Clifford sits up, plumps his pillow, leans against the wall then draws her to him. He runs his fingers over her back.

CLIFFORD
You're in Chicago next week, right?

OLIVE
Um huh.

CLIFFORD
When you get back, take Sheila to dinner. Soak up a few carafes of Eau de Chateau Clifford. Tell her everything.

Olive gets off the bed. Clifford grabs her hand.

CLIFFORD
Where are you going?

OLIVE
To call Sheila.

CLIFFORD
It's two o'clock.

OLIVE
She'll be awake.

CLIFFORD
Does it look like I'm finished with you?

He pulls her back on top of him.

INT. A CAFE. LATE AFTERNOON

Olive enters. In the sunlight, she SEES Sheila at a table wearing a BLOND WIG. Olive HESITATES, but Sheila waves her over. Olive sits, lays her purse on the table. She fiddles with her skirt, adjusts the purse so it's square to the edges of the table.

SHEILA
What's so important?

OLIVE
I have a confession to make.

SHEILA
Can we have coffee first?

Olive grips Sheila's hand. She sees dark circles under her eyes despite the thick pancake makeup masking her skin.

OLIVE
Sheila. Please listen to me.

SHEILA
All right. If you've been really really bad I'll take your confession. Did you get skewered again in a cheap hotel?

OLIVE
Before I ran into you at the bank--I went to a bar, I let a man pick me up.
(long pause)
All I can say is that I'm sorry. It was stupid, but how could I know?

Sheila touches her lips with her index finger.

SHEILA
Slush. I know.

OLIVE
You know?

SHEILA
Can't we just not talk about this? I don't need you clearing your conscience on an empty stomach.

OLIVE
How do you know?

SHEILA
Daniel told me. I knew the way he looked at you the minute you came in. When you left, I cornered him and I squeezed the confession out of him.

Sheila smiles wanly. Clears her throat. Looks at Olive and pats her hand.

SHEILA
You are so naïve. You always were, but now I see you're like some little crusader trying to clean up the world after you've spread your legs.

OLIVE
I'm trying to protect you.

SHEILA
You? Protect me? I should be angry with you so stop before you make me mad.

Sheila smiles.

OLIVE
You have to leave him.

SHEILA
Did you hear me? I should just claw your eyes out right here. Would that make you happy? Is that what you want? You want me

to shout at you and pull your hair? Call you a slut?

OLIVE
He's dangerous, Sheila.

SHEILA
If you really care about me, you won't say one more thing.
(beat)
You will just drink your coffee and eat your stupid pastry.

OLIVE
Sheila. He doesn't use any protection.

SHEILA
Maybe he wants to die.

Sheila clutches Olive's hand, raises it and covers it in both of hers.

SHEILA
I don't need protection, Olive. I need a friend.

OLIVE
He came to my apartment. I threw him out after he offered me
money to sleep with him again.

Sheila pulls the wig off. Olive is STARTLED. Sheila lays the wig on the
table. Her head is shiny, bare. She rubs her hand over her head. Tears bud
in her eyes.

SHEILA
Will you just shut up? I can't leave him, honey, because I need his
god-damned medical insurance.

OLIVE
Oh...for...Oh my...What?

SHEILA

The cancer's metastasized to my breasts and it'll be just a while till it's in my spine. I'm beyond surgery now so I'm left with chemo. Do you have any idea what the treatments cost? I have another treatment on Wednesday in Houston. It will cost six thousand dollars. Will your little confession pay for that? No. You want absolution but I'm no priest but I know what's next for me. Paralysis. Paraplegia. Without his medical, I'm dead in six months. Leave him? Oh, no. Olive. He's going to pay to watch me die. Leave him? I don't think so.

Sheila opens her purse and jams the WIG in it. Snaps the purse closed. She LOOKS at Olive. Tears stream down her face.

SHEILA
I'm trapped. So. I don't need your protection but do I need a friend and I really don't care if he sodomizes his little whores. Is that what's so unspeakable? That's his favorite style. It always has been.
(beat)
You're not special, Olive. Just one of so many I don't even keep count anymore. I hope your tests were negative.

OLIVE
Oh Sheila. What have I done?

SHEILA
We're sisters silly. You see?
(beat)
Daniel's not very big, is he? I'll bet Tim has a huge cock though, doesn't he? You know you're crazy to leave that on the farm. But Tim's a man and men think their penises are magic wands and all they have to do is wave it at you and you orgasm. Did you orgasm, Olive? I never could that way. It always just felt uncomfortable. Maybe if Daniel had been bigger.

A waitress comes carrying two glasses of water.

WAITRESS

279

What can I do you ladies for today?

Sheila looks at Olive and she SNIGGERS.

> SHEILA
> (to the waitress)
> What's the richest, creamiest, fattest most obscenely gorgeous pastry you serve?

> WAITRESS
> I guess that'd be the double éclair with crème brulée filling topped with whipped cream and coated with candied pecans. It comes with a dose of insulin.

> SHEILA
> We'll have two of those. Oh. And two cups of hot chocolate with whipped cream and those candied...

> WAITRESS
> Coffee beans?

Sheila smiles and pats Olive's hand.

> SHEILA
> Just like when we were in school...

INT. A GOTHIC MANSION. A WEEK LATER. DAY

Standing at one of the bay windows, Olive WATCHES Tim, her husband, walk up to the house. He stops to adjust his belt, touches his Stetson. Shiny new boots. He knocks, takes his hat off, holding it in front of him. Olive OPENS the door.

> TIM
> It's been a while, Olive.

> OLIVE

How are you doing?

TIM
Could be better. Didn't get much of a harvest 'cause the rain beat down the wheat.

OLIVE
Can I get you a cup of coffee?

Tim pulls an ENVELOPE from his pocket, hands it to Olive.

TIM
Can't stay long enough to drink it. Gotta see a banker and as I recall you didn't make such hot coffee.

OLIVE
I've learned a lot. In the kitchen.

Flicking the envelope in her fingers, Olive leads him into the French Provincial kitchen. She lays the envelope on the table. Tim STANDS in the doorway. She POURS two cups, hands him one.

TIM
I tell ya. You sure wormed you way outa that prairie dog hole you fell into back there in town. What'dja have to sell to get this place?

OLIVE
You didn't come here to chit-chat.

Holding his coffee, Tim sits and lays his hat on the table.

TIM
Tell the truth? I met a woman, Kate Younger, a widow gal, a reverend. She's got two kids just about Nan and Toby's age. And. Well, Olive, she's moving out to the place with me. I want a divorce and I'm keepin' the kids.

OLIVE
No you aren't.

TIM
Open that envelope and read it.

Olive opens the envelope, reads the LETTER. As she reads, the heat of confusion rises in her face. Holding the letter, she FLOATING AGAIN, SWIRLING, SPINNING DOWN INTO THE WATER FROM THE TOP OF THE WINDMILL, DIVING INTO A BLACK HOLE.

TIM
The lawyer says that's a temporary writ, all legal and everything, and he says it gives me sole custody. Law's pretty clear here, Olive. You abandoned your babies and you ain't seen'em in a year. That's what the line there, 'wilfull abandonment' means.

Tim sips his coffee.

TIM
I don't aim to do you harm, Olive, so I'm making you an offer.

OLIVE
(disoriented)
What?

TIM
Lawyer says I can give you a lump sum for the equity you got in the farm 'cause we never signed no per-nup. So, you take this deal and we don't go into court with the unfit mother stuff. You see? You left'em same as if you dumped'em on a street corner.

Olive COLLAPSES into a chair and the letter flutters onto the table. Tim plucks another letter from his pocket, THRUSTS it and A PEN at her. Olive TAKES the pen. She looks at Tim, then at the paper, but she still confused. Instead of signing, she STANDS, wobbly, and STAGGERS to the sink.

Tim follows her. He lays the second letter on the drainboard.

> TIM
> (menacing)
> Better sign it.

> OLIVE
> What is it?

> TIM
> (overbearing)
> You just god damn sign it.

Olive scribbles her signature on the letter. Tim folds it, pockets it. Olive GRIPS the sink ledge, her back turned to Tim.

> TIM
> You hurt me real bad, woman. Some nights I thought I might as well take a twelve gauge to my head, but Kate, she's showed me the true path 'cause she was grieving too and we share a lot of pain and now we've got Jesus Christ and he's showing us the way. I wanted the lawyers to deliver this, but Jesus told me I had to look you in the eye 'cause you're poison.

Tim goes to the table, polishes off the coffee, puts on his hat.

> TIM
> Yeah, well. I gotta run. You're right about the coffee. You did learn something.

He heads for the door. Stops. Turns. Olive SEES him reflected in the kitchen window like he's floating there.

> TIM
> Oh. Just sos you know. That paper? You signed off on the mineral rights.

Olive watches tim as he SPIRALS INTO A WHIRLPOOL AND THEN DISAPPEARS. Olive, on automatic, picks up Tim's coffee cup, dumps the dregs into the sink then, turning, SLAMS the cup into the FLOOR.

INT. ROSE'S OFFICE. DAY

Olive stands at the window WATCHING the beer truck driver unload his cases. She SEES the Black SUV in the sun. She turns to Rose who CROSSES her legs.

> OLIVE
> I had a dream two nights ago. Right after Tim came to lay the bomb in my lap. I was up on the windmill looking out over the fields and the entire wheat crop had turned black and there was an irrigation wheel spewing red water over the wheat but it didn't do any good. In the distance, the air looked like it was on fire and I had trouble breathing, but I wasn't spinning and when I woke up I was sweaty. I haven't had a sweat dream in a couple of months.

Rose takes notes using a bright yellow fountain pen with a red clip on the cap.

> OLIVE
> That's new, isn't it?

> ROSE
> What's new?

> OLIVE
> The fountain pen.

> ROSE
> Yes. A...a friend gave it to me.

> OLIVE

Why?

Rose LOOKS at the pen, then at Olive.

> ROSE
> Why did a friend give it to me?

> OLIVE
> Why did you change to ink?

> ROSE
> I kept breaking the pencil.

> OLIVE
> Do you think your clients worry about a broken pencil?

> ROSE
> A broken pencil means more to some than to others.

Olive sees the beer truck driver finish his work. He leans against the shady side of his truck smoking a cigarette. He opens a can of beer, foam shoots out of the can in a shower of white that the driver sips while leaning over.

> OLIVE
> She's been gone a long time. That's unusual.

> ROSE
> Why does she interest you so much?

> OLIVE
> She might be someone I'd like to know.

> ROSE
> Are you hunting for a friend?

> OLIVE
> Maybe. I've got Eileen and Janey.

ROSE
Let's get back to the dream. What does it...

OLIVE
I know what it means. It means the end of my old life. That's what
it means.

Olive turns to face Rose who wears a bright red dress, bare legs crossed,
red high heels and no afghan.

OLIVE
I've started over and the icing on the cake--Clifford Kissner wants
me to marry him.

ROSE
Is that what you want?

OLIVE
Yeah, that's what I want. He's a beautiful man. I didn't see that at
first but now, my stars. He's strong as an ox in every way a man
should be.

ROSE
He makes you happy?

OLIVE
And he makes me laugh.

Olive glances at the black and white paintings on the wall.

OLIVE
The paintings, Rose? What are they supposed to mean?

ROSE
You tell me.

OLIVE
(laughs)
I see a woman with her lover reaching across an empty space and
the lover is handing the woman a yellow fountain pen. Right? Did
I get it right?

ROSE
At my age?

OLIVE
You're writing everything in ink, Rose. You haven't worn your
gray uniform for a month and I'll bet you've got some sexy
underwear stashed in your drawer. Do you make love naked?

Rose spins the yellow fountain pen in her fingers. Olive's fixated on the
spinning. Then Rose closes her notebook and caps the pen. She SMILES
and, crossing her legs, bounces one bright red high heel up and down.

INT. A GOTHIC MANSION. BEDROOM. NIGHT

Rain beats on the windows. Olive on her side facing Clifford rests an arm
on his hip.

OLIVE
Stop. You make me nervous when you stare.

CLIFFORD
You know I can't get enough of you. When you're on the road,
you're all I think about. My company's going to hell because of
you.

OLIVE
No it's not.

Clifford runs a finger to her neck.

CLIFFORD

I like your neck. I like your belly button. I like your ankles--
(faster)
Your hair your ears your legs your--

OLIVE
Stop. I have to tell you something.

Clifford closes his eyes.

CLIFFORD
Okay, I'm not staring. What?

OLIVE
I didn't tell you everything about when Tim was here.

CLIFFORD
You told me he wants a divorce and he's going to marry what's her
name, the minister. He won't get the kids.

Clifford opens his eyes. Sits up, takes Olive's hand. He caresses her for a
long time.

CLIFFORD
What?

OLIVE
I signed something but I don't know exactly what I signed.

Clifford gets up. He's not FAT at all but muscular, solid, very fit. He
PULLS Olive to her feet, lifts her by the waist and CARRIES her to the
window. Naked, facing the window, he runs his hands over her.

CLIFFORD
Don't worry about the writ. The lawyers are gonna iron all that out.

Clifford kisses her neck, still holding her.

OLIVE
It's not the writ. I think I signed away the kids' mineral rights.

CLIFFORD
Look at me, babe.

Olive turns to face him, wraps her arms around his neck.

CLIFFORD
You think they're gonna need mineral rights when your name is
Kissner?

EXT. WHEATLAND MARKET PARKING LOT. DAY

Olive sits in her Chrysler beside the black SUV just as the RED SPORTS
car pulls back into the lot and the woman, wearing dark glasses, gets out.
She leans in and kisses the man behind the wheel. He drives away. The
woman heads toward the market. Olive gets out and runs to her.

OLIVE
Excuse me. Can I talk to you for a minute?

WOMAN
Who are you?

OLIVE
I used to see a psychiatrist
(pointing)
just across the street and I'd watch you shopping here.

WOMAN
(nervous guilt)
What do you want?

OLIVE
Well, I was wondering if I could buy you lunch.

The woman cocks her head, looks at Olive. She SEES the SHORT BLACK SKIRT, SCOOP NECK COBALT BLUE BLOUSE, BLACK HAIR, CHIC SUNGLASSES, BLACK HEELS, SILVER NECKLACE.

> WOMAN
> Who does your hair? It looks great.

EXT. A GOTHIC MANSION. ONE WEEK LATER. NIGHT

Olive gets out of a TAXI. The driver sets two SUITCASES on the ground. Olive pays him.

> DRIVER
> Whoa. Thanks. That'll keep me in coffee for a week.

INT. A GOTHIC MANSION.

Dropping her keys on the lowboy by the door, Olive answers the ringing phone.

> OLIVE
> Hey there.

> CLIFFORD
> How did it go?

> OLIVE
> Your company isn't going to tank.

> CLIFFORD
> (laughs)
> I tracked your flight, but I got held up. Still okay for dinner?

> OLIVE
> I smell like airplane so I'll need time to change.

> CLIFFORD

Eileen called me while you were in the air.

OLIVE
Oh?

CLIFFORD
She'll meet us there a little late.

INT. BATHROOM. MOMENTS LATER

Olive in the shower, shampoos, rinses, dries off, checks her short cropped hair in the mirror.

INT. BEDROOM. MOMENTS LATER

Olive opens A WALK IN CLOSET with A MAN'S CLOTHING on one side, OLIVE'S on the other. She runs her fingers over a double row of dresses, suits, pant suits, coats and jackets, skirts, blouses all arranged by color and style.

She chooses an ELECTRIC BLUE PANT SUIT and a CHROME YELLOW SILK BLOUSE and tosses them on the bed.

She opens another closet and from the rows of pumps, sandals, boots, strapped high heels, strapped spiked heels, sneakers, flip-flops, she selects a pair of RED SPIKED HEELS.

Olive stands in front of the full-length mirror. Her pubic hair is trimmed into a small V. She runs a FINGER over the BUTTERFLY TATTOO on her belly that seems to perch atop the V.

She DRESSES. The electric blue makes her skin glow. The chrome yellow silk brightens her face.

At the VANITY MIRROR, she strokes on just a faint touch of eye shadow.

Finishing her make up, she SEES the two photos of Nan and Toby in their

291

heavy silver frames next to a PHOTO OF CLIFFORD and OLIVE in front of the Aston-Martin. Olive lifts the kids' photos from their hooks and fondles the faces and then she goes to the bed and pulls out the BATTERED LEATHER SUITCASE with its steel buckles. She opens it and lays the pictures on her old 501 Levis and the chambray shirt, the denim skirt, sandals, the brocade blouse--all the old clothing from her former life.

She closes the suitcase and slides it back under the bed.

She then opens and unpacks the smaller of the two SUITCASES she carried in and lays out an array of CHILDREN'S CLOTHING--Hello Kitty t-shirts and Thomas the Train pajamas as well as dresses, jeans, an ELECTRONIC GAME.

She carries the children's clothing to a BEDROOM done up in LITTLE GIRL style. She switches on the light and lays the girl's clothing on the bed. Olive looks around the room, touches the mirror of the vanity, does a Mother-straightening job on the bed before turning out the light.

In the room next door, she switches on the light to show a BEDROOM done in LITTLE BOY. She lays the boy's clothing and electronic game on the bed, smoothes the covers then turns off the light and leaves.

EXT. CLIFFORD'S ASTON-MARTIN. LATER

Clifford stands beside the car WATCHING Olive walk down the steps of the mansion. As Olive approaches, she FLOATS like a Blue, Yellow and Red flower.

Clifford opens the door. Olive kisses his cheek.

> OLIVE
> You smell good tonight.

He closes her door, goes around, gets in.

INT. THE ASTON-MARTIN.

Clifford buckles his seat belt. Olive CARESSES his neck. He TOUCHES her face. LOOKS at her for a long time. She faces him.

> OLIVE
> You look tired.

> CLIFFORD
> I'm okay. You?

> OLIVE
> Okay. I bought them some things in LA. I was thinking...

> CLIFFORD
> Yeah?

> OLIVE
> I have to get new portraits of Nan and Toby.

Olive's hand migrates to his shoulder.

> CLIFFORD
> I talked to the lawyers. They say we'll have them here for our first visit next Friday.

> OLIVE
> What if they've forgotten me?

> CLIFFORD
> They won't. You're their mother.

Olive touches his hand. He starts the Aston.
The tail lights disappear into the dark canyon of the sycamore-tree-lined street.

> FADE OUT